THE DEPTHS

SOLYPSE: BOOK 1

PAUL NESLUSAN

Formatting by www.ebooklaunch.com

DEDICATION

To my lovely wife Christine: Thanks for all your support. You are truly amazing.

Isabella, William, and Griffin, let this be a lesson to you: never forget your dreams, and never stop following them.

ACKNOWLEDGMENTS

I would be remiss if I didn't thank some folks for their help along the way, so here it goes: first and foremost, Robin, profound thanks for all of your support and feedback, now as ever. Joe at the diner, thanks for giving me 180 cheeseburgers; my word count and cholesterol are both higher because of you. Christine, thanks for being patient while I jousted at this windmill; you are simply amazing. Ted, thanks for suggesting this in the first place, and encouraging me to get going. The rest of my family, thanks for supporting my writing over the years. Lastly, thanks to a friend who passed away, reminding me that life is too short to put things off until they are more convenient (because they never will be).

PROLOGUE

A lonely funeral barge, long forgotten by those who tearfully urged it onward, made its way downstream. Rivers met rivers, feeding and growing into a broad expanse of water flowing urgently forward. Bits of debris, logs, honored dead, and other flotsam converged until a unified flow came together into what was known as the River of the World. At the base of a ring of mountains, it all tumbled into a massive crater, known as the End of the World. Loved ones, carefully prepared for their journey, plummeted into the abyss.

Thousands of feet below, the immense flow of water came down in a waterfall that spanned the width of the broad cavern, concealing a bustling city carved into the side of an underground mountain. The six tiers of Solypse, for that is what the city was called, worked together to make the city a ceaseless juggernaut of trade, exchanging goods from the shadowy races of the depths for the treasure of the overworld. The descent to the city was treacherous and long, and even moreso for those who elected to stay; for Solypse was also a city of those who wished to be forgotten, and with that came a willingness to make others disappear.

1. DEATH BEGINS

He shrugged his cloak closer around his frail body, absentmindedly daubing pus from an open facial sore with a dirty handkerchief. The cold stone catacombs did nothing good for his humours, but it was the only place where he could study his art without interference. He re-read the page in the dim candlelight, trying to make sense of the arcane runes as shadows danced across the page. Though the elven half of his heritage allowed him to see quite well in the dark, this capability did not extend to reading. In his mind's eye, the figures on the page began to make sense; their meaning, emblazoned in an impossible array of colors and permutations, began to weave together until they formed unified figure.

Smiling, he closed the ancient tome, the dry pages mottled with mold making a faint crackling noise as he did so. As he gently caressed the cover of the spellbook, he saw his hand highlighted by the candle glow. Thin, pale skin stretched over the long skeletal fingers of the sickly man, the flesh mottled with brown spots and lesions. His hands were nearly as cold as the room itself. He balled his skeletal hands into fists and pulled them into the heavy, warm recesses of his dark robes. He had been a sickly child countless seasons ago, and little had changed. His father had convinced the clerics of the temple to have an audience with them and begged them to help. Neither that, nor countless cures brought in from distant lands had worked.

Though those illnesses had never subsided, their effects were superseded by more recent, much more prominent diseases and infections. His work often required handling the dead, bloated corpses floating in the waters near Solypse, and they occasionally had surprises of their own. The dry, burning cough was a product of being in the cool, dry stone tunnels beneath Solypse. His frail constitution was a willing host for any and all ailments that drifted in his direction; and many did. Cockroaches scurried up his sleeves and out of the neck of his robe, occasionally crossing his face.

He turned his attention to the dead body behind him. It was

bloated, the person's tongue swollen like a gag in its voiceless mouth. One eye socket lay empty, a hollow cave left as a reminder of what was once there. The socket's partner, with an eyeball bulging, threatened to match it with little effort. The hair was dry, but matted, having been fished out of the waterway a few days prior. Shy of the venous grey shade of the entire body, the straw blond hair was the only color associated with the corpse. Beyond that corpse lay two dozen others, neatly laid out in rows.

He took a deep breath and tried again. He swiftly muttered an incantation, weaving his hands together, finalizing with a gesture towards the corpse on the dais. The corpse sat up stiffly, a gagging moan slipping past its constricting tongue. He uttered another phrase, and made a chopping gesture with his hand. The zombie fell back on the stone slab with a wet crunch, as its head made impact. He gestured again and cast his spell, slightly varying his intonation and his gestures. The dozens in the room began to stir, coming to their feet. As they rose, he smiled, baring his muddled collection of teeth and empty sockets. He was pleased; he had improved upon a spell he had learned for the creation of one zombie and extended it to over twenty.

The wizard walked slowly into the cavernous room next door, steadying himself on a tall onyx staff topped with an intricately carved likeness of a beholder. As he clutched the staff tightly, he surveyed the rows upon rows of corpses stacked on top of one another, extending off into the darkness of the room. A solitary gnome scurried about, dragging the corpses and trying to neatly stack them in rows, six bodies high. The dark robed figure exhaled slowly. A few dozen today was nothing; the real test would come very soon.

2. A JOURNEY OF FAITH

A whitish glow emanated from the top of the Veil, indicating that morning had once more graced Solypse. The city covered six tiers, carved into the front half of a small mountain protruding from the canyon wall. It spread several miles wide, with a population as diverse as the wares of the merchant quarter. As dawn broke, hundreds of fishermen guided their skiffs and larger fishing vessels into the rippling black waters at the front of Solypse, while caravan ferries pushed off for their day-long trip to the Over-Tunnel. The fishermen dared not get too close to the roaring waters of the massive waterfall, lest their vessels be crushed asunder. The waterfall, or the Veil as it was called, fell from miles above and spanned the entire width of the cavern. Blocking view of the city from above and occluding the sun from the residents below, the Veil was aptly named.

Coal smoke began to rise from chimneys as innkeepers began cooking the morning meal for their guests. Shopkeepers stepped outside to sweep the debris from the city's nightly revelry from smooth stone roadways in front of their stores and stalls. Solypse was a town that lived on travelers and transience; it was a nexus of trade for any and all things imaginable. From the fishermen on the first tier, to the temple to the god of Trade on the sixth tier, the entire city was geared towards the generation of capital in various forms.

Light filtered past the columns on the temple grounds, playing across the stone altar in front of the frustrated acolyte.

As Lethos is a light unto my mind, let this be a light unto my path.

Nothing.

He had recited the prayer over a hundred times, trying to vary rhyme, meter, and inflection; it was no use. In theory, he should be able to light the candle with the prayer in mind, without even vocalizing the words. He tried clearing his mind and beginning again, but his clarity was getting pushed aside by his frustration.

Pash's youth had been spent in a walled garden, every step along his path predetermined by his father. This, his appointment to the temple, was a final brutal execution of his father's political will.

He knew he wasn't to be groomed for his father's position, as his father didn't intend to vacate his seat for several hundred years yet—but there were only two other professions befitting the child of a council member, and his father had all but laughed off the notion of him pursuing magecraft.

The Brothers stood in the temple grounds on the top tier, out of sight of the acolyte, watching him go through his morning rituals. The acolyte was trying, and failing, to light the candle in front of him.

Larrik's bright amber eyes narrowed. "He is weak, Brother Kern."

The high priest of Lethos nodded. "His weakness in execution reflects a weakness in devotion."

"Perhaps he isn't the one."

"You doubt prophecy?"

"Prophecy always needs interpretation. Perhaps we need to look again."

The high priest shook his head. "I'm certain of it. Something about him practically radiates energy."

Larrik looked back at the acolyte and watched him repeatedly try to light a candle, to no avail.

Larrik allowed a grim smile. "Indeed. Ye should be careful, he'll burn down all of Solypse if ye don't put a leash on him." He paused a moment, his eyes still on the acolyte. "Perhaps he needs his faith tested in the crucible of conflict. There are very few left faithless after a week in the depths."

Brother Kern tilted his head to regard Larrik. The surly, grey-skinned dwarf had a point. In fact, it was a conclusion that he himself had come to several days ago. "I received word of a small settlement, two day's journey off of the Path. I was thinking he would make a fine emissary to negotiate a new trade route."

Brother Larrik shook his head. "Off the Path? He'd never make it alive."

Brother Kern sighed casually. "That's why I planned on sending you with him."

Larrik turned his head sharply. "Am I now a babysitter to whelp-lings? Is there no one else to send?"

"Well, there is Brother Mindel; you could take his place on the water purification detail..."

"Are ye daft? Mindel is barely better than the boy." He threaded his stubby fingers through the front of his beard, tugging on it for emphasis. "They'd both be dead before the Veil glows!"

Brother Kern folded his arms across his chest, regarding him passively.

"Fine," Larrik grumbled, "I can respect yer wisdom, but I don't have to like the answer."

Brother Kern smiled, and thumped him on the back. "That's the spirit!" He turned to face the acolyte. "Acolyte Pash!" He yelled, "come here, that you might learn of Lethos' plans for you!"

As the acolyte stood up and began in their direction, Larrik sighed.

"Are ye going to tell the council, or am I?"

Brother Kern shifted uncomfortably. "I'll tell them first thing tomorrow after morning feast."

"When am I leaving?"

"At first light."

3. THE ASSIGNMENT

Five tiers below the Brothers in the Temple, the north side of the harbor was bathed in foul smells. Multiple tiers of offal and human waste emptied from a canal into the river that flowed along the north side, far beneath the temple in the northwest corner of the city. Down the river also floated trash and corpses, cast-offs from funeral boats and other detritus in the rivers that drained from the overworld into the Veil.

Several hundred paces into the tunnel, shrouded in the darkness, glowing hands rapidly gestured at one another. Thalen accepted his assignment with a small measure of excitement; he had been personally selected by the head of the guild for this mission. He signed his thanks to the master and made a gesture to darken his enchanted gloves.

The head of the assassin's guild, by tradition, was unknown, even to the most senior members of the guild. *"Someday"*, he thought, *"that will be me."* Thalen slipped away, and padded silently down the tunnels toward the guildhall. Tonight was going to be an important night.

4. THE PATH

Pash met Larrik at the gates of Solypse, just as the town began to bathe in the morning glow. Pash looked up at the stone walls of the cavern, thousands of feet high, that surrounded the town. Larrik squinted at the young acolyte, watching him crane his neck towards the roof of the cavern.

"What're ye lookin' at, boy?"

Pash blushed, and turned his attention to Larrik. "It's hard to wrap my mind around it, Brother Larrik. We're surrounded by water, we have sunlight, and the roof of the cavern is so far up that we can't even see it on foggy days. It's hard for me to think of this as being below ground."

"Aye, but we are. The Veil doesn't give light—there's something from above that does that. Up there, it's so bright yer eyes'd burn out of your head, and it blazes for thrice as long, every day. Be thankful you're down here! Now, double-check your kit one last time, before we head out. There's no turning back once we've left."

Pash looked at the Veil, and silently gave thanks to Lethos. The Veil, a massive waterfall that fell from the sky and spanned the miles across the width of the canyon, effectively formed a solid wall of water a few miles from the shore of Solypse. Standing at the back wall of the canyon, next to the gates to the Path, Pash was as far from the Veil as he had ever been in his entire life.

Pash fidgeted uncomfortably, checking his pack and pockets one last time to make sure he hadn't forgotten anything. "I guess I just always thought of underground as, you know, over there, beyond the bridge, in the tunnel and beyond. We seem too...civilized."

Larrik grinned wickedly. "Aye, uncivilized it is, and still deeper underground as well. Be that as it may, the Path is at least maintained, and well traveled. Where we're going...well, let's just say—oh ho, what's this?" Pash turned, and saw a tall, muscular woman striding purposefully towards them, dressed in tightly woven black chainmail. Pash blushed. She was undoubtedly both attractive and deadly, her long black hair and striking features contrasting with the battle scarred scabbard hanging at her side.

As she reached them, she nodded toward the grey dwarf. "Brother Larrik?"

"Aye?"

"The Council sends their regards, as well as their protection. I'm Cillan; I'll be accompanying you for your safety."

Larrik arched an eyebrow. "Well met my lady, but we won't be needin' any protection. Please be sure to give the council our thanks though." He started to turn away from her. Cillan swiftly stepped around Pash facing Larrik.

"I'm afraid the council insists, Brother Larrik."

Larrik sighed. "Of course they do."

Pash looked at him quizzically as Larrik, waved curtly at a gate guard. Pash noted that the guard was young and looked to be his age. At the moment, Pash wasn't sure if he'd rather be manning the gate or passing through it.

The guard removed the bar and hauled the heavy door open. Pash hesitated for a moment, then stepped through the stone archway. Pash looked around uncomfortably while clenching his fists. Though he was only steps outside the city, he felt enormously vulnerable. He stood on the stone bridge, water to either side and the yawning maw of the tunnel to the depths looming ahead. The three travelers crossed the bridge, while matched pairs of translucent skinned elves in ink-black chainmail silently stood watch at regular intervals.

"What are they here for?" Pash whispered.

Cillan strode past him, taking point. "They watch the Path", she said, gesturing at the massive tunnel. "Just in case."

5. A MEETING OF MINDS

From his balcony in the tower on the fifth tier, Ellias Tirth watched the merchant district wake up. He could see innumerable vendors preparing their wares for the day, in hundreds of streets throughout the district. This was his favorite time of day. The early, lighter hours were dominated by elven and human traders from the overworld, and he still felt a kinship with them. Though he had lived in Solypse for nearly sixty summers, the half-elf had lived in the overworld for nearly as long. He turned from the greyish light of dawn, remembering the sun's golden fingers reaching out to caress the forests and towns of the overworld. He sighed, casting his eyes around the opulent Councilman's quarters. There were benefits to his life in Solypse, to be sure, but there were some things that all the gems in the depths couldn't purchase.

As he turned from his window, his indentured servant, Narhal, entered the room. "Honorable Councilman, there is a gentleman from the Temple here to see you. Something about a mission to a new settlement."

Brother Kern strode in behind Narhal, with a serene look on his face. "Lethos' blessing be upon you, Honorable Councilman."

Ellias made a slight bow at the waist. "And upon you also, friend cleric. To what do I owe this honor?"

"Lethos graced us with the knowledge of a settlement, about two days from here, down beyond the Path. As is my duty and pleasure, I wanted to ensure that the council was made aware that the temple was sending out missionaries to establish relations, and perhaps a trade route. I thought it to be a worthy mission for one of our aspiring acolytes."

Ellias feigned surprise. "A new settlement? Two days' journey beyond the Path? Surely the Council can help keep your acolyte safe. I shall have a guardian party assembled at once!"

Brother Kern shrugged off the Councilman's concerns with the wave of a hand. "He left at first light; I sent Larrik with him. He should be fine."

Ellias snickered. "That old fool? Certainly you could do better than that."

Brother Kern stiffened. "Brother Larrik is a fine guide, and a more than worthy defender. I'm sure they will not have any problems."

Ellias smiled. "Yes, well, I'd hate to see the old dwarf oversleep and forget to protect his charge. I've already sent someone to mind their safety; they should already be well on their way, no?"

Brother Kern's face turned red. "I suppose so. Thank you for your time Councilman."

As Brother Kern turned to leave, Ellias interrupted him.

"One more thing, *Brother.*" Brother Kern paused in the doorway.

"Please do not try to sneak members of your order out of the city again. People might get the wrong impression." Ellias laced his fingers together. "Don't worry, I'll not tell the rest of the council of your sloppy coordination...this time."

Brother Kern nodded curtly. "As you say, Honorable Councilman."

6. IN THE BEGINNING

*G*rowing up surrounded by frippery left a bad taste in his mouth for anything that bore any resemblance to the effete lifestyle of the upper tiers. He had been raised to be seen and not heard, and that left him to hear plenty; enough to know that he was surrounded by people who didn't so much have personalities as they did individual collections of overwrought affectations. Everyone on the council hated one another, yet pretended to be the best of friends. He knew this from the various private meetings held by his father with his political allies. Never did they have a good thing to say about another whilst the other wasn't present, except where they might need something of such a person at a later time.

For years he assured himself that he would never become as false in character as the socialites of the upper tiers. He scowled at the irony, knowing full well that he had rarely expressed a personal opinion in the presence of his father, or dared to challenge the social fabric from which his entire life was woven.

He could remember his first major confrontation with his father like it had happened yesterday. It had started with a carnival, the joy of every child in Solypse. Pash had gone to the merchant district to watch, along with the rest of the aristocrat children. He had been delighted by the mysterious performers and their amazing feats. He was particularly taken with the carnival magician.

As the children filtered in and out, distracted by midway games, he stayed for show after show. He watched a rabbit disappear into a hat, only to be replaced by a bouquet of flowers, and watched the magician float above the ground. After one performance, the magician's assistant went on a break, leaving just Pash and the magician in the tent. Pash seized the opportunity to ask the Magician if he would teach him some tricks.

The magician reeked of alcohol and stale body odor. His wide, thin moustache curled around his mouth like a permanent frown, and he shook his head. "Sorry kid, the tricks are mine. Trade secret y'know."

Pash produced a handful of golden coins, and begged him. The magician snatched the coins, and began weaving his hands into complicated gestures.

"Magic good, Magic here, make these coins DISAPPEAR!" He clapped his hands together, and Pash's coins indeed were nowhere to be found.

"Where did they go?"

"I told you, trade secrets, kid."

"But that was my money."

"Not anymore."

"But I gave it to you so that you would teach me magic."

"I made it disappear, didn't I?"

"How?"

"Trade secret."

"Give me my money please."

"No."

"GIVE. ME. MY. MONEY. NOW."

The Magician laughed, and pushed Pash backwards.

"Kid, go cry home to daddy. I have real things to deal with."

Pash stood up, his fists balled at his sides.

"Oh, you're going to hit me now?"

He hadn't thought about it; he had just lashed out. He had felt the anger burning in his mind, and then throughout his body. Still, before he even made contact, the look of surprise on the magician's face told Pash that something unexpected had just happened.

7. THE JOURNEY BEGINS

They walked along the Path without talking, the creaking sound of Pash's new leather armor breaking the silence. Occasionally, a merchant caravan or a group of travelers would pass by on their way to Solypse from Bruemarrar, the city of the Deep Dwarves. The Path, as it was called, was actually a massive tunnel, four cart paths wide and a height far enough to allow a small giant to pass. Hewn magically and manually from solid rock by Dwarven craftsmen, it was the first direct trade-route between the overworld and the depths. Hundreds of merchants and travelers traversed the road on the march between cities, trading exotic overworld goods for rare gems and minerals, while dozens of side tunnels led to untamed depths. Indeed, it had earned its reputation as being "paved with gems and lined with swords."

A globe of light floated just above the trio. Larrik had urged Pash to cast a simple light spell to guide their way; red-faced and flustered, he tried repeatedly to call upon the simple prayer, with no results. Larrik summoned the globe in moments.

As they trudged on, hour after hour, Pash sighed in angry frustration. Months of practice, prayer, and meditation had yielded nothing for him. His father, whose reputation was partially tied to Pash's success, would have been furious if he knew of Pash's failure in this simple task. *"Well,"* he thought, *"Yet another way that I can disappoint Father."* After several hours of trudging in silence, he reached for an apology. "Brother Larrik-"

The dwarf cut him off. "Don't ye call me Brother Larrik out here. Just Larrik."

"But Brother Kern said-"

The dwarf glared at him. "Just. Larrik."

"Apologies B-... Apologies Larrik. I have been diligent in my studies, but I still lack the skill to conjure light. I will work harder. I'm sorry I haven't proven myself worthy yet."

Larrik shook his head. "Studies got nothin' to do with it. It ain't up here", he wrapped his knuckles on his iron helm "it's here" he said, as he thumped his chest with his fist. "Methinks you should spend less time studying, and perhaps some more time searchin' yer soul."

"Is that how you did it, *Brother* Larrik?" snickered Cillan, baiting the temperamental dwarf.

Larrik glared at her. "Aye. Methinks that perhaps ye could use a bit of it yourself." He abruptly moved to the right wall, the sloping shadows giving way to the floating light, revealing a passage on the side. "We descend here. Acolyte Pash, ye oil yer leathers as soon as we set camp for the night, or every creature in the depths will hear us coming," muttering "if they haven't already smelled us coming."

The passage narrowed until they had to walk single file, occasionally needing to duck their heads as the tunnel roof got lower and lower. Larrik took point, with Pash behind and Cillan guarding the rear. Cillan walked cautiously, following the impotent acolyte and the cantankerous dwarf. She had been on many jobs more dangerous than this one, but few as distasteful. It wasn't the work that bothered her; she was good at what she did, and had no misgivings about that. It was working for the council that was the problem. She had spent her life fiercely independent. No matter how she tried to assure herself that it was just another job, she knew that once the council got their hooks in her, they wouldn't let go easily. With each job she gained private accolades, greater rewards, and a greater understanding of the hidden world of political intrigue within Solypse. The more she learned, the dirtier she felt, and the harder it was for her to break free. *"This is the last one"*, she vowed to herself. She had sworn that oath before, but this time she aimed to keep it. She sighed inwardly. *"If only the money wasn't so good..."*

Larrik continued to guide them as they descended, occasionally pausing to place a hand on the ground, sniff the air, or press an ear to the wall. After hours of walking, the trio came to a spot where the tunnel widened out. "We'll set up camp here." Pash looked around the dimly lit cavern. Though it widened out to nearly thirty paces on a side with stalactites, stalagmites, and large rocks scattered about, it was otherwise barren.

"Do most deep dwarves and elves carry coal when they are adventuring?"

Larrik looked at him curiously. "For emergencies I suppose. Why?"

Cillan laughed softly. "The young man has never been out of the city before. Acolyte, those who are from the depths need no light to see. In fact, many of the creatures in the depths would be blinded if they even saw the light that passes through the Veil."

"What about cooking fires?" Pash questioned.

"When they cook the meat," Cillan paused, looking at Larrik for emphasis, "*if* they cook their meat, they often cook with a dark flame." Pash cringed in disgust.

"We cook our food plenty," Larrik said, clearly offended. He turned to Pash. "Many creatures down here are likely carrion feeders," he explained. "They'll carry a sickness from a long dead creature, then pass it along when something eats them. An entire bloodline could be erased from something like that...or if they survive, the cook's entire bloodline."

Cillan gave a gentle bow. "Pardon my ignorance, friend of the depths. I clearly do not know such things as well as you. Nonetheless, I think we can all agree that a bright fire will probably keep unknown creatures from areas below at bay, yes?" Larrik grunted in agreement, and Pash smiled, privately relieved. Cillan grinned at him conspiratorially. "Being stuck in this mere human's body, I'm bound by the trappings of convention." Pash looked at her quizzically. "I can't see in the dark, so I brought campfire materials" she explained, opening her pack. As she finished building a pyramid of sticks on a small bed of coal and reached for her flint, Larrik waved her aside. He squatted over the sticks and moved his hands slowly, as if warming them over the fire. Embers began to glow in the coal. He continued his quiet invocation, and soon they had a roaring fire. "With Lethos' blessing, we shouldn't need any more fuel for the fire. He nodded in Cillan's direction. "It's best if we save the fuel anyway. Never know when we might need it."

They sat around the fire, feasting on their provisions. Pash was relieved that he hadn't decided to travel too lightly—he was starving after walking for the entire day. Cillan finished her meal, took a long pull on her waterskin, and let out a contented sigh. "Acolyte Pash, this is your first time outside of the gate, is it not?"

"Indeed. And just call me Pash." He furrowed his brow as he took his last bite of food. "Acolyte is just a term the Brothers use. I don't think it has any meaning outside the Temple."

She raised her eyebrows in surprise. "But it does, Acolyte Pash. It distinguishes you as a member of the clerical order of the god of Trade. Lethos would certainly find value in your rank, no matter how lowly, no?"

He shrugged. "I suppose. Larrik won't allow me to call him Brother, and this fire alone proves that he's in greater favor than I."

Larrik shook his head, dismissing Pash with a wave of his hand. "That's different."

Cillan looked at Larrik, arching an eyebrow. "Is it?"

Larrik appraised Cillan's look. He had an aversion to the council, though he didn't have a particular reason why—other than their meddlesome ways, such as her in their midst.

He was usually a pretty good judge of character, but Cillan remained a mystery. Throughout the day's march, she had often struck up conversations about Solypse, the Temple, and other topical things; however, whenever a question was directed towards her, she artfully deflected it into other topics.

Cillan turned to Pash again. "So what did you think of the trek outside the gate? Not as frightening as they would have you believe, is it?"

Pash nodded. "The Path really makes it seem as if there is nothing to fear; it's certainly impressive. How did the original missionaries ever make it in the first place?"

Cillan cocked her head, surprised. "They don't teach you the history of Solypse at the temple? I would have thought memorizing such a thing would be required, considering the missionaries came here because of a vision from Lethos."

Pash gave a quick nod. "They taught us the history, but not of the tunnel. They taught us that Solypse had been founded hundreds of years ago, by missionaries of Lethos." Cillan nodded, and gestured for him to continue. "As it grew into a major trade hub, it gained notoriety as the locus of trade from the overground, underground, overworld, and underworld. Anything could be gotten for a price; but managing such an extraordinary city required a strong rule of law, which came with a heavy price tag; thus, the council was born. The council of Solypse was formed to manage the daily governance of the city. The temple used to be in control of the city, but then had to cede much power to the council. Over time, a rivalry grew between the temple and the council."

"They teach you of political rivalries?"

"I added the last part", he confessed, "but everyone knows it's true."

Cillan nodded; she couldn't disagree. "It is interesting that they teach about it becoming a trade hub, but they don't explain how it happened. I would think that the temple of Lethos would preach about heavily."

"Don't presume to understand Lethos' will for the temple", Larrik said sharply, "There are reasons for everything."

"His or yours?" she queried.

Larrik grunted noncommittally in response.

Cillan smiled warmly at Pash. "The tunnel wasn't made by human hands; anyone with eyes can see that. No, legend has it, the original tunnel was just wide enough to allow a man, in some cases sideways, to pass. As the story goes, the missionaries of Lethos had been given a vision of the Veil and the ground upon which Solypse is founded, a vision from Lethos himself. When they arrived, they found plentiful fishing, but found no obvious signs of other civilization. For twenty days and nights, the missionaries prayed. Finally, a vision came to them, that they needed to make contact with the deep dwarves, and only then would they be able to fulfill the vision set before them. Guided by their faith, and bearing few provisions, seven of them set off into the dark tunnel at the edge of town."

Larrik interrupted Cillan with a wave of his hand. "Yer just going to tell it wrong. Let me." Larrik cleared his throat, and began where she had left off.

"For countless days, the missionaries walked, crawled on their bellies, slid, and crept down into the depths of the depths, until at long last they reached the Dwarven city of Bruemarrar. By the time they reached the gates, they were weary from hiking and battling the denizens of the deep, and had lost three of their number. As legend has it, the guards were so surprised to see fair-skinned creatures that deep in the depths, they brought them before the council to decide their fate."

Larrik paused, staring into the fire. "The council had scoffed at the missionaries' request to build a massive road between their fair city and the missionary's tiny temple, rejecting the prophecy shared by the missionaries. The whole council, save for one house. A house of lower nobility, House Gaerrorn saw an opportunity to make a name for themselves, should the prophecy come true. The missionaries presented the leader of house Gaerrorn with a rare artifact, an enchanted mattock, as a symbol of their gratitude and pledge of friendship.

"Aided by the magical digging tool, and encouraged by dreams of riches and grandeur, House Gaerrorn and their workers began by widening the tunnel enough to begin trade, and continued to work for six-and-thirty years.

"In the meantime, the missionaries and the workers had also built paths to the surface, where the missionaries spread the word of Solypse to daring merchants. By the time the tunnel was complete, Solypse already had a booming trade business, with the Path attracting merchants from all over the depths. Gnomes, deep elves, and others gathered in Solypse in a temporary truce, to trade goods, information, and stories. Solypse flourished, and began growing into what it is today."

Larrik stared intently into the fire. "House Gaerrorn, on the other hand, was not as fortunate. When their gamble began to pay off, the other houses became angry. The others asked fer a cut of the profits, which was understandably ignored by House Gaerrorn. Jealous and greedy buggers, the council declared war upon House Gaerrorn. Before the last pick had even cooled from hewing stone, the entire house and their workers were slaughtered."

"Every last one?" Pash looked at the two of them in disbelief.

Larrik didn't respond. Cillan watched him intently.

"So the story goes."

Larrik continued. "When House Gaerrorn was under attack, a battle raged in tunnels around and beneath Solypse, out of the view of the people above. The artifact was stolen from House Gaerrorn and used against them. The head of the House, Lord Gaerrorn himself, recovered the artifact and hid it, telling no one of its location. He intended to recover it after the battle died down, but he—as with everyone in his house—was struck down before it could happen. Methinks the Temple is embarrassed at the loss, and concerned that it may come back to haunt them."

Cillan inclined her head towards Pash. "I can see why your friend here wouldn't want to talk about it either. It isn't quite the sort of story I would want to share about my people, especially if I were the lone dwarf at the temple in Solypse."

Larrik looked fiercely at her, fire in his eyes. "You council lackeys are all the same. Ye sit up and beg for yer masters, hopin' for table scraps, and it makes ye think ye can tell everyone else their business. I'd thank ye to leave myself out of it. Ye don't know me, I don't know you, and I don't have much interest in changin' that. Ye weren't invited and ye certainly weren't invited to share yer opinions."

Cillan stiffened. "I am not a council lackey. I work for them of my own free will, when I choose."

Larrik snorted. "When ye choose, aye, up until they choose for you and ye haven't got a choice. If you don't realize that, then yer either stupid or ignorant. You may not see the collar around your neck, but the leash leads back to the council. Even a pup thinks he has a choice, until he tries a choice his master doesn't like."

Cillan's face flushed furiously. "And what of you, half a brother?

You have a collar around your neck too, do you not? Are you a temple lapdog? A mascot that they won't accept into their ranks?"

Larrik's face contorted in rage, and his voice raised to a shout. "I live of my own choosing! I am not a Brother because it is my will! I have no need to kiss a ring!"

Cillan laughed, mocking him. "So you live of your own choosing? But amongst a city of humans, outcasts, and transients?" She gestured toward the path they had taken. "Your people are up there, at the other end of the Path. Perhaps we should make a visit, and ask them what they think of this fine dwarf, free of encumbrance!" Cillan's face turned to abject horror, as she saw Larrik reach for his belt. Before she could react, the mattock at his side was in his hand, and then hurtling towards her.

The mattock flew over her shoulder and beyond, into something dangling from the ceiling. The mattock buried itself deep in the creature's face with enough force to penetrate the back of its skull. As the large humanoid creature fell from the roof of the cavern, a frenzied clacking and clattering erupted from the room. Cillan dove to the ground and tucked into a roll, coming up into a crouch with a dagger and a short sword. Pash had lept to his feet, an onyx staff in one hand, and a torch in the other.

"By the gods, what ARE they?" he shrieked.

"Death, lad, if you aren't quick! Stay alert! And keep an eye out for the ceiling!"

Pash kicked a pile of tinder and wood into the fire, stoking the flames into a blaze. He could see creatures on the ceiling and walking on the ground in front of them. Nearly ten feet tall, with blades for claws at the ends of their long arms, they looked as if they could grab and gut in one fell swoop. Their prismatic insectoid eyes gleamed in the reflected fire light, and they shrank back from the brightness.

"Their eyes!" Pash yelled to his companions. Cillan loosed her dagger in the air towards one and dropped her short sword. Her hands moved in liquid symmetry, drawing a dagger from either side of her belt and hurling them into the faces of the two nearest creatures. Pash dropped to a knee and spun his staff over his head, terminating his momentum with a jab up under the bird-like jaw into the brain of one of the creature. He used his momentum to rise to his feet and push the creature away from him. Freeing his staff, he spun it from an extended arm into the head of a nearby creature lumbering towards him on the ceiling of the cave.

Larrik, having retrieved his weapon, had waded into the midst of the creatures on the ground. With his diminutive height and his speed working on to his advantage, he deftly parried attacks with his mattocks, planting a spike in the back of one head and in the chest of another. A bladed hand lashed out from the ceiling, impaling his left shoulder and causing him to drop one of his weapons. Without missing a beat, the dwarf spun to face his attacker, and once more launched a mattock. The creature fell, it's bladed hand twisting, then snapping off in the dwarf's shoulder.

Larrik yelled in rage, and lunged to retrieve his weapon.

"Drop!"

Larrik dropped, just in time to see two more of Cillan's daggers embed themselves up to their hilts in the faces of two more of the creatures behind him. Pash bounded over to Larrik as Cillan retrieved her first pair of daggers. A loud chittering noise erupted from the corner, and the three adventurers turned at the same time to regard the new threat. A single creature rushed from the darkness, wildly brandishing its arms and claws. Pash brought his staff in a tight arc, swinging it into the side of the creature's neck, killing it instantly.

Cillan leveled her gaze at Larrik. "Well met."

Larrik returned the gaze. "You as well."

8. A FATHER'S WRATH

*W*hen Pash dropped his arm, he could see five small purple and blue shards embedded in the magician's stomach where his hand had been. The magician fell to the ground, the shards melting away with the sound of ice sizzling on a hot griddle.

The magician looked up at him, astonished. "They were...just...tricks." The magician tumbled to the floor, and the coins fell out of his sleeve and clattered to the floor. Pash ran out of the tent, as fast as his legs could carry him, nearly bumping head-first into the magician's assistant.

"Hey, watch where you're going!" she exclaimed. Pash ignored her, darting out as fast as he could. Moments later, a scream erupted in the tent; He broke into a run, and didn't stop until he reached the upper tiers. By the time his little legs had carried him there, the news of the events had reached the council guard. That had not been a good day.

Pash was discreetly escorted to his father's official chambers. He stood on the carpet facing his father, his father sitting behind his massive wooden desk. The desk had been carved from a single tree in the overworld; intricately inscribed with scenes lifted from the history books of Solypse, dyed dark, and shone smooth and lustrous from years of use. His father continued writing on the sheet of parchment; deliberate and beautiful letters detailed a trade arrangement for a museum as if the agreement itself were a work of art.

Councilman Hielan set aside the parchment delicately to allow it to dry, and closed his eyes. He took a deep breath and exhaled slowly.

Pash watched his father take a deep, cleansing breath. Gillas Hielan's eyes snapped open, and he slammed his fist down onto the table, impacting it with enough force to impale the desk with the metal tipped quill.

"Do you know how long I have been on the council?"

"No sir."

"Longer than you have been alive."

"Yes sir."

"So you can imagine that if it is that long, that it is perhaps, of importance to me?"

"Yes sir."

"At least, say, equal or greater in importance to something that has been a part of my life only since you were born?"

Pash swallowed. "Yes sir."

Gillas' voice began to escalate. "So you can understand that when I find out that my career is in jeopardy because you had a temper tantrum, I find myself in a quandary. You eat my food, you wear my clothing, and you consume my wealth, all with the promise that someday you will prove yourself worthy of this resource sink-hole that is your life. And then this."

Gillas stood up from behind his desk, his pointed ears juxtaposed with his towering, muscled six-foot frame.

"At some point in a businessman's life, one has to wonder when an investment is no longer worth pouring money into. When one is finally done chasing bad money with good money."

Gillas paused, ensuring he had Pash's full attention. "Your brother is dead. Dead because of power he could not control, and because he could not control himself. I will ensure that you reach the same inevitable conclusion, if you prove that you similarly lack control. Have I made myself clear?"

Pash nodded.

"HAVE I MADE MYSELF CLEAR?"

"Yes sir!"

"Get out."

9. A SURPRISE IN THE TEMPLE

In the near-perfect darkness, Thalen perched easily on a window ledge hundred of feet above the ground. His practiced eye could see the telltale shifting shadows of assassins and thieves on rooftops, hoping to get their jobs done and disappear. Thalen smiled. Daily, he saw members of the assassin's and thieves guilds; he watched them as he watched his marks, sizing them up and assessing their capabilities. In every one, he saw the same thing: weakness. He silently shook his head as he watched another shadow disappear down a distant wall. *They all were fleeing from something, or climbing toward an unreachable goal, trying to escape what the fates had laid before them in their early years.* Thalen had no such misfortune. He didn't chase wealth; he was born into a family of comfortable resources, and wanted for little. He wasn't making up for a lack of affection; his parents had given him plenty enough while he was growing up—not that such things were ever of great concern for him. No, he came by his profession honestly.

He started as a child, first with strays running through the street, then with pets left behind homes. He remembered the tingling rush of excitement in his breast as he watched their life slip away. His parents had caught him, of course, and he had wept and promised them the he would "never kill animals again." They worried and fretted, and sent him to the priests, who declared him 'dispassionate'. The reality couldn't have been further from the truth. There was passion, more than he would have expected they could understand. The feeling of power, of holding the strings of death over life, was an intoxicating call. Still, he was young, and had made his parents a promise, and wanted to keep that promise. He exercised restraint, furious amounts of restraint. As time went on, his unvented passion became an itch that he couldn't scratch, a nagging irritation that would never go away.

All this went on until a bully of a boy in his class gave him a reason to scratch. By all accounts, it was the other boy that had provoked it. Thalen snapped, throwing punches in a blind rage until he was pulled off of the other boy, but it was too late. He eventually discovered that the boy had succumbed to his injuries. Thalen's parents assumed his classmates were the cause of his emotional distress; that the animals, the bully, all of it would go away if he was removed from that environment.

They decided to educate him at home, bringing in tutors for all his subjects. His isolation fueled his imagination, and his ample free time was spent fantasizing about the work that would one day become his profession. He studied warfare, politics, and religion; ultimately deciding that they were all roughly the same in thought execution. He slipped out of his reverie and focused at the mission at hand.

The assassin gently eased the window open. As expected, the window latch wasn't fastened. Though it was on the second floor, it was hundreds of feet above the ground. The living quarters for the clerics of the temple to Lethos were one of the first things created in the town. Carved into solid stone and flush with the face of the ledge overlooking the council tier, the dormitories were meant to allow the clerics to look out upon all of Solypse first thing in the morning, and last thing at night. *"More like look 'down' on Solypse"*, he amended silently. Normally, the dormitories, like the temple itself, were considered unreachable without a formal invitation. He, however, did not trifle with such formalities. He slid through the window, and gently pulled it closed behind him. He surveyed the room and froze. Something was amiss. A candle on the bedside table had burned down almost completely, leaving a cold puddle of wax frozen to the folded leaf hanging down from the side of the table. He stepped cautiously forward toward the bed and felt resistance as he pulled his foot up from the floor, a sticky noise accompanying the motion.

Alarmed, he swiftly crept up to the bed, his thin leather shoes growing damp as he did so. He looked down onto the bed, and swiftly bit the side of his hand to suppress his gag reflex at the smell. He had killed many men and women, and even tortured a few, and this... this was fascinating. The priest's body -or what was left of it- was spread across the entire bed. He had literally been ripped open; from the look paralyzed on his face and the grip of his fingers on the bedsheets, it looked as if it had happened while he was still alive. He looked around. If it were done by a person, they didn't appear to have taken anything. He did a quick count; all the organs appeared to be there, which virtually ruled out an animal.

Thalen slipped back out of the room quickly, not bothering to latch the window behind him. He had never seen anything like it.

10. SHOAL

Therrien yawned, and stretched his sore limbs. Though he still slept deeply, the bed he had constructed left much comfort to be desired, though it was enough to prepare him for the night watch. He had left Solypse with the expedition, his curiosity piqued at promises of riches and adventure. The adventure of the trip had been short, compared to the many months of boredom that followed. He soon realized that the riches were to be made by the merchants, and that his value as the settlement's magician faded as the settlement fortified and became more secure.

He walked over to a polished bronze bowl on a pedestal, and intoned a few words over the still water in the basin. Something had tripped the wards that he had placed along the path to the settlement; though it was likely just some wandering creature in the night, he was still duty-bound to check. As a blurry image came into view, his jaw dropped. After months of glimpsing oversized slugs, man-sized spiders, and other creatures he intended to research another day, he now was staring at an exquisitely beautiful woman. Her black hair pulled tightly back under a small, dark helm, her piercing eyes reflected dancing flames from a blazing fire. Though he couldn't hear the words she was speaking, he could see that she was addressing an acolyte from the temple in Solypse and a dwarf dressed in well-worn leather armor. But he wasn't paying attention to them. Perhaps he had been away from civilization for too long, but he had the feeling that she wasn't a stranger to such attentions, wherever she went.

He straightened himself up and pulled on the robes that he wore for his official duties. He tucked his walking staff absent-mindedly under his arm, and headed out of his home. Though his staff could serve as a light source if necessary, one of his first official duties was to ensure there was continual light around the residents and walking paths of the colony; as such, there was rarely a need for it within the walls of the fortification, unless he was indoors. The walk to the Nar'el's quarters was a decent distance. Originally, the colony had occupied a small encampment; as they began to settle in, however, they chose to take up an entire cavern. Truth be told, the cavern was nearly ideal for a colony; the location left them with only two tunnel entrances to guard, an underground river nearby, and a massive cavern to themselves. *Massive Indeed*, he thought to himself. They had picked a large cavern to ensure that there was room enough for new residents, with the hopes that the colony would one day become a trading city.

Their meager compliment of a hundred or so men and women were scattered about a space that could hold over a thousand, and it had taken him over a month to connect all their homes with decently lit pathways. In time, a magician in the depths was a very valuable resource. They were depended upon for opening portals to distant cities, protecting colonists from danger, and acting as trusted advisors to colony and city mayors. He shook his head as he trudged toward the Mayor's house. All those things required intensive studying, and there were no libraries in Shoal. And so, he instead was in charge of lights and warning the guards when his wards were disturbed.

He arrived at Nar'el's home after a while, slightly out of breath. The home, larger than most in the colony, was adjacent to the town hall in the middle of the cavern. Though the nearby river and the odd menagerie of flora and fauna that surrounded it provided most of the settlers with the materials that they needed to fashion homes, Nar'el had a home burrowed into a mound of rock in the middle of the cavern, the privilege of his station. It was spacious, with three bedrooms, a study, a brightly lit great-room, and a private entrance at the rear. Therrien knew all of this because Nar'el had convinced the colonists- and subsequently him- that as the Mayor, Nar'el needed quarters that would be suitable for entertaining guests. When Nar'el had pointed out that the magician's ability to soften and mold rock was far more suited to this task than the colonists' ability to gather and construct such a home, they readily agreed.

Therrien rapped on the front door with his walking stick. After a few moments, the heavy door eased open a crack; a moment later, Nar'el's portly face appeared in the crack. When he saw Therrien, he broke into a wide grin. He opened the door wide, and ushered Therrien in.

"Come in my friend! I was just thinking about you!"

Therrien raised an eyebrow skeptically. "You were? Do tell."

"I was just thinking that perhaps I should ward the back entrance. Just in case."

Therrien shrugged. "I wouldn't worry too much my lord. I already concealed it from view."

"I was just thinking...a man can never be too careful. If we grow, this could become a much coveted position."

Therrien gave a faint smile. "Certainly, I will take care of it this week. This doesn't have anything to do with that misunderstanding about the blacksmith's wife, does it?"

Nar'el's face turned scarlet, and he waved Therrien's concerns away with a pudgy hand. "No, no. It's not that, I'm just...worried about making sure that we are prepared for the future."

"Right now, we have more pressing matters to attend to. It seems that Lethos smiles favorably upon us. A small group has triggered the wards, and it appears they should make it here by mid morn."

Nar'el's face lit up. "An expedition? A merchant caravan perhaps?"

"Better; it appears as if there is at least one acolyte of Lethos, which means that there is likely a brother to mind him. I would assume that is the dwarf, as the woman clearly cannot be."

"You come to me excited about THREE people?" Nar'el exclaimed, exasperated.

"Yes, Lord Mayor," he said patiently, "I think it is worthy of your attention. If they are of the temple, then it is possible that she is of the council. This could be the first true trade link with Solypse."

Nar'el grunted. "Please attend to them, and bring them to me in the eve. I have other matters to attend to today."

"Yes, Lord Mayor."

Therrien bowed slightly at the waist, and excused himself. As he walked towards the guard hall, he smiled, thanking Lethos for his good fortune. A beautiful young woman, from Solypse, and *he* was to escort her. Normally he would have cursed Nar'el's laziness; this time, he was thrilled.

11. A LONG WALK

They sat around the campfire, which was now stoked brightly. The energy of battle subsided, Larrik appeared to have sunk back into his normal quiet, contemplative stare. Pash glanced at Cillan, who appeared lost in thought staring into the flame.

"So, uh, you are really great. Fighting I mean. Thanks."

Cillan glanced up at him, startled. "Yes, well, when you've been doing it as long as I have...it's just one of those things."

Out of the corner of his eye, Pash saw Larrik gently nod in agreement, without looking up.

"You don't look old enough to be that good," he blurted, "I mean, not that you're too young, you just look about my age, and you're a woman, and-"

"So that means I can't fight?"

"No, it's not that. I just mean that I can't even reliably conjure a light, which is a basic skill for even the newest faithful of Lethos, and you fight like a seasoned warrior." He paused. "And you look like a *woman*, not an elf, which means you truly are young. I guess I feel blessed by Lethos to have you as a friend and a traveling companion." He blushed.

Her face hardened. "I'm glad you feel that way," she said indifferently, "As for me, this is a job. I'm here to watch over you because you can't look after yourselves. Blessings and friendship have nothing to do with this arrangement. You'd best remember that."

Larrik glanced up, surprised at the sharpness of her tone. Pash looked as if he had been struck across the face. Pash stood up swiftly.

"I'll take first watch. You two had best get some sleep." With that, he walked off toward the edge of the ring of light cast from the fire. Cillan wordlessly walked to her bedroll and lay down.

Pash could feel the blood rush to his face in embarrassment as he walked to the edge of the firelight. She was right; he was weak, and he knew it. It wasn't his physical strength, or even his knowledge. He felt a hard knot in his stomach. It was his faith. He knew it; more embarrassingly, he knew that Larrik knew it, even if he never stated so. Conjuring light was a simple task, little more than a parlor trick. To him, however, it was the world; with his inability to call upon his faith enough for such a simple task, he felt worse than a fraud. He shivered, staring off into the cold darkness, alone.

Pash cursed the luck that had led him there, the honor of the Temple thrust upon him. He stared off into the darkness, his head swirling with bad memories.

Ah yes. His coming of age celebration. Gillas Hielan was part of the ruling class; as such, there was a certain expectation of fanfare surrounding auspicious occasions. Pash, by extension, was required to play along. By the time he had reached his coming of age celebration, Pash was more than ready to be on his own. He had spent decades watching the subterfuge that actually made the gears turn in Solypse, and he wanted none of it.

When his birthday gala was announced, he nearly jumped for joy; it was the first birthday that he had truly looked forward to since he was a young child. Normally opposed to all the gaudy glitz and glamour, he relished this opportunity with reckless abandon. He supervised the choice of the decorations, the provisioning of the hall, and personally selected the meal. His father, usually vacillating between disapproving and dispassionate, actually smiled when the event was broached in conversation.

On the night of the festivities, Pash dressed in his finest, and waited at the door of the hall with giddy anticipation. He greeted his guests with genuine enthusiasm. Each one had earned their ticket to the event with their position and reputation: the wealthy, the powerful, and the well connected. His father played the part as well, smoothly in his element. Gentle greetings, half smiles and warm handshakes were his tools, and he wielded them like a master craftsman.

Tradition dictated that a courteous gathering would give way to dinner, a speech from his father, and revelry until the early hours of the morning; the next day was usually painful for all the revelers, if not a complete loss. The meal wound on uneventfully. As he reached the end of his plate, his father gave him a long look, and patted him on the back.

Gillas stood and drained his metal goblet. Inverting the cup, he held the base and rapped it on the table to call the room to attention. Conversations quieted, and he cleared his throat.

"Thank you all for coming this evening to celebrate this auspicious occasion. It has been a long time coming. Truth be told, I'm not sure who has looked forward to this more, Pash or myself." He gave a thin smile, and waited for the polite laughter to die down. "In all honesty, I am certain it was Pash. From an early age, I could sense that he was different than most children. Quieter. Content to spend his time in his head, rather than running about with the other children. As he got older, it be-

came obvious that he was not cut of the same cloth as his peers. Don't let this grand event fool you—the finer things in life are not his passion; they never have been, nor will they ever be."

Pash blushed uncomfortably, not sure whether he should feel embarrassed or complimented.

"And so whether you are elven and call it becoming a senior, or human and call it becoming a man...today, we acknowledge my son officially crosses the bridge from childhood to adulthood. To him, I ask all of you to raise a glass." Gillas raised a glass, leading the toast. He paused, then cleared his throat loudly.

"I have one last gift for my child-come-adult." He held up a hand to quiet the crowd, ensuring he had their full attention. "As many of you know, his elder brother passed away while he was in the charge of the wizards of the tower. For that, I would never think of sending another child into their care. But much like his brother, Pash is exceptional in mind. Because of this, I can think of no finer choice than to send him to the temple to become a Brother of Lethos. As you wish him congratulations on his passage in time, you may also wish him well on his next chapter in life. He will walk up to the Temple in two days time."

The crowd murmured their astonished approval. The temple rarely accepted acolytes at such a young age, with so little experience in life. Either Pash truly was exceptional, or Gillas wielded considerably more influence than was previously thought.

Pash was struck speechless; he and his father had met with the brothers of the Temple many months before. The original audience had been granted out of courtesy and deference to Gillas' seat on the council, with little expected outcome. They had nodded politely and moved them along from office to office; at the end, they had sent him off for testing. Pash had made it clear, or so he thought, that he held little interest in the Temple, intentionally fumbling even the most basic of tasks. He assumed that would be the last he would hear about it. But none of that passed his mind in that moment; all he could thing about was that Gillas' last official act as his father was to remove all remaining choice from his life.

12. SERVITUDE AND AMBITION

Nanong hummed quietly to himself as he worked. Though he had never been one for manual labor, he had never been one to shy away from work that needed to be done. "It doesn't get done until you get doing", as his father used to say, and that included the grunt work associated with his craft. His hard work and talent had already been rewarded, and that encouraged him. Nanong snagged the gaff hook from where it leaned against the stone wall, along with the ropes to the sledge. He trotted merrily down the dark corridor, the light of the vaulted room fading away; his sight was quickly replaced with vision of equal clarity in the pitch black. As a people, the gnomes had physically adapted to living in utter darkness long ago, and it wrapped around him like a comfortable old blanket.

Nanong came to the end of the corridor and ran his hands along the stone wall until his fingers sensed the depression for the hidden catch. He pressed on it, and swung the door inward.

In the distance, he could faintly hear the sound of the Veil crashing into the massive underground sea; though Solypse had been enchanted to deaden the sound coming from the outside, it was impossible to completely drown out the sound of hundreds of rivers pouring from the sky. He spread his feet wide, leading a little with his right, and swung the gaff hook into the underground river in front of him. It connected with a satisfying wet smacking noise; success on the first swing was always a good thing. Sometimes he would come up with logs, boat debris, or old fishing nets; any of which would slow him down and sometimes require him to waste even more time disentangling his tool.

He leaned back, pulling the hook and his quarry up against the rock ledge at his feet. He reached down and felt a belt. This was good. When the corpses were naked, or their clothes had mostly rotted, pulling them up required unconventional handholds that were both inconvenient and ran the risk of damaging the bodies. He pulled the body up onto the sledge, carefully shut the door, and headed back up the corridor. It was a shame that he wasn't strong enough to drag more than one at a time, though he had perfected a sort of rhythm to it after many months of practice. As it turned out, he had a natural knack for organization, and a nearly compulsive ability to count and manipulate numbers. He chalked it up to his proud gnomish heritage. As of this snag, he had stacked 2,643 corpses in the main chamber, and one in his own quarters for personal uses. This snag was also his last of the evening, which meant he could now focus on his true passion. He dragged the sledge over to the most recent pile, the drenched body now leaking from a hole in its stomach where the hook had punctured it. He tipped the sledge on its side. The body rolled neatly into place, where it would function as the bottom of a new pile. He swiftly re-placed the sledge and gaff hook in their positions by the tunnel en-trance, and rushed off to his quarters.

Stripping off his leather apron, tunic, and breeches, he replaced them with a simple black robe. He lit a candle at the corner of his desk, and looked down in the warm glow at his spellbook. Though he had been studying and scribing in it for over a decade, it still seemed new. He smiled and traced a hand over the stack of un-scribed pages on the right side, imagining it as a tome as filled and complex as the one owned by Gerrus. He looked next to the desk, at the makeshift cot that he had built for the corpse—the one that Gerrus had graciously allowed him to keep in pursuit of his studies.

He had been a simple illusionist when he and Gerrus first met, but back then he yearned for something more. Nanong came from a long line of engineers that focused on automatons, but he had lacked the artistry needed to follow their craft. His embarrassing lack of skill left a great distance between him and his family, and his parents had en-rolled him into the Academy of Wizarding. This simultaneously of-fered him a chance at new skills and divorced him from the family, as was the custom of the school. Though he quickly discovered that he had a natural talent for the illusory magics and rock transmutation spells that were the mainstay of the Academy, he was left feeling unsat-isfied. He still remembered the wonder he held as a child, watching his father breathe life into a small mechanical creatures, powered by a steam. Not wanting to stay, and knowing he could not return home, he set out for Solypse.

When Gerrus had found Nanong, he had discovered him hidden near a pile of corpses from a recently slain expedition. Gerrus had set about dragging the bodies away, when he discovered the little gnome napping in the pile. Recognizing a kindred spirit, Nanong described his vision to Gerrus, who agreed to take him as an apprentice. Nanong was thrilled to finally have the opportunity to learn the art of animation and reanimation, from a master of the art.

"*We complement each other well*", he thought, "*with his focus on quantity, and mine on innovation.*" He looked down at the corpse, and the collection of parts he had sewn into it. Two additional arms protruded from the chest, and an extra leg protruded from the torso. The stitches on the extra leg were beginning to tear where they joined the body; he was going to have to replace the body soon. Still, this one had provided valuable research in the meantime.

13. A WELCOME ARRIVAL

Larrik woke Pash and Cillan, and they packed their camp with few words between them. Larrik took point, padding silently ahead of the other two by several hundred paces.

Pash glanced quickly at Cillan, his head down. "Look, about last night-"

Cillan shook her head. "Forget about it."

"No. I mean, if I offended you, I'm sorry. I know this is a job for you, but there's no reason we can't still be friends. If I was too forward in my speech, I apologize." He exhaled heavily.

"No, we can't." She put a hand gently on his arm. "My job—my life—doesn't work that way. This is a business arrangement. It's best that you understand that."

"What about once our business is concluded? Surely the council can't care what you do after we are done here?"

Cillan let her hand drop. When it was clear that she did not intend to respond, Pash sped up his pace, leaving her alone to her thoughts. She knew she was right; her life did not work that way. *"But why not? Why couldn't it?"* Pash was, undoubtedly, a failure as a cleric. That aside, he definitely was a good person, the kind with whom she could imagine being friends. *Hm. Friends.* His boyish innocence was refreshing in its contrast to her hardened perspective on life, and his easy conversation made him pleasant to be around, but his naiveté contrasted starkly with her all too aware view of the world. She shook her head to clear her thoughts. *"After this job,"* she promised herself, *"I'm going to walk away."* She ran her hand absentmindedly over her scabbard. *"Will I? What else can I do? This is all I've ever known."* She was sick of the killing; if only she wasn't so *good* at it.

They arrived at the gate to the colony with little incident. Therrien had already alerted the guard to expect visitors, and they were received warmly, and brought to the mage. Therrien bowed low to them. "I am Therrien, chief wizard of the settlement. To whom do I have the pleasure of meeting?"

Larrik spoke up. "I'm Larrik, of the Temple of Lethos" he jerked a thumb towards Pash "This here is Acolyte Pash, and the young lady over there is Cillan, working fer the council."

Therrien bowed again, to Cillan. "It is always a pleasure to meet a representative of the council. I look forward to building an alliance that will last." Cillan stared back at him coldly. "Are you in charge?"

"I-uh, no; uh, That would be Lord Mayor Nar'el. We will meet with him for evening feast. You can negotiate and discuss terms with him then."

"I am not here to negotiate. Leave that to Brother Larrik over here."

Larrik nodded. "Cillan was sent to escort us; this is a mission trip on behalf of the Brotherhood of Lethos. We look forward to the meeting."

Therrien nodded in understanding. "Of course, my apologies. As you have some time before evening, please, make yourselves at home in my quarters. You may walk freely around here, the town is quite safe. The cleared walkways are well lit, and it should be easy enough to find your way around."

***

The adventurers unloaded their packs in the guest quarters attached to Therrien's home. Therrien walked out of his bedchamber to find Cillan alone in the great room, studying a map of the colony on the wall.

"We are quite lucky, you know." Cillan spun quickly at the sound of his voice, her hand swiftly moving to the hilt of her dagger.

Therrien put his hands up in mock surrender and chuckled. "Sorry to startle you. I was talking about the colony." He gestured at the map. "We have only two entrances to the colony, which are easily defended. We have much space, which will allow us to grow as trade grows. There is a river at the far end, outside the gate," he pointed to the left "and it provides us with water, food, a way to dispose of waste, and more. This really is a fairly ideal location."

Cillan studied the map. "It looks quite large. She pointed at a marker labeled 'blacksmith', and another labeled 'mayor'. "It looks quite spread out. Why don't you just settle close to one another?"

Therrien gave a feeble smile. "Nar'el—Lord Mayor Nar'el, that is, believes that once we establish a trade route, we will have many more people joining us, and advised us to stake our claim early."

He gestured to the middle of the map. "The mayor's residence, where we will be dining, is a decent walk from here, but in the center of the town. From there we have our blacksmith up against the north wall, and —gods be praised—some form of natural chimney takes smoke out of the cavern." He made a shooing motion with his hand. "There's a hole up there, that much I know; I set wards on it, and nothing has come through it, so it must end up with cracks too small for creatures to fit in."

Cillan cocked her head to one side. "Wards? Most impressive, Chief Wizard. Is that what you tend to?" Cillan looked at him with feigned awe; Therrien, missing the subtle sarcasm, blushed with pride.

"The wards on the paths, the lighting, that sort of thing. I supply whatever the colony needs."

"But the cavern is huge—how can you possibly set wards on all the paths? You must be quite a magician."

He waved his hand in protest. "Oh, no no no. We don't actually have wards in the city. I meant the outer paths. We don't have any crime here; there are so few of us, we're like family, and we have very few visitors."

"Perhaps I'm an overly cautious person; I just can't believe that you wouldn't even have a lock on your door, or on the Mayor's at least."

"Most folks around here only know enough about magic to be afraid of it; I don't think they want to risk the consequences with me. As for Lord Mayor Nar'el, there's nothing in his home that is overly coveted by another." He grinned. "Well, except for Cael, the black-smith's wife."

Cillan snickered.

He smirked, pouring a beverage into cups for the two of them. He handed her a cup. "He had me put in a hidden passage that just happens to open near her home. It's enspelled to look like a pile of rock debris, so no one ever sees her go near his home without her husband around. He said it's for safety." He grinned, winking conspiratorially.

Cillan arched an eyebrow. "So this is how you seek your fortune as a wizard?"

"Well, there really isn't much to attend to these days, except his personal wishes."

"Sounds exciting."

"I actually have had my fill of colony life", he admitted. "I might consider asking Larrik if I could join you on the way back to Solypse, if you don't think that would be too much of an imposition."

She shrugged. "You would have to ask Larrik." She paused. "But I would like that. Perhaps later...you could show me around a little?"

"Ask Larrik what?" Pash walked into the room, and glanced at the other two.

Therrien's face flushed. "I was, um, just talking to your lady friend here about journeys in the future."

Pash glanced at Cillan, and looked back at Therrien. "She's not my friend," he said flatly, "she's here doing her job."

Cillan blushed, and smiled warmly at Therrien. "My apologies, Chief Wizard, for taking up your time. I should attend to my things. I look forward to talking to you later." Cillan slipped out of the room, leaving Therrien flustered, and Pash confused.

Pash took measure of the magician. He was of average height, with a sturdy, somewhat muscular frame. He looked to be a few, but not many years older than Pash. His hair was completely grey, causing him to appear slightly more advanced in age, and revealing his human heritage.

Therrien cast around the room, searching for a new conversation topic, avoiding eye contact with Pash. "So... I understand you are an acolyte of Lethos, yes? Do you have much experience with clerical magics?"

Pash bit his lip. "Well, I'm still an acolyte, so I'm not very good."

Therrien nodded encouragingly. "Yes, it takes a while to get the hang of things, doesn't it? It seems like it took me forever to learn my first cantrip, but now..." Therrien made a series of hand gestures, and whispered *"lechte!"*. A small glowing ball floated lazily in the air between them. Therrien caught it in his hand, and it disappeared. "I imagine it's much the same with your discipline, yes?"

Pash shrugged. "Not exactly. Hand gestures and words are easy, or at least what I'm studying. It's trying to get Lethos to listen to an acolyte asking him for a bit of glowing fuzz that makes it difficult."

Therrien smiled, and patted him gently on the shoulder. "I'm sure he's listening; perhaps you aren't asking the question right!"

Pash shrugged again. "I suppose. I have been an acolyte nearly three years; soon I will be a full Brother, and I think things will be different. How about you? How long have you been working with" he gestured at the study desk in the alcove, with the book laden pedestal beside it, "...your art?"

Therrien thought for a moment. "I suppose it has been about ten or so, though I admit it took nearly half that just to understand enough to make that little 'glowing fuzz', as you call it. It gets easier over time though."

Pash smiled. "I sure hope so."

"It does. Speaking of which, would you pardon me a moment? I do need to attend to some things before dinner."

"Certainly. Well met, my friend."

"And you as well."

Therrien stepped out of the room, and started towards his chambers, the image of Cillan fading into the back of his mind. He stopped short, realizing he had left his spell book in the great room. He turned and saw Pash still in the room, looking away and doing something with his hands. Therrien squinted, and walked quietly toward him, trying to get a better look. What he saw made the breath catch in his throat.

"*Lechte!*" Pash whispered, and a small glowing ball appeared, floating lazily away. Pash followed it with his gaze, and caught sight of Therrien. Pash's mouth gaped open in wordless horror.

Therrien looked back at him, expressionless. "Perhaps we should talk a bit more," he said in a low tone.

14. THE TEMPLE REVIEW

*A*fter Pash and his father had left the Temple, Brother Kern called Brother Prival into his office.

"*Assessment?*"

"*His memorization skills are high. He is athletic. He is good with his hands.*"

"*And?*"

"*He is poor at figures. He appears to lack interest in the brotherhood; actually, in all of the faith.*"

"*Did he say as much?*"

"*He said as little.*"

"*I see. So what are your overall thoughts?*"

"*He's another spoiled Council brat who was granted an audience out of deference to political station. The best we could hope for him is that he could be a scribe. He has no business being at the temple, except in one regard.*"

Brother Kern cocked his head. "*Go on.*"

"*When I read his aura, he radiated with an energy that I've not seen in a decade of testing.*"

Brother Kern leaned back in his chair. "*Send him to the Tower then. It sounds like a nice fit.*"

"*His father won't let him.*"

"*That isn't our problem.*"

"*His father won't let him because his brother died at the Tower.*"

"*An unfortunate circumstance, but still not our concern.*"

Brother Prival cleared his throat. "*His brother.*"

Brother Kern looked at him quizzically, then sat up with a start.

Brother Prival continued. "*I think we should go down to the vault and review what we know.*"

"*Hm. We might just have a new scribe.*"

15. ANOTHER DAGGER DRAWN

Thalen wandered back through the city, melting instinctively into the shadows. Stealth and survival was no longer simply a skill; it was an instinct, honed since the beginning.

His mother had died just as he aged from a boy to a man. Thalen had been home at the time; his father, out. He had been upstairs when he heard the commotion, and had quietly descended the stairs to see his mother tied to a chair in the kitchen, a man forcing a rag into her mouth to gag her. She snapped her gaze towards Thalen, causing the man to whirl around. At first, Thalen didn't dare move. Then slowly, he slid his hands into his pockets and leaned against the bannister. His mother's eyes went wide; the assassin's eyes also registered surprise. The killer stood to the side of Thalen's mother, so that she was in full view. Locking eyes with Thalen, the attacker plunged a dagger into her left breast twice, once high and once low, repeating the procedure on the right. Thalen matched the assassin's gaze, the outline of his mother struggling in the periphery of his vision. The assassin looked at Thalen's mother, struggling for a breath through the fistful of rag in her mouth. He pulled the rag out, and she panted for breath, her punctured lungs slowly crumpling as her chest cavity filled with air.

The assassin looked back at Thalen, who remained coolly leaning against the stairwell. As his victim finally stopped struggling, the assassin casually wiped his dagger on her blouse, then sheathed it. The assassin walked toward the back door, then paused. He quickly turned and tossed something at Thalen. Thalen glanced down at the object, then back up again, but the assassin was already gone.

His father had howled when he had returned, but it was clearly more out of fear and rage than of sorrow.

Thalen slipped out of his memories and back into the present, checking his room for signs of intrusion. Finding none, he settled in for the night; he was going to need his rest to deal with Ellias.

"Have you looked for him? What do I pay you for? You know I am expecting someone!" Councilman Ellias shoved his servant roughly between the shoulder blades and went back to staring out over the balcony. He was annoyed, though truly it wasn't with Thalen. The Temple's outdated sense of entitlement was troublesome. True, they had founded the Solypse many moons ago, but their claim on the city, much like his interest in the temple's opinion, had long since past. Though the temple had ceded administrative control over Solypse to the council, it retained honorary voting positions on the council. Unfortunately, the brotherhood seemed far more interested in their own agenda than in the interests in Solypse. Recently, a temple representative had taken a very firm stance against some of the council's policies. Ellias smiled. If all had gone according to plan, Brother Prival wouldn't be a problem anymore. Ellias strode out onto his balcony and looked out over the dark grey evening, pinpoints of light springing up to greet people at their homes or at the inns. The top of the wizarding tower, shrouded in perpetually glowing purple fog, stood out prominently over the city. From his position, he could just barely see gryphons and their riders landing in the aviary at the top as they changed out the guard.

"Councilman."

Ellias whirled around. Seeing the assassin lounging in the chair behind him, he quickly regained his composure. The assassin was frowning. "Thalen. Give me good news."

The assassin shook his head. "I wish I could. It seems you may have a problem."

"Does Brother Prival live?"

"Oh no, he is quite dead, I assure you; but not by my hand." Thalen related what he had seen in the temple dormitory. Ellias' eyes grew wide.

"You were supposed to make it look like he died in his sleep!" He exclaimed.

"As I said, this was not my doing. To be honest, I'm not sure what might have done it; it was as if a wild animal snuck in." Thalen waved his hand casually in the air. "There were pieces...everywhere."

"They're going to accuse the council, do you realize that?" He paused. "However, Cillan will get her job done, unlike some people..." He narrowed his eyes at Thalen, then relaxed and stared off into the purple cloud, watching another gryphon take flight. "Yes," he said wistfully, "this might actually work out better than I had ever expected."

Thalen grinned wickedly. Having apprenticed under Cillan, he knew just how deadly she could be.

16. POWER AND CONTROL

He leaned on his desk for a moment, his eyes closed. "Nanong come here. I have something interesting to show you."

The gnome quickly scurried from his chambers to the Necromancer's side. "Yes, Gerrus? What can I do to be of service?"

"Observe. You already have seen this," the necromancer turned to the corpses and uttered a brief phrase, and one stood up.

Nanong stood with his mouth agape. Though he had indeed seen a corpse reanimated, it normally was a complex series of gestures and intonations. Gerrus had simplified and refined it down to a mere phrase; truly Gerrus' power was more formidable than even he had realized. Nanong forcibly regained his composure.

"Yes master, I have."

"And you have seen this," Gerrus made another intonation, slightly longer, and the rest of the group rose to join the one already standing.

"Yes master."

"But now observe what happens when I do this." Gerrus made another intonation, longer and more complex. The zombies began milling about, then settled in a formation, with one at the front.

"You taught them to be soldiers?"

"No; better." He held up a closed hand, and opened it. A cockroach scurried down his sleeve and disappeared into his robes. "So little intelligence, yet they work together. They are like a hive."

Nanong instantly grasped why his master was sharing this. His flesh golem was little more than a collection of independent parts sewn together, and animated. There was no cohesion, no common aenima. This could change all that.

Gerrus handed him a scroll, loosely tied shut. "Study this in your free time, and see what use you can make of it. Also, I have need of some items from the traders above." Gerrus handed him a pouch and a list.

"Yes master, my thanks." Nanong's excitement was almost palpable as he hurried off to his quarters. Once Nanong had left, Gerrus spoke a quick word of command, and all the zombies fell to the ground, lifeless once more. He looked past them, regarding the dingy room, the piles of corpses, and the ornate door behind them. The door had been carved with intricate carvings and inlaid with gemstones, making little effort to conceal the value of what once lay within. Soon, it would contain something far more precious.

17. THE COMPANIONS DINE IN SHOAL

Larrik rolled out of his cot, his muscles complaining as he rose to his feet. Though he enjoyed the journey, he hadn't been in combat in a long time, and he felt it in his bones. He opted to keep his traveling leathers on.

He hadn't traveled much in recent years, but there was a long time where that was all he did—sleeping in caverns, eating what he could hunt, and drinking water that he foraged from underground streams. It all came to him as second nature now, and his leathers still fit him like a second skin. It felt good to be out again.

Larrik stepped into the great room.

"Ah there you are Brother Larrik, just in time. We still have some time, if you want to freshen up."

Larrik raised a bushy eyebrow at the magician.

"Yes, well, perhaps not then...Is there anything I can get you? Water perhaps?"

"Ale perhaps?"

"Begging your pardon, Brother Larrik. I didn't think you were allowed to imbibe. Certainly."

"If I were a Brother, ye'd be right."

"I apologize; I didn't realize-"

"Ye didn't ask."

The magician squirmed uncomfortably. "My apologies."

"About that ale?"

"Indeed, right away." Therrien hustled to the pantry.

Therrien came back with a tray with three mugs on it for his guests, and offered them around. Pash and Cillan passed. Shrugging, Larrik downed all three.

"So, should I call you..."

"Just Larrik."

"Larrik it is then."

Larrik looked hopefully inside the third tankard. He sighed heavily.

Therrien took a steadying breath. "We should get started, I think."

Larrik ducked into his room and retrieved his pack.

"You can leave your things here; I assure you they will be safe."

Larrik smirked. "We've come bearin' gifts for our courteous hosts."

Pash and Cillan regarded him curiously.

"We do?" asked Pash.

"Aye."

They set out on the path from Therrien's home, while Therrien cheerily described the various sights and highlights of the colony. Pash's ears burned hotly as he listened. Cillan seemed to happily eat up every word, asking about the roads, the people, the lights, and seemingly everything she could come up with. He was an acolyte, which meant a vow of celibacy, but the contrast in her affections still stung.

Larrik, meanwhile, followed and listened in sheer amazement that the mage could talk as much as he did. It seemed as if the young human knew the intricate details of everything in the colony, and was intent on sharing all of them before they arrived at their destination.

They arrived at the Mayor's house, not a moment too soon for Larrik or Pash, and seemingly far too short of a journey for Cillan or Therrien. Therrien knocked; before he could announce their presence, the Lord Mayor swept the door open grandly.

"Come in, my honored guests!"

As Larrik and Pash crossed the threshold, they were met with handshakes and armclasps from the rotund man. Cillan received a meaty kiss upon the back of her hand, and Therrien simply received a strong clap on the shoulder. Inside, the great room had a roaring fire in the fireplace that illuminated the magnificent feast that had been laid out on the table.

Pash cleared his throat in surprise. "I must admit, I wasn't expecting such a grand presentation. I- We are flattered and honored."

"Oh, think nothing of it. We humble colonists of Shoal are the ones honored. It isn't every day that we are visited by Brothers of the temple, or representatives of the council." He gave Cillan an exaggerated wink.

As they sat down to the table, Nar'el nodded toward Larrik. "Brother Larrik, would you do me the honor of blessing the meal?"

"I appreciate the thought, Yer Mayorness, but I'd rather pass that along to Acolyte Pash here. And it's just Larrik, not Brother Larrik."

Nar'el's voice dropped. "I see. Very well then." He said flatly.

As they dined, they discussed the origins of the colony, the wild dreams of creating the new frontier, and the unique challenges of the uncivilized wilderness.

Larrik's eye twinkled. "How do ye know what time it is?"

Nar'el laughed. "You know, we don't. We all generally sleep at the same time, and all generally get up at the same time. We don't have the Veil here; it's just sort of a community agreement. Which," he admitted, "can cause problems sometimes."

"Did ye ever stop to think that if you trade, then you're going to have to have some sort of time keepin'?"

"I suppose you have a point." He laughed. "Then again, if we get traders to show up, I'm sure we'll make a point of being awake to greet them."

Larrik smiled. "Well, that's mighty sportin' of ye, but it shan't be necessary, methinks." He reached into his pack, and pulled out a stone pyramid the size of a cook's large bowl. "The temple wanted me to bring you a gift as a symbol of a lasting partnership."

Nar'el looked confused. "That's, um, very thoughtful. Thank you."

Larrik shook his head. "It isn't just a pretty rock. Do you have somewhere around here that is dark?"

Nar'el nodded, and hesitantly led Larrik towards the passage at the back of the great hall. Curious, Therrien, Pash, and Cillan followed behind.

As they got further from the bright room, it became clear what Larrik was talking about. The pyramid was glowing with a low blue color.

"I...see." Nar'el said hesitantly.

"It's a day-rock. It's dark blue because it is night in Solypse. When morning comes, it will glow orange, and be bright white at high sun. Shoal will always have a day and night."

Nar'el nodded thoughtfully. "I suppose I should keep this in my quarters, or in the town hall, for safe keeping."

Larrik shook his head and turned the pyramid upside down. "See these words? When you are ready, you have but to read the inscription, and it will rise in the air, and burn with the brightness of a thousand candles and the warmth of Lethos' blessing. The whole of the colony should be able to see it from wherever they might be."

Nar'el bowed low. "I'm - we - are flattered by your temple's thoughtful gift."

The gathering returned to the table. Nar'el seated himself at the head of the table, insisting that Cillan and Larrik take the adjacent seats. "Therrien, make yourself useful, and fetch some wine from the far room, would you?"

"Certainly, Lord Mayor" he replied stiffly, and excused himself from the table.

Nar'el turned his attentions toward Cillan. "Now dear, what can I do for the council?"

"I'm not sure I am the one to address that, Lord Mayor."

"If there is anything..." He squeezed her leg under the table, causing her to take a sharp breath. "Anything at all that I can take care of for you, or anything I can do to make your stay more comfortable, just let me know."

Therrien set the bottle down between them with a loud thunk. "I am sure, Lord Mayor, that the lady is more than capable of taking care of things herself."

Nar'el removed his hand from her leg, only dropping his gaze to look her over once again. "Yes well... If you need anything, you know where to find me."

Cillan stood up quickly. "Sir wizard, weren't you going to show me around the colony a bit?"

Therrien nodded, and extended the crook of his arm to her, ignoring the glare from Nar'el.

Larrik struggled to keep his composure, a smile tugging at the corners of his mouth. "So, let's talk about establishing a trade route."

Cillan walked along the glowing path, the curling smoke of the blacksmith's house in the distance, disappearing into the darkness. "You know I could have handled that myself."

Therrien gave her a sly glance. "The question in my mind wasn't whether you could handle yourself; it was whether you would come with me."

Cillan furrowed her brow and pursed her lips like a petulant child. "Yes, well, it was for the best anyway. I don't have much stomach for politics."

"Surely you realize that the point of a sword is simply the sharper edge of politics? Being in the hire of the council simply means you are a tool for them to use or discard."

"Well," she said hotly, "coin in my pocket still beats a fool's errand into the wilderness. Or is fetching wine for the Lord Mayor answering some higher calling that I am not aware of?"

Therrien stopped in his tracks. "Perhaps you are right."

"I - Look, nothing personal. I just can't fathom why you would willingly be, essentially, his servant."

Therrien resumed walking. "I'm not sure either, anymore. I wanted to travel, adventure, be away from Solypse... But I'm starting to realize that there's enlightenment to be had without traveling the entirety of the depths. Or even if there isn't, that wandering around doesn't necessarily provide it either."

"Perhaps you had to wander off to figure that out."

"Perhaps." His face lit up. "Want to see the Lord Mayor's 'Love Tunnel'?"

She grinned wickedly. "That sounds...exciting."

18. THALEN RETURNS HOME

Thalen was relieved; the meeting with Councilman Ellias had gone far better than he had expected. Granted, he had only walked away with half the fee, but the whole job was botched. Also, he hadn't actually had to do any work. His only concern, and an increasing one, was what the guild master would say. This wouldn't have been guilded work; they never crossed marks at the same time, lest they cross their customers. *Unless he was being set up.* He pondered this for a moment, then dismissed it. There had been no one to receive him. Though the guild did occasionally extinguish its own, it was usually gruesome, and was always successful. Last moon, a half-orc with a penchant for ale had spent one coin too many in the tavern. Caught sneaking into a window, he was apprehended, and confessed under interrogation. Before he was released, the guards found him in his cell, dead. Though it was clear from his wounds that he had been tortured to death, it wasn't clear how his killers had gotten into or out of the jail.

Thalen glanced around to ensure that no one saw him, then slipped down an alleyway in the merchant district. At the end, marked by the raised stones around it, was a wide pitch hole used for garbage and relieving bowels. He walked up and grabbed hold of the stones on either side of the hole, lowering his legs and torso down the middle. He swung his legs forward until he felt the rugs of the ladder. He hooked his feet into the rungs and felt for the hand-hold on the underside of the pitch hole. Grabbing the ladder, he climbed down the hole several lengths, until he felt rough scrapes cut into the ladder rungs. He tensed his body, crouching down on his legs, and jumped across the hole. He landed in the tunnel entranceway. He glanced down into the hole and grimaced. Many a new initiate into the guild had missed the leap, and ended up plunging into the fathoms-deep river of sewage below.

He wound his way through the maze of tunnels, slipping past traps set to dissuade anyone either curious or foolish enough (perhaps both) to continue on. He stepped into the Assassins' Guild Hall, and glanced around for familiar faces. Of the dozen or so members that loitered in the main room, most were human or half elf. It seemed that humans took well to the profession. Their blood coursed with a certain level of ferocity, as if they all tried to cram as much experience as a centuries-old dwarf or elf into sixty summers.

Nodding at the barkeep—an old blade who had since retired—he headed to the corridor at the back. At the end of the corridor, was an ornate door that led to a big open room. Finding the door unlocked, he stepped in, closing the door behind him. He murmured the word of locking; he paused, and set a trap by the door, just in case. The room of assignment supposedly would alarm if anyone other than the guild master entered; still, he didn't like to take chances.

He looked around at the vast library filled with boxes of job ledgers, each numbered. Each assassin had a number assigned to them that only they, and presumably the guild master knew. He stepped in and locked the door behind him, and headed down the aisle towards book 36128. He located the book box, and brought it to the table at the front of the room. Carefully, he enunciated the words that would release the wards on the box. His book box, like all the others, was enspelled to secure the books from everyone, save the owners and the guild master.

He lifted his ledger out of the box and set it on the table. Opening the book, the pages opened limply. Though he wasn't at the end of his ledger, he was well past the halfway point. He was young, and he was both talented and ambitious; his volume of work spoke for itself. At the end of the last page, there was already an annotation for the job he had begun, and the initial date. Beneath it, he wrote:

Arrived unseen at location to service target. Target was already dead upon arrival, body in pieces. Left without incident. Not seen on departure. Lack of actual servicing of the target decreased payment by half.

He laid the book back into the box, and laid several of the coins in a small compartment at one end of the box. Fastening the lid on it, he uttered the phrase of locking, then put the box back on the shelf. A good meal was coming up: even at half, murder paid well; when it was the council, it was even better.

Payment was fine, but the thrill of it was what made it worthwhile. Thalen smiled at the memory of his first kill. *After his mother had died, Thalen resolved to put an end to his father, before his father's dealings could put an end to him. He waited that night until after his father had fallen asleep, sorrows putting him several cups into a deep intoxicated slumber. Thalen stole into the basement where he knew his father concealed his wealth. He filled two large bags, quietly making a trip up to the hall. Finally, he filled saddlebags with what money he could carry, and set them by the front door.*

Ascending the stair, Thalen quietly eased open his father's door. The drunken snoring continued, unabated. Thalen eased his new dagger from its sheath, and surveyed the old man. His father's passions—gambling and drinking—had finally caught up to him. Thalen wasn't about to let them turn him into another casualty of his father's weakness.

He reached over and turned up the oil lamp beside the bed, staring at his father one last time. His father stirred, rolling over and squinting in the bright lamplight. His brow furrowed. "Thalen? What are you doing in here?"

Thalen responded with the dagger, the four swift symmetrical cuts mirroring those on his mother. His father wheezed at him in confusion, attempting to sit up. Thalen planted his hands on the old man's shoulders, flinging him back on the bed. His father's breathing became more rapid and shallow; he struggled to sit up, but lacked the strength the second time around. Thalen stepped out into the hallway and retrieved the bags of coins. As his father lay dying, he poured the coins onto his father's body, the gold and silver reflecting in the lamplight as it rained down on his punctured chest like a tarnished waterfall. By the time the second bag was empty, Thalen's father was still. Thalen wiped the dagger on his father's shirt; re-sheathing it, he tucked it back into his belt. He turned heel and walked to the door, scooping up the saddlebags behind him, not once looking back.

He wasn't a child anymore, though he was not yet a man. Though he grasped that life on his own would be difficult, he still remained possessed of youthful optimism. He was convinced that he would land on his feet, never dissuaded by the fish flayers in shanty town, or the begging urchins that filled the streets and alleys of the merchant district. His coin-filled saddlebags did little to dissuade him of this perspective. Accordingly, he set himself up in a nice inn room, slipping out in the evenings and conducting 'business.' He had an innate talent at sneaking about, coupled with his casual indifference to the value of human life. This pairing of talents found appreciation from people with money and a need for discretion, and whispered word of mouth spread his client list, occasionally even overlapping his client list with his target list.

19. CILLAN GOES TO WORK

Cillan woke with a start. *How long had she been asleep?* She delicately moved Therrien's arm from across her body. She rolled out of the bed quietly, catching herself on her fingertips and the toes of her boots. She stood up and smoothed out her rumpled clothing, and tiptoed out of the room.

The fire had died to low embers in the fireplace. She crept through the low glow towards Larrik's room. Seeing him asleep, she gratefully tiptoed to her quarters and quietly packed her things. She slipped out of the house and headed across the shortcut that Therrien had thoughtfully shown her the night before. Weaving around the rocks, she found her way to the mayor's back-passage, and slipped in. She glided quietly down the length of the passage, until she reached the end—an entry way concealed by illusion to appear to be part of the mayor's chamber wall. She stepped through the entryway into the room, quickly scanning for traps. An oil lamp cast dim flickering shadows from the mayor's sleeping form onto the wall, the leftover smell of wine effervescing from his pores and breath. She crept up beside his head and slipped her dagger from its sheath, leaning down low enough to feel his hot breath on her cheek. The mayor's eyes flicked open, and went wide. She instantly clutched a hand over his mouth and nose. He struggled to free his head, but she pressed down firmer. Reaching down with her free hand, she drew her blade across his throat. He struggled a bit longer as she kept her hand firmly on his face, a low frothing and whistling noise emanating from his throat as blood crept into his lungs, until at last his body was still.

As she relaxed her grip on his face, she heard a quiet strangled cry. She squinted into the shadows, and saw what she had missed in the low light before: a young woman, not much older than birthing age, tears streaming down her cheeks. Cillan's eyes narrowed into slits. "Go home to your husband." The woman frantically nodded, and gathered her clothes as she ran into the tunnel. Cillan cleaned the blade on the blanket, and re-sheathed it. She glanced around at the room. Mayor though he was, there weren't many possessions to be had in Shoal. She grabbed a pouch of coins and started for the tunnel, then paused. She swiftly backtracked into the great hall, and spotted what she was looking for. "You might be useful", she mused, and slipped the object into her pack.

She headed for the tunnel. It was time to disappear.

Therrien woke to a guard gently shaking his shoulder. "Sir, there's been trouble," the guard whispered. "Lord Mayor Nar'el has been killed."

Therrien sat bolt upright. "Where are the outsiders?"

"The dwarf and the cleric are still sleeping. The girl is missing."

Therrien cursed quietly.

"Where? How? Who found him?"

"It appears that someone took him by surprise while he was sleeping, and slit his throat. Smith Ragern was the one who spoke to the colony guard. He claimed he went to talk to the Lord Mayor about issues of indiscretion, and he found him that way."

Therrien winced. "Where is Smithy now?"

"We have him in custody," the guard said hesitantly, "given...well, we thought he might have had a reason to be upset with the Lord Mayor."

"Come with me. Leave a guard posted here; if the other travelers wake, have them escorted to the Lord Mayor's house."

Therrien hurried out the door, guard in tow. By the time they arrived at the Lord Mayor's home, a crowd had gathered outside. The guard parted the crowd, Therrien in tow. Therrien looked around the great room, noting that nothing looked disturbed. Stepping into the bedroom, he saw the corpse still lying in bed, the head rolled to the side at an unnatural angle. He noted the blankets were disturbed on the other side of the bed. He tapped his chin. He leaned down over Nar'el, and picked up the scent of a familiar musky perfume, the same that was wafting up from his shirt. He turned to the guard. "Wait here. I have to talk to someone."

"What should we do with Smithy Ragern?"

"Wait until I get back, then let him go."

The guard cocked his head to one side. "Let him go, sir?"

"Yes. But not until I get back." Therrien turned and walked swiftly through the false wall into the tunnel. Once out of sight, he broke into a run until he got to the Blacksmith's house and pounded on the door. "Cael!"

He pounded again. "Cael! It's Therrien! Open up!"

Cael opened the door a crack. Her eyes were bloodshot, and rimmed in pink from crying.

"Yes?" she asked, barely managing a whisper.

"Who did it?"

Cael's lip trembled. "Did what?"

"I don't have time for games right now. Who did it?"

Cael began to sob, and let the door open.

He put his hand gently on her shoulder. "I won't tell anyone I spoke to you. But I need to know."

"I- I don't know who she was. I heard this awful noise, and when I looked-" Cael started sobbing. "He wasn't dead yet, but his throat was cut, and there was an awful noise coming from his throat."

"Did you love him?"

"No. I mean, I don't think so. But still-"

He sighed, and gave her a gentle hug and a kiss on the forehead. "I think you have a lot of thinking to do." Therrien left the homestead, less hurried in his return. There was no doubt it was Cillan; he felt like a fool. *"But what of the others?"* He wondered.

He arrived back at the Lord Mayor's home to find the crowd, the outsiders from Solypse, and Smith Ragern standing outside. Smith Ragern was red faced in a mixture of embarrassment and rage, confined by shackles he had forged himself.

Therrien walked up to the smithy and leaned over to whisper in his ear.

"What's done is done. You can't fix the past, but you can fix the future."

Ragern moved his head back, regarding Therrien with sorrow. He said nothing.

Therrien addressed him in a low tone. "Remember that 'what has been' isn't always as important as 'what will be'."

Therrien tilted his head back, and said loudly, "Let Ragern go. It wasn't him." A murmur passed through the crowd. The guards released the shackles, and Ragern bowed his head towards Therrien.

Therrien turned to look at Larrik and Pash.

Larrik looked at Therrien, his brow furrowed. They weren't shackled, but the compliment of guards who had escorted them there was a clear indication that they weren't quite welcome to leave. It was his responsibility to bring the boy out on the road and give him a chance to test his spiritual devotion; if this didn't push the boy, then he wasn't sure what would. He looked over at Pash, pale as a ghost and trembling. *We all start somewhere*, he thought.

"How well do you know Cillan?" queried Therrien, looking directly at Larrik.

"Not well at all. Begging your pardon, yer mageness, you may actually know her a bit better than we do at this point."

Pash's eyes opened wide, his lips pressed into such a firm line that they were almost white. Therrien blushed furiously, and turned to address the crowd, in a loud voice. "I have very strong reasons to believe that your female companion may have been responsible for the events that transpired last night. Though I do not wish for Shoal to be unhospitable to guests, most especially clergy, I must—for the good of the colony—establish what your role may have been."

A murmur passed through the crowd. Therrien waited for it to die down, and then he continued. "I know from the wards that I placed, that you did not leave your quarters last night, and that she acted alone. What we need to establish is why Brothers of the temple of Lethos would escort an assassin into our midst."

Pash broke his silence. From a squeaking shout, he addressed the crowd. "We didn't even know she was coming until she showed up that morning. I don't even know how she found out we were going!"

Therrien clasped his hands behind his back, addressing the crowd once more. "Though this is a fine tale, how do we know the truth of it?"

Larrik locked eyes with Therrien, and glared, his voice rising so that all could hear. "What the boy says is true. I know that yer magic has us tellin' the truth; there's no use denying it. There's no reason to continue askin' questions. Acolyte Pash and I would like to offer our humble services as servants of Lethos, that we might give Nar'el his last rites." He paused. "Yer welcome to observe, to make sure we don't steal anything, if you like."

Therrien stared at the dwarf, his mouth slightly agape. "Ye-yes. I see the truth of what you say. The colony appreciates your offer, and is grateful for your services, if it wouldn't be too much trouble." A murmur of approval passed through the crowd. Therrien hesitated. "I think- I think that given the circumstances, however, that it would be best if we sent an escort with you, for your return." Larrik furrowed his brow fiercely at Therrien. Therrien held his hands up in front of him. "For your safety", he added hastily. "We are wary of what lurks in the tunnels most days. Today, there is an assassin added to that. We are only concerned for your safety."

Larrik scoffed. "Will it be another squad of armed guards? I think we will take our chances."

Therrien shook his head. "I will personally escort you. I pledged to keep him safe, and I failed. His death is nearly as much my responsibility is it was the assassin's blade."

Larrik contemplated his words, and relaxed a touch. The encounters with the creatures on their descent to Shoal had been a close call. Without Cillan, they might already be dead. *Cillan.* Anger crept back into his mind, this time directed at the traitor that had been in their midst.

A gasp went up in the crowd. A shout of "No!" came from the back; from the middle, a stout shouldered dwarven maiden spoke up. "Who will lead us if you go?"

Therrien gestured downward with his palms, attempting to quiet the crowd. "Tallen, as Captain of the Guard, is nearly as familiar with the running of Shoal as Nar'el or myself. He is a fine choice for a leader. He will take good care of Shoal."

The half-dwarf swiped the air with her muscular arm. "I'd trust a staff before I would trust yer wigglin' fingers. I'll go. Someone needs to be watchin' you."

Therrien contemplated this for a moment, then shook his head. "Halail, I appreciate your support, and your company would be much welcomed, but your place is here with Mikkel and the dwarflings. We will be fine."

Halail's face purpled with rage. Mikkel, standing next to her, giggled. He knew what was coming.

"MY PLACE?" she bellowed. "Yer talkin' to me, and ye think ye can tell me MY PLACE? Riordan as my witness, if you say that again, TeeTee, you will know where my PLACE is!"

Therrien blushed at the sound of his childhood nickname. He hadn't forgotten that she was the one who had taken him under her wing in his misguided youth. Clearly she hadn't forgotten either. Mikkel grinned ear to ear, the twin braids of his beard quivering as he held back laughter. "Thank you for yer concern Therrien! But I think you'll be takin' the lady!"

Therrien held up his hands in protest. "Please! Her skills are too valuable to pull away from the town right now. We need her here." Mikkel contemplated this. Halail was not only the primary healer in town, she was also the person who knew best how to heal hearts and minds. If anyone could help the townsfolk through this time, it was her. He conferred quietly with his wife.

"Fine then!" he said to Therrien, raising his voice. "Ye can get away from her, but not away from me and me hammer!"

Halail harrumphed, and wrapped her arm around Mikkel's, and rested her head on his shoulder. She nuzzled her beardless cheek against his worn tunic. He turned his head to the side and kissed the top of her head.

Therrien sighed and allowed a slight smile. They were a unique couple, well known and loved. She had been a wandering depths druid when she had caught Therrien trying to steal from her, many years ago in Solypse. Rather than turn him over to the guard, she elected to take him in. She taught him the ways of Riordan, and soon thereafter they met Mikkel. They all became close friends, becoming inseparable. As time wore on, the dwarf and the half-dwarf fell in love, and were married. Four dwarflings later, Halail had continued to follow and practice her druidic ways, while Mikkel focused on tending to the children. All three had joined the caravan to Shoal together, in hopes of adventure. Though Halail wouldn't be joining them, there was no way that Mikkel would let Therrien go without him.

"As you desire, gentle dwarves. I suggest you go prepare your things; we will be departing with all due haste, after these gentlemen see to our dearly departed leader."

20. THE DEVOURER

The creature stirred, feeling something tugging at its consciousness. Buried in the deep primordial layers of the ethereal sea of darkness, time was of little consequence to the creature; but it knew that it had fed recently. It had been good. The creature slid across the identical fields of uniform darkness, unable to resist the call. It wasn't sure it wanted to resist—not yet anyway. It had already spent an eternity feeding on cursed souls floating by, but this was different. This had been *fresh*. It had never experienced the sheer joy of bathing in warm viscera, inhaling a soul as the soul escaped its vessel. More importantly, the creature had never felt such a surge of raw power before. It felt the master tug at him once more, and faster it climbed, toward a pinprick of light in the distance. The master had ripped the soul back out of the creature; oh, how that had *enraged* it. Still, it had tasted, and that was almost enough. Even now, it felt stronger. Hungrier.

In the crystal cavern, Gerrus continued the incantation, focused on the swirling portal before him. He stood in a circle, surrounded by mystic runes carefully circumscribed around the circle. Lights from candles danced in a thousand reflections, making the room glow with brightness. He coaxed at the swirling blackness, willing the creature to come forward. After a long while, a shadowy figure became visible in the hazy view through the portal. He continued intoning his spell, the staff in his hand glowing furiously. Finally, the devourer emerged from the portal, floating in mid-air. Forged from nightmares, it was black as an oil slick, with twelve legs attached to a bulbous body, not unlike a squid. The devourer's mouth comprised the entire bottom of its body, wide enough to fit a man over his head, past his shoulders. The double rows of teeth would part occasionally, and a set of four elongated arms would reach out, casting about for whatever they might grasp. Gerrus telepathically communicated his wishes to the devourer, and the devourer spirited off, passing through the rocks as if it were flying through air. Exhausted from the summoning ritual, he leaned heavily on his staff, his body wracked with pain in his joints, his lungs, and his skull. It was an extraordinarily difficult ritual, but it was worth it. He looked the at his staff, and grinned. It only had one soul at the moment, but soon it would have hundreds, perhaps thousands more, feeding power back into him. He had only just begun collecting for his transformation. Each spirit captured would bring him more power; power that would last an eternity.

21. LAST RITES

Therrien clasped his hands together in front of his waist, and stood back from Pash. Pash was methodically preparing the body for last rites. Larrik stood beside Therrien, directing Pash in the ritual.

Pash had already laid Nar'el out on a white sheet, covered only by a loin cloth. He reached into the satchel, and withdrew the proper oils—one for the legs, to prepare him for the journey to the spirit world; one for the arms, to symbolize the strength of the gods, and one on his head and breast, symbolizing the soul itself.

"Larrik, I'm not sure I understand why we do this. He is already dead, is he not?"

Larrik regarded him curiously. "Aye...yer point?"

"If he is already dead, then how can we prepare his soul for the journey? Wouldn't it make more sense to do this while someone is alive?"

"Aye lad, if it were for him. The worms and the wild things would just as soon eat him without the oils."

"But I thought this was to bear his spirit to the next world. The prayers, the rituals...if not for him, then for who?"

Therrien looked Pash over. In some ways, it seemed strange to him that Pash had chosen clerical life as his profession. Then again, though Pash only appeared to be a few short years younger than him, Therrien's years working with the colony had taught him more than he would have ever expected. "Pash, it's for everyone else. Nar'el's closure came with a blade to the neck; the rest of the colony is confused and upset. Even though he wasn't the most popular person in Shoal, he was still like family. Rituals like these help people have some closure, some finality."

Pash stopped for a moment, and contemplated Therrien's words. "If that's the case, then why am I preparing the body with you two? Why are we not doing it in front of everyone, with everyone?"

Larrik spoke up. "Because it's our job, lad. Because our job is to provide that closure to those fine people, and doing this reminds us why we are doing it in the first place."

Across the cavern, Mikkel was carefully preparing his pack. Though he had willingly volunteered to undertake the trip with Therrien, already he felt mild pangs of regret. He gently put down the blanket he was rolling, and gazed out the window. Halail was playing with their youngest, Teagan. He already knew he would miss Halail terribly, and the four children as well. However, this journey, and all the journeys like this, were why Riordan had graced them with life. At an early age, Mikkel had felt the calling to wander. Riordan, the patron father of deep druids and rangers, had provided him with ample opportunity, and blessed him with excellent companions as well.

Mikkel turned from the window, and cast a look around their home. A wall by their bedroom stood half-finished, toys lay scattered about. He wished he had time to finish the wall, or clean up the toys. He sighed. There was never a good time to leave. Though every departure yielded a new beginning, there were some that he disliked more than others, especially those that didn't include Halail. Mikkel packed the last of his things, and pulled on the grey-black travel cloak he had worn for many years. With an air of finality, he plucked a fine steel warhammer, nearly equal to his four foot stature, from its resting place over the fire mantle.

Mikkel stepped outside, watching the four children giggle and tackle Halail. He opened his mouth to say something, but the words stuck in his throat. He cleared his throat noisily, causing Halail to look up.

Mikkel gazed upon his wife. She was truly the balance between strength and beauty. Though her barren chin whiskers were considered ghastly by most dwarves, he found it to be one of her best features. The four children clung to her as he looked on, her blinking back tears, while he prepared for his trip. She put on his best and biggest smile for him. "Don't be lookin' sad at me, dwarf. Ye' were built for walkin, not for tendin' fires and playing nursemaid!"

He gave a sad smile. "But the children-"

She waved his concerns away. "Pah. The children'll barely know yer gone. It'll do 'em some good to do some things on their own."

He exhaled deeply. "And you. We haven't been apart in a very long while."

She put a hand on his arm, and held him tight. "All journeys we take, we take together, whether we be near or far...."

He smiled, reciting the rest of their wedding vows. "in life, or even in the journey beyond." They embraced tightly for several minutes. "I must go," he whispered.

Halail released him, and bowed her head with a slight smile in return. "So it must be, my love."

Halail kissed him gently, and beckoned the children over. The children ran to embrace him; they overwhelmed him, nearly knocking him to the ground. He giggled in spite of himself and hugged and kissed them all goodbye. He walked down the path toward Therrien's home, glancing backward at Halail waving. The last thing he saw as he dipped out of sight at the last hill was her madly grinning visage, so far away that he didn't see the tears streaming down her ruddy cheeks.

By the time he reached Therrien's home, Therrien was already packed, as were Larrik and Pash. Pash marveled at the small satchel perched in the middle of Mikkel's back, and cast his eyes at the ground out of embarrassment. The pack on his own back was nearly big enough to tuck Mikkel in, satchel and all. Likewise, Pash was surprised at the relative speed at which Therrien deftly selected the key items that were needed for their trip. Pash was dressed in his clerical leathers, though not squeaking quite as much as when they had first set out, gods be praised. Therrien donned a set of blue robes that flowed gently around him as he swept around his home. Therrien swiftly picked up sachets of herbs, vials of various unknown types, and other small trinkets and stuffed them into a seemingly endless array of pockets in the robes.

They walked the short distance from his home to the gate, where he exchanged brief pleasantries and goodbyes with some of the colony guard. Larrik fell into his normal role on point; Mikkel padded quietly behind him. Larrik glanced back over his shoulder at Mikkel, then resumed his swift pace.

Trailing behind, Therrien tilted his nose to the air and drew in a deep breath. Truly, he had missed the open road. Pash plodded along next to him, lost in his own thoughts.

"Tell me Pash, why the Temple?"

Pash bit his lip. "I think that serving others is the highest calling there is."

Therrien eyed him warily. "Is that so?"

"Absolutely!" Pash insisted, "Why else would we forge alliances, friendships, or marriages, but to commune with one another?"

Therrien considered this for a moment. "This is true, but one does not have to devote one's life to Lethos for that."

Pash blushed. "Yes, well,,,this was the option that presented it self."

Therrien persisted. "Pash, the life of a Monk of Lethos is the life of one completely devoted to his work and teachings. One should not choose to devote one's life to options that simply 'present themselves', wouldn't you agree?"

Pash stared off at Larrik in the distance. "This is about the other day, isn't it?"

Therrien nodded. "You need to understand what you did."

"I just repeated what I heard from you, and had the same result; that is all. Moreover, I committed heresy, according to the edicts of the Brotherhood." He paused. "Please- Please don't tell Larrik about what happened."

"Pash, learning magic isn't just repeating what you have heard. Understand, it took me over three years before I could cast even that simple cantrip. It takes studying, understanding the meaning behind the rhythm and the intonation, and getting the inflection exactly right."

Pash shrugged his shoulders, scuffing his feet along the ground.

"Pash, what I'm saying is that you may have a natural gift. I want to try to teach you a bit more, if you are willing to learn."

Pash contemplated his options.

"Pash, you lack faith. The brotherhood is not your calling."

Pash whirled to face him; the words stung as painfully as if he had been struck. "How dare you presume to question my devotion?"

Therrien matched Pash's gaze and held out a hand. "*Lechtë*", he whispered, and a small ball of light danced in his palm. He spoke in a low voice. "Then show me *your* light, my friend of faith."

22. FLIGHT

After Therrien had thoughtfully shown her the layout of the colony security, and the location of the wards that he had placed, slipping out of town was simple. She stopped for a second and rested a hand on a rock, and tried to catch her breath. She guessed that she had at least a couple hours' head start before they discovered the body, assuming the blacksmith's wife didn't speak up. She silently cursed herself for her weakness; she should have eliminated the girl. It was a wonder that she had progressed as far as she had, all things considered. True, she had nerves steely enough to take care of business when she needed to; but there was no joy for her in her work. She had found early on that she was good at what she did, and she far preferred to take care of a problem person quietly, rather than face them head on. It was, for her, a business arrangement of sorts. The others though... Thalen, for instance, took a perverse amount of pleasure in stalking and killing his prey; he was a natural born predator.

Thalen had proved to be as resourceful as he was feral. He had once faced an assignment to eliminate a well-guarded merchant, commissioned by a rival. The target was thought to be untouchable, surrounded by a phalanx of guards, with a home woven out of a web of traps and alarms. Rather than go directly after the merchant himself, Thalen tortured the merchant's neighbors to death. And then the families of his guards. And then the local grocer. Eventually, it became publically known that everyone that came into contact with or supported the merchant became a gruesome corpse. He was shunned into solitude, and eventually forced to close his business and return to the surface world. It was brutal, but it was incredibly effective.

Cillan breathed easier, and looked around her surroundings. She had just stepped through a narrow passage into a broad cavern, one that they had passed through on their way to Shoal. She searched the room for a manner in which to block the passage. Her normal compliment of equipment included all manner of things for dealing with things inside Solypse; being in the wild, she felt a bit disoriented. She looked around again, and saw a stand of massive mushrooms on the far side of the cavern, partially obscuring the cavern's exit passage beside them. They appeared to have been there for some time, having grown taller than a man. Some had already fallen to the ground dead, and others sprang up from around them.

Cillan walked over to one of the fallen mushroom logs. Balancing a torch in her left hand, she wrapped her right arm around it, and heaved. As she struggled to pick it up, the she felt dampness on her skin, followed by a foul odor. Liquid dripped into a puddle on the ground beneath where she had squeezed the mushroom. As she leaned her torch close to the puddle to look at it, the puddle erupted into bright orange flames, causing her to stumble backwards a few paces. After a few moments, the flames subsided, and eventually went out.

Cillan carefully set aside her pack and propped up her torch. One by one, she dragged several of the man-sized mushroom logs over to the narrow passage and stacked them up. By the time she had the last of the logs piled in the passageway, the stack was over waist-high. The logs leaked their fluid from where she had grabbed dragged them; a puddle was forming underneath her pile. Carefully, so as not to get too close to her torch, she took a spare shirt from her bag and thoroughly wiped down her hands and arms. When she was sure she had removed the fluid from her body, she held the shirt near her torch, until it erupted into a blazing ball of fire. Quickly, she tossed the shirt into the puddle under the pile of logs. The puddle ignited, and soon the entire pile was ablaze. Thick smoke poured in every direction. She shouldered her pack, grabbed her torch, and ran for the opening at the far side of the cavern.

She ran until she had put some distance between herself and the blaze. Though it wouldn't burn forever, it would slow them down, which would give her a bit more time. She slowed to a brisk walk, and contemplated her plans upon her return to Solypse. She needed to report in one last time to get paid, and let Councilman Ellias know that she would no longer be available for employment. She also needed to retrieve her belongings from the guild hall. After that... She hadn't gotten to that part. Solypse might not be the safest place for a retired master assassin; unfortunately, the only other major city in the depths was Bruemarrar, and she would stick out like a beacon in the night in the dwarf city.

She had amassed enough coin to either retire to a frugal life, or live very well for a few years. This was a tidy sum, though not uncommon for members of the guild. The guild members were paid very well for what they did, along with the requisite discretion. Most retired quite young, assuming they lived long enough to retire at all. Working for the council, she had been paid even better; however, the jobs had been far riskier.

Safely on the other side of the fire and smoke, she allowed her pace to slow, and her mind to wander. The cavern she was in now was filled with stones that glowed with bright purple and blue hues, with small transparent lizards darting across the rocks from time to time. In her few ventures outside of Solypse, she was always amazed that nature seemed to always need light to show its beauty. Many of the creatures of the depths could perceive with no light whatsoever, which was of course necessary. Because of this, nature hadn't deemed it necessary to grace many of them with colors. Indeed, most of the depths were monochromatic, which made rooms like this all the more dazzling. The dwarves of Bruemarrar seemed to understand this better than most; she recalled the city being a wonder of ornate carvings in darkness, and incredibly colorful ornamentation near the fires and forges.

Oh, how long ago that had been. Her trip to Bruemarrar had been a gift, of sorts, from her mother, when she wasn't much older than the blacksmith's bride. When she grew past her first ten-year, her mother gave up her former profession as a lady of the night, and vowed to raise Cillan "right". Her mother had raised her alone, slaving away on the docks, gutting fish from the moment that the first fishing boat pulled in for the day, until hours after the last vessel had docked for the night. Her mother had always tried to teach her that hard work would pay off, and some day she would be able to pull herself up to the next tier. All Cillan had seen was her mother work harder for the same paycheck and abuse, with no opportunity to leave Wallenbrook. Wallenbrook, better known as Shantytown, was where she had grown up, a subsection of Solypse known best for the massive river of sewage that separated it from the rest of the city. Thousands lived in Shantytown, mostly dockworkers and fishermen and other people who would prefer to be left alone. When her mother had arranged for her to apprentice to a merchant for a trip to the Dwarven city, she had jumped at the chance. She had met Corad on that trip, and they became fast friends. When they arrived at the Dwarven city, she was dismayed to see the merchants at work—for all their finery and flash, they made their coin by cajoling and groveling, always grumbling quietly about how it should have been more. The Dwarves were friendly, but treated them like servants—they knew the merchants survived on their trade, and that without the Dwarves, they would go home penniless. She confessed her dismay to Kith, and Corad had offered her another option, one that would shape her future.

His simple explanation had made much sense to her as a young girl at the time. "There are those who have things," he had said, "and they know how to keep things. There are those who don't have things, and they can't figure out how to earn enough to get things. And there are the others—those who realize that the only way to get things is to take them from those who keep them."

She told her mother that she was apprenticing to a merchant—which Corad actually was, though the bulk of his profits were realized elsewhere. He introduced her into the world of elaborate, high-value thieving. As she quickly showed her skill at the trade, he had brought her all the way into the fold. "You see," he had told her, "the people who keep things, will never give them away, even if others suffer, or even perhaps die. The people who suffer and die, they keep faith that they will succeed, but never rise above their station. The wealthy would put you under without remorse; why then, would you mourn their passing? If an assassin is sent, that assassin is sent by someone, and the blood is on that person's hands. An assassin is a tool, nothing more." She had wanted to believe him, and it made sense. Even now, his words had a certain poetic elegance about them, though she had grown to understand much more about the world. Though she still felt little remorse about doing her job, she realized that it wasn't for justice; it wasn't for social equality; it was simply for money.

She passed out of other side of the glowing cavern, her torch once more illuminating the path before her. The quiet was comforting, though she did feel a pang of regret. Therrien had been courteous, friendly even; she had forgotten what it felt like to be comfortable enough to enjoy herself with the company of another, unguarded. She sighed, the sound lost in the caverns ahead and behind. She felt badly for having used him; still, it was the job. *It was always the job.* No longer; it was time to start living.

23. HALAIL'S STRENGTH

As Halail watched her life-partner disappear over the crest, she smiled through her tears. He was an amazing creature; no doubt about it. Their love was as deep, and as simple as truth; she worked hard at supporting their family, and he worked hard at caring for it. She laughed. He was oft fond of telling people that she was simply too good for him. In her eyes, that couldn't be further from the truth. They fit together. She turned to the dwarflings, already playing in the dirt around her feet.

Their resiliency always amazed her. It wasn't that they forgot—no, they always remembered mamma and da, and knew when they were gone—but they possessed that wisdom reserved for only the very old and the very young, the deep innate knowledge that everything would somehow end up okay in the end. She tousled Teagan's hair as Teagan stood on one of Halail's stubby feet, clinging to her leg. She looked up at her, beaming. "I love you mommy!"

She looked down at her, a stern look in her eyes. "That may be so, lassie, but how can I love ye back, if ye don't have a beard?"

Teagan pouted. "You don't ha' a beard! Ne'er do the ground-lings!" She pointed at her brothers, using the nickname Mikkel had given to the rough and tumble boys. Halail laughed out loud. One was chasing the others with a toy battle hammer that Mikkel had made for them; another had taken paint and drawn lines all over his face. All three running and screaming... She supposed she should put a stop to it. She smiled. Perhaps in a moment.

"Yer right, little one. But how do I know ye ain't an elf? Yer so tiny!"

Teagan roared at her and leapt up, climbing her belt and buckles until she clung to Halail's hair, erupting into giggles. Halail hugged Teagan with all her might, pulling the child down to chest level. "Aye lass, yer definitely yer father's daughter."

"Get inside, you beardless cretins!" she hollered. She knew Mikkel had endured a lot of abuse, good natured and otherwise, for being the parent who tended the fires and reared the younglings. She knew that, truth be told, Mikkel would have liked to do a bit more on the side. She just hoped he understood how much she truly valued his dedication to the family. Nothing would distract, or come between him and his family; for that, there was no end to her appreciation or love. They couldn't leave the children alone at their age; not that she could see him wanting to if he could. Try as he might, she had never seen him as satisfied in any job as he was with this one.

Mikkel, not gifted in tradecraft, was left with the option of mining or leaving Bruemarrar; he chose to seek his fortune elsewhere. He had left Bruemarrar for Solypse, where he had met Halail. At first he sought acceptance in Solypse. When he realized that would never fully happen for a dwarf who neither crafted nor traded in Solypse, he simply sought peace for himself and his family. Both wanderers by nature, Halail and Mikkel jumped at the opportunity to join the colonists, and left Solypse for Shoal. So far, Shoal had provided the peace they sought. Halail had settled right in, her druidic tradecraft providing the colony with a mixture of care taking and counsel. Mikkel had even picked up a few tricks of the druidic trade, though he often used scrolls that Halail prepared for him. The younglings had taken a shine to Shoal—as they had everywhere else—and quickly turned it into their playground.

24. FAITH AND MAGIC

"**S**o what's your story?"

"My story?" Pash looked at Therrien quizzically.

"Everyone has a story. You got here somehow. What's yours? How did you end up at the Temple?"

Pash gave a slight nod. "I guess so. Nothing terribly exciting, I'm afraid. I grew up on the fourth tier; my father is a councilman. When I came of age, my parents sent me to the Temple to study."

"He didn't want you to follow in his footsteps?"

Pash shook his head. "I remember that he said 'This family needs balance, not political rivals', whatever that means."

Therrien pondered this for a moment. "So you've never studied the magical arts?"

Pash shook his head again. "I had mentioned it to him before I went to the temple; he refused to even entertain the notion."

Therrien nodded in understanding. Though the Wizards Tower held a prominent place in Solypse, they were ill-understood, and oft regarded with suspicion. In a town where deep dwarves and deep elves mixed freely with humans and surface dwellers, the citizens had formed a common bond of superstition towards the inhabitants of the tower. The lower ranked magi were mocked as charlatans or dreamers; the higher ranked magi were simultaneously feared and revered. As a child, he had been fascinated by the stories he had heard of them: planeswalkers, dragon-whisperers, men who could fly... He had aspired to become one of these gods among men. The process of getting accepted as an apprentice had was arduous for everyone; worse still, it didn't come easily for him. His master had taken a chance with him, noting that what he lacked in skill, he made up for with effort.

As time progressed, he had discovered that being one of their number required a level of zealous fixation that he lacked. With his teacher's blessing, he took a leave of absence to join the expedition; it had been a welcome break. Unfortunately, he wasn't sure he wanted to go back, though he wasn't sure what else he would do.

Therrien looked ahead. Larrik and Mikkel were several paces ahead, but their torch clearly marked their location. He paused mid-stride. "So you're telling me that you have *never* studied under a wizard? Cantrips perhaps? An old friend who taught parlor tricks?"

"No," he said hesitantly, "Father... father said that magi were worse than followers of Dark Orders."

Therrien let out a low whistle. "That's a pretty serious dislike."

"He said that at least followers of the dark gods believed in something; Wizards only believed in power."

"Hm. I suppose there is a grain of truth in that. But truth isn't measured in grains, is it?"

Pash shifted uncomfortably. "I suppose not." He looked ahead at Larrik and Mikkel. "We should start walking again."

"I suppose so." Therrien began walking again, slowly. "Pash, did you know why I wanted to talk to you in private?"

"Because you bore witness to my heresy?"

"Heresy?" Therrien queried.

"Heresy. As a follower of Lethos, I'm forbidden from calling upon magic. I am supposed to rely upon Lethos to give me my spells, and trust that he will provide what I need."

"Ah, I see; no, that's not it. But my apologies for leading you astray—It was never my intention to cause you to stumble in your faith."

"You cannot be responsible for my actions; only I am responsible for my choices."

"If you had the choice, would you do it again?"

Pash considered this for a moment. "Yes, I think I would. I am, after all, an acolyte. Though an acolyte is a student of a profession, one cannot choose faith; one simply must have it.

Therrien looked at Pash, mildly surprised at his admission. "I want to teach you some of what I know," he blurted out. "We have a couple days' journey before we arrive at Solypse. I can't teach you much actual magic in that time, but I can teach you about magic. There is no need to fear it, and rarely a reason to fear those who wield it.

"What about Brother Larrik?"

"*Brother* Larrik? I suspect *Larrik* will not mind. What you do when you return to the temple, however, is up to you."

Further ahead, Larrik found himself surprised to be enjoying his new company. Perhaps it was because it was a dwarf —craft-skilled or not—, or perhaps simply because Mikkel had seen a bit more of life than most members of the temple; he wasn't sure. Mikkel had an affable, but non-invasive way about him. His family's role as he saw it, he explained, was to help steady and mentor the colonists, and bolster their spirits as needed.

"Many haven't been away from Solypse much," he had said, "and over time, they may need some comfort or guidance. I suppose you could say that we try to help them make the right decisions; and when they do not, we help them pick up the pieces and glue them back together. Mostly, it's Halail; but it helps to have extra hands, minds, and hearts with situations like these." Larrik contemplated this, glancing back over his shoulder at Pash, several steps behind him. *Had he guided him right?* He sensed that this journey, which was meant to be a journey to strengthen faith, had done little for Pash.

Mikkel saw the expression on his face. "Yer thoughts, Brother Larrik?"

"Just Larrik."

"Aye. Larrik it is. I had ye figured for a ranger of the depths on sight."

Larrik looked at him quickly, surprised. "What do you know of such things?"

Mikkel reached inside his collar, tracing a leather thong from around his neck, and fished a hammered symbol of Riordan from beneath his leather breastplate. "I know many things."

Larrik's face changed from surprised to shocked. Riordan was the Dwarven god of the wandering path, the patron saint of deep druids and rangers of the depths. Given the strong family and community ties of Dwarven communities, Riordan and his followers were worse than ignored; they were shunned. Dwarves weren't meant to wander; they were meant to forge grand edifices and cities with the help of their community. Dwarven society had neither place nor interest in wanderers.

"Aye, that's right. Halail and I both. Ye didn't think you'd find a pair of Dwarves roamin' around the depths with Kerrick's blessin' did ya?"

"Riordan be praised; I'd have never expected such luck. The Brothers took me in long ago, but I never took a gleam to their ways."

"Do ye know of any other Danites?"

Larrik shook his head. "I knew one, long ago, but it has been a long time. What little I know I know from him, and a couple of his traveling companions."

Mikkel's eyes sparkled. "Well you've met one more. Two, in fact;

we'll have to have some good long conversations with Halail when we get back. She'll be thrilled!"

"So I see you aren't a craftsman; you are both practicing druids then?"

Mikkel shook his head. "Nope."

"Then a Ranger perhaps?"

He shook her head again. "Nope. Days gone bye, aye, but I'm a bit rusty. These days, I tend the Dwarflings, and the home."

"So ye don't work then?"

Mikkel's brow furrowed. He closed his eyes tight in frustration, then finally settled on a more relaxed expression. "I tend the children, the home, and the hearth. Everything we do, we do t'gether. True, I tend the fires, but we adventure together, and we raise a generation together."

"I- er, nevermind. I didn't mean it that way." Larrik blushed.

Mikkel took a deep breath. "I'm sorry. I forget that you too know what it is like to be an outcast of Dwarven society."

Larrik flinched. Though he had never contemplated it that way, there was a certain amount of truth to his words. "Indeed. I'm an outcast even among those who have adopted me and pledged to shelter me. I profess to follow Riordan, but I know little of the ways of the wandering path."

"I led the boy on a pilgrimage to bolster his faith, yet I cannot demonstrate my faith either. In his god, I have none. In mine, I have no knowledge. You called me Ranger, but I'm little more than a dwarf who lost his way in the wilderness." Larrik stopped speaking abruptly, pressing his lips together. He wasn't one for talking about himself, and never about his faith, if indeed he had such a thing.

Mikkel placed a reassuring hand on his shoulder. "Well met, Ranger Larrik. All of Riordan's people are those who wander in the wilderness. The secret is understanding that when you wander, you aren't lost; you are found."

25. CILLIAN AND ELLIAS

Cillan sat in the antechamber of the councilor's quarters. She smoothed her hand through her hair, and shifted in her seat, uncomfortably. Ellias' manservant opened the double doors, ushering her in, shielding his mouth and nose as she passed. Cillan sniffed experimentally, and realized that she was indeed foul. In her haste, she hadn't stopped to bathe or strip off her travel leathers; she smelled of sweat, smoke, and a variety of other indistinguishable scents.

She paused a moment, then thrust her shoulders back and strode purposefully into the room. Ellias was in his usual place, out on the balcony gazing down at the city. The manservant stepped outside of the room, and drew the doors closed behind him.

"It is done then?"

"Yes."

"Any...complications?"

"Nothing of import. The Temple Brothers are likely about a day's journey behind me."

"Good, I will have the guards pick them up at the gate. We can't have rogue clerics roaming about, killing anyone who refuses to deal with them."

"No sir."

"While you were gone, we had a slight problem. It seems someone decided to eliminate one of the Brothers."

"Anyone of interest?"

"Brother Prival. He was one of the more vocal opponents of the council."

"Well that's convenient at least."

"Unfortunately, it may look as if there were sinister motivations behind it, and people may think that the temple is involved. His pieces were spread around like the contents of an ale mug dropped on the cobblestones."

"But with Nar'el gone, it may look as if there are some problems within the Temple itself. This is good news for you, yes?"

He looked at her, as if considering something, then looked back out over the balcony.

"I need you to take out Aerun Firelight next, followed by Gillas Hielen."

"Firelight? I- I'm sorry, councilman, I can't."

Ellias turned and faced her, arching a delicately maintained eyebrow. "You're the best, or so I hear. If anyone can do it, I would think that you could."

"No, I mean that I am not interested in the work at this time. I appreciate it, but I have other obligations."

Ellias set his jaw firmly. "If it's more payment that you want, I assure you that it was already in consideration."

She exhaled heavily. "No, Councilman, I mean that I cannot do the job. There are others who are capable; Thalen, for instance-"

Ellias eyes narrowed into slits, and he leaned in towards her. "So is it that you *can't*, or that you *won't*?"

She matched his gaze defiantly. "I won't."

Ellias turned once more to face the city. "Your payment is in the salver by the door."

She stared at his back for a moment, then turned on her heel towards the door, grabbing the purse on her way out.

"Cillan!"

She turned her head, her hand resting on the door latch.

"You don't quit working for me. I will let you know when we are done."

She left angrily, tucking the purse under the guard's tunic that she still wore. She wanted a measure of relief at putting the gilded doors and the grey monstrosity of the Council compound behind her, a sense of finality. Instead she felt frustration and anger. She could walk away, alright, but then she would spend the rest of her life as a fugitive. She walked casually down the tightly cobbled paths, weaving through meticulously maintained gardens. Though Solypse didn't receive enough sunlight for garden growth, the city planners had added bright points of light in each of the city gardens. She shook her head. *The cost of such opulence...and they didn't even grow food.* There were small farms in the lower tiers, but they grew weak crops under the natural light provided through the Veil a short few hours every day. She strolled through the last garden, looking at the detailed statues of the council members. This garden was the first thing that visitors saw when they ascended to the fifth tier. It was an homage to the council members, past and present, with plaques scattered about extolling the good deeds and virtues of each. She neared the end of the garden on her way to the top of the stairs to the fourth tier, relieved to have both Ellias and his statue behind her at last.

As Cillan stepped out of the garden, two well-dressed gentlemen stepped from the landing to meet her.

"Cillan?"

She felt a knot in her stomach. "Yes?"

"We were hoping that perhaps you would like to have dinner with us again."

"I'm sorry," she said blithely, "I'm afraid I have plans for this evening."

The gentleman rubbed his face, appearing chagrined. "I'm afraid I must insist. We need to discuss some of your work here with the city guard."

She shook her head. "I'm sorry, I'm not looking for more work at the moment."

He stood there, staring at her. She opened her mouth to continue, but stopped. One of his fingers was adorned with a ring, the top of which was an eye inset with an iris fashioned out of emerald, displayed as a gentle reminder.

"My apologies, kind sir, where would you like to go?"

"There is a nice, discreet pub on the far side of the Second. Hopefully Dwarven fare suits your tastes."

She nodded. When the secret police invited you to dinner, it wasn't really a choice.

26. THE DEVOURER FEEDS

It was time for things to start dying. The devourer glided through earth and stone as if it were floating through air, until it reached the city. The core of its being, driven from a deep, abyssal requirement and unceasing demand to consume, began to overload in desire. The smell of flesh and souls surrounded it, threatening to drive its supernatural essence into a frenzy of madness. It tore itself from its paralysis as the necromancer's command compelled it forward, towards its goal. It drifted through the docks, then up through the merchant quarter, invisible to the distracted crowd all around. If it had sported hair, it would all be standing on end; if it had a heart, it would have nearly exploded with the excited rush. It had neither; instead, it had a word of command, which forced it forward with a compulsion that only a master necromancer could impart. It floated forward and up the ramps, its repressed core screaming inside, as it passed through person after person.

The devourer was nearing the tower. It could see the auras of the magical wards that surrounded the tower, wrapping it in defensive magics. The devourer slowed its approach, and allowed itself to settle onto the ground, then into the ground. It was as it had expected—no one had thought to ward the solid rock at the underside of the tower.

The devourer floated through the rock until it was beneath the massive tower, and willed itself to ascend. As it floated up through the tower, it slipped past carefully warded chests and cautiously locked doors, few enspelled smartly enough to include their floors. It floated higher and higher, and slowed his ascent as it felt itself get close to its target.

It was early, but Lak'ail was tired. Today, much like nearly every other day for the last decade, he had been teaching aspiring mages about the finer points of wizardry and conjuration from the time the docks woke, until evening meal. Lately however, he had been spending his evenings trying to advance his own studies. True, he could remain in the tower respectably as a teacher for years—many did—but he had greater ambitions. The wizards who ascended to the top floors of the tower were borne there by hard work and the most prized skills in all of Solypse: they crafted permanent teleportation nexus locations. With these portals, they were able to teleport dignitaries, wealthy merchants, and goods—saving several days or weeks of travel between cities. If he could master these skills, he would begin to ascend past the teaching ranks which he had been banished to many years ago.

He was a bright student, and had shown promise from the start. He was made a teacher after three short years, and was expected to move on to better things sometime in the three years following that; and then something happened.

He remembered it like it was yesterday. In his first year of teaching, he was young, exuberant, and impetuously dedicated to "experiencing life" in Solypse. One morning, after having spent the evening prior far too deep in his cups, he was late to his morning class. When he had arrived at the classroom, the students were huddled in a circle. Some were giggling, amidst cries of "eww!" Unnoticed, he walked up and looked into the middle of the throng. In the middle, there was an open space on the floor, where two rodent like creatures, nearly waist high, stood on their hind feet and battled. One was missing an eye; another, a paw. Both had severe gashes across their chests and bellies, and one had its innards spilling outward on the floor. He cleared his throat noisily; as soon as he did, the animals collapsed to the floor, and all eyes turned to him. He remembered casting about, looking for the culprit. He locked eyes with a young sickly looking boy, no older than ten.

"Did you do this?"

The boy had nodded his head.

"You know that necromancy is strictly forbidden." It was a statement. The boy shrugged his shoulders, and stared fixedly at the corpses at his feet.

"Clean it up." Lak'ail had immediately sought his superiors, and recommended immediate dismissal. Though they had nearly consented to his punishment, which was in line with the rules of the school, the boy was the child of a someone with much power. The boy was retained, but the family demanded that something be done to atone for the embarrassment foisted upon their family name; and so it came to pass that Lak'ail was bound to the teaching ranks for decades before he would be allowed to try to ascend. Now that his teaching tenure was nearing a close, he spent every spare moment studying, until he was near collapse.

It was in this state, worn and weary, that the devourer found Lak'ail. Though the human looked fatigued, both his life force and his magical aura blazed like light from the sun. The devourer hovered above Lak'ail, allowing itself to slowly come back into view. It could have swallowed Lak'ail without the wizard even knowing; however, there was something delightful to the nether beast about tasting the fear and panic that erupted from the victim when they saw it. The devourer floated over the wizard. It opened its mouth wide, and reached down for him.

Lak'ail glanced up, just in time to see two arms reach out of a gaping maw, and pull him in. He felt the mighty jaws slam shut at his waist, and then he felt no more. The devourer felt a surge of power, and then excitement: the night was just beginning.

27. SMOKE; A DELAY IN TRAVELS

The companions wound their way steadily through the caverns, the Dwarves scouting ahead while Pash and Therrien followed behind. Pash's hesitance to discuss magical studies had subsided rapidly, and he devoured the information offered by Therrien. They discussed the subtle differences between transformation and transmutation, shaping energy, translocation, and the commonalities between the summoning of elementals and demons.

Several hundred paces ahead, Larrik listened intently as Mikkel described the details of being a true follower of Riordan, punctuated with colorful stories of him, Halail, and their children as they adventured through life.

"Good companionship leads to light feet," Mikkel observed, and indeed they moved at a rapid pace for several hours. So engrossed in the conversations were they, that they failed to notice the smoke that was beginning to fill the tunnel, until it became as dense as a light morning fog.

Larrik held the torch away from his face, and inhaled deeply through his nose. "Fireshrooms! The blasted girl must have lit the cavern on fire." They turned around and trotted back to the other two, and explained their discovery. "We need to backtrack and take one of the side tunnels. It's only going to get worse."

"Fireshrooms?" queried Pash.

"We passed through the cavern on our way down. They're mushrooms filled with some kind of oil; they're good at burnin', hours at a time, but they smoke terrible." Larrik looked at Mikkel. "Actually, can ye do anything about this? It might'n save us quite a bit of time."

Mikkel shook his head. "Halail might be able to put 'em out, but I'm of little use here."

"So much for light feet," grumbled Larrik.

Therrien piped up. "I may be able to help, actually."

"Ye can purify where a Ranger cannot?"

"No; but I can lead us around. I had the caverns and tunnels between Shoal and Solypse mapped as best we could, so that I would know where to place wards and such. My information is far from perfect, but I should be able to get us to where we need to go. I remember a route not far back down the tunnel that should add a little over a day to our journey."

"A full DAY?" Larrik tugged on his beard, clearly displeased with the notion.

"I'm afraid it's the best you can hope for, unless—well, there's one other option, several hours shorter. I wouldn't recommend it though, unless you feel like trying to sneak through a city taken over by Clutchers."

Larrik shuddered.

Mikkel shook his head emphatically. "No thank ya. I'd rather walk fast instead."

Pash coughed. In the short time they had been discussing their options, the smoke had nearly doubled in thickness, threatening their ability to see and breathe. "I don't know who the Clutchers are, but you should probably make a decision before we run out of air trying to pick something."

"On to the long road then. Follow me!" Therrien walked swiftly back down the tunnel, the other three companions in tow. They walked for several minutes, winding through tunnels, until they came to a crevasse that disappeared into inky blackness below.

"Blast!" Therrien punched his fist into his palm. Larrik added his own colorful invectives, looking around the edges for a path.

Pash peered over the edge of the hole. "I thought you knew where you were going?"

"I do—or, at least, I did. In the tunnels, it's possible for a sinkhole to open up, just as there's always a possibility for a cave-in, if the conditions are right."

"How far down does it go?"

Therrien shrugged. He tossed a loose stone over the edge, listening for an impact; he heard none. "There's no telling. What's worse, that means..."

Larrik groaned. "Clutchers."

Pash looked at him quizzically. "What's the problem?"

Therrien sighed. "Pyrric Symbiotes, also known as Clutchers, attack from behind, wrapping themselves around their victim. Their arms have barbed claws that wrap around a person's arms, and they have a ribcage that opens up and wraps around someone's midsection the same way. Even the underside of their heads are hollow and barbed, so they can slam them down on top of a victim. Once they grab you, they are almost impossible to remove."

Pash took a step back, horrified. "What a terrible way to die."

Larrik shook his head. "Oh no lad, you don't die. They jam a stinger into your spine, and take control of you. You are their host; they keep you alive."

Pash looked at Therrien. "You're sure there's no other way?"

Therrien held up his hands in a pleading gesture. "I wish there were. In fact, there might be; there are many days' worth of tunnels that have gone unexplored. We stopped mapping after we stumbled on the Clutchers. Finding out about the infestation cost the colony a couple good people." He paused, and added softly, "really good people."

Larrik picked up his pack. "We need to get going. Discussion time is over; Therrien, lead the way."

Therrien led them back through the twisting tunnels, past the acrid smoke-filled passage, and down a steep path that wound through a forest of underground flora.

"When we first came across the town, we were excited. We had never expected to find another settlement so close, let alone one that was so well established. When we reached the town though, we were ambushed. They must have seen us coming; by the time we realized what was going on, Kale and Shel had been grabbed. We wanted to save them, or at the least put them out of their misery, but-" Therrien's voice cracked, and he looked away. "There were just too many of them, all charging straight at us. Must have been dozens." He exhaled deeply. "Anyhow, that's what happened. We ran out of the other end of town, and eventually found ourselves up on the Path. After that, we decided to focus more on defenses, and cut back on exploring."

They walked onward; Larrik, relieved of scout duty, fell back to keep an eye on the rear, once again in the company of Mikkel. Pash walked beside Therrien with careful, measured steps, reading as he walked.

"You have a mind for it, there's no doubt. What would your temple say though?"

Pash looked up from the book. "I have decided that I don't much care. I don't think I want to return to my studies at the Temple once we return to Solypse. Lethos may well be a benevolent god to his devout followers, but I am simply not one to put my faith in anyone else—even a god—to determine my fate."

Therrien looked sidelong at him. "You mean to tell me that you went on a pilgrimage for your temple, and lost your faith instead?"

"Not exactly. Nothing has changed; that's the problem. I thought this would bring me closer to Lethos, increase my understanding of the mission, somehow bind me tighter to his fold. Instead, I woke to the realization that I don't need Lethos; I can shape my own destiny, wield my strength from within, rather than above."

Therrien shook his head. "I'm not sure I agree with you. I pray to Lethos every day for strength, guidance, and wisdom. At the end of the road, alone in the darkness, you are left with nothing...except your faith, and the love of your god.

"Oh, I disagree." Pash grinned at him from the other side of an outstretched palm. "*Lechte*." Pash's eyes glimmered from the light dancing in his palm. "Actually, this friendship might be more fortuitous than we had originally imagined."

"How so?"

"Would you like to borrow my Codex and anthologies? You might find them to be an interesting read. The anthologies chronicle the history of the worship of Lethos, from hundreds of years ago, up through contemporary times. Texts of faith will clearly not be lost upon you."

"I...would like that very much. Thank you." Therrien gave him a light smile and a slight bow. "So, how are your studies with magic progressing?"

"Amazing, actually," he exclaimed. "It simply makes sense. The way the words come together, the intersection of ley energies, the subtle hand gestures used to manipulate and bind energy... It is like a complex puzzle, but one that is a joy to figure out."

Therrien clapped him heartily on the back. "Would that faith in Lethos came as easily, eh?"

Pash shook his head. "The one thing I have come to understand about the Temple's doctrine is that understanding it, explaining it, reciting it...even *practicing* it doesn't give faith, or the things that go along with it. If there were a way to explain it or construct it, I would have by now, trust me on that."

Therrien laughed gently. "And so it is. The funny thing is, faith actually *is* something that I 'just know'. Magic on the other hand..." He shrugged. "I left the tower for a reason."

Larrik was thoroughly enjoying himself. He had spent years being a guest at the Temple, always welcomed but never quite fully accepted. Mikkel had proven to be a good travel companion; a strong, able-minded dwarf. On top of that, he was a font of knowledge about Riordan. Danites, as the faithful of Riordan were known, were solitary wanderers by nature. Among the faithful, it was oft joked that they found Riordan on their own, because Riordan himself likely couldn't find half of his followers.

Mikkel, for his part, was delighted at his interest. "Ye seem to have taken a shine to the teachings. Don't tell me yer thinkin' of becoming a druid now?"

Larrik snorted at the thought. "Lethos or Riordan, I'm not one to be preachin'; I'll stick to wanderin'. That suits me fine."

Mikkel nodded. "Do what suits thee; Riordan ain't one to push either way. Yer Rangerin' skills though... I'd put you toe to toe with some of the finest Rangers I've met. Who trained ye?"

Larrik laughed. "Riordan himself, as much as anyone. I spent a very long time in the tunnels. I learned what I needed to, to stay alive."

"All without healing magics," he mused. "Would you like to learn some of what you have been missing out on?"

Larrik flashed a rare grin, and rubbed his hands on the front of his breeches. Though Dwarves were rarely fond of magic, godly blessings were a different thing altogether. "I-do you think I could learn such things?"

"T'aint about learnin'. It's about trustin' that Riordan has yer back. Here, let me show you." Mikkel grabbed one of Larrik's hands, and murmured a quick prayer. Before Larrik could ask Mikkel what he was doing, Mikkel thrust the hand into the torch flame, and held it there, refusing to let Larrik pull it out. Larrik stopped struggling. Amazed, he watched the flames dance around his hand, not even singing the hairs on it. Mikkel let go of Larrik's elbow, and the hand dropped out of the flame. "Now it's your turn to try."

Larrik's eyes went wide. "My hand will catch on fire if I tried!"

Mikkel chotled. "Don't worry. You're going to try it on *my* hand."

Larrik shook his head vigorously. "You ask too much. I know far too little."

"You are favored, that is clear, or you would not be alive today. Listen to my words; better yet, listen to my meanings. It isn't about what ye know; it's about *knowing*." As Mikkel spoke, his voice took on a warm, bold tone, and his Dwarven inflections subsided. Larrik listened intently, and gripped the back of Mikkel's hand. He intoned the prayer with as much fervor as he could muster, to ensure Riordan knew that he meant it in earnest. When Larrik completed the ritual, Mikkel pulled his hand free and thrust it into the flame. Larrik cringed. Mikkel continued to hold his hand in the flame; it did not burn. Larrik's face lit up in childlike amazement; Mikkel's, one of tranquility.

They were so engrossed in their exchange that they almost bumped into Pash and Therrien.

Larrik looked at Pash quizzically.

"We're on the outskirts of the city", Pash said softly.

"Can they hear us?" Larrik whispered.

Pash shrugged and held up his hands. "Do you really want to find out?"

They surveyed the city before them; truly, it had once been quite formidable. A broad main boulevard ran the length of a long, narrow cavern, lit overhead by a cavern roof completely covered in the subtly shifting colors of luminescent crystals. What once had been homes and businesses had been carved into the rock faces on either side of the cavern, three tiers high on either side. Stone ramps led up and down the levels on both sides.

"They had cross-bridges too, look-" Larrik pointed at pairs of stone pillars set at intervals on the upper tiers. "The bridges would anchor to those. There's pretty much nothing left there though; this place has been here for a long while."

Therrien looked puzzled. "Larrik, how long would it take to carve a city of this magnitude?"

Larrik looked around the cavern thoughtfully. "The work could be done in a decade or two. What's interesting is that it was done at all. Look at the ramp intervals, and notice how they set in front of the upper paths, all seamless cuts. Now look how the buildings set back from the paths. Dwarven craftsmanship is peerless, but this sort of work takes many years of planning, even for Dwarves."

Therrien furrowed his brow. "How is it that no one talks about this place? It's half as big as the merchant tier in Solypse; such a thing would have been of considerable note, at least at some point."

"It could be a settlement from a different Dwarven clan." Larrik furrowed his brow. He knew that wasn't right. There was something very distinctive about the craftsmanship, but he couldn't put his finger on it.

Pash sighed, voicing what no one else wanted to. "Shall we go in?"

28. THE CLUTCHES OF CLUTCHERS

The long, narrow road in front of them conjured up different terms. Pash conjured up images of a bustling main street from days gone by. Therrien saw the long, narrow corridor, and thought both "ambush" and "alley" simultaneously. Larrik simply thought it looked like a bad idea.

"I thought we were done with such foolishness when we got to Shoal," Therrien muttered.

"We'll be adventuring until we're dead, ye know that," snickered Mikkel, pulling his heavy warhammer to the ready, and poking him with the end of it. "Ye ain't dead yet, are ye?"

They walked forward cautiously, four abreast with Larrik to the left, Mikkel to the right, Pash and Therrien in between. The path sloped gently downward, leveling off as it reached the first buildings in town. They peered into the doorways as they crept past, but the swirling red and purple hues above did little to illuminate the doorways to either side.

"It all seems very quiet," Therrien muttered.

They walked forward for several more minutes, peering into doorways at a distance, the ceiling shifting into bright bursts of blue and aquamarine. As they came closer to the center of the main road, a bright shining crystal came into view, reflecting the ceiling's colors on the building and the road. The crystal sat above the third floor level, the center of the town a broad open circular space. The walls on the left and right had been carved back to make way for the space, rather than populating the sides with buildings. Graceful stone bridges on the second and third floors arched over the carved out stone below, connecting the rows of buildings before and after the town center. They approached the center cautiously, barely daring to breathe.

"We're halfway through, no sign of anyone. Maybe they've abandoned the town," Pash whispered.

"Let me tell ye somethin' about attackin' on a bridge," Larrik growled in a low voice, "ye don't attack when the enemy is at the beginnin' of the bridge."

As if on cue, the cavern erupted in a cacophony of sound, from all directions. Therrien groaned. "You wait until they are in the middle!"

From their position in the middle of the town, the crystal blazed orange light in every direction, casting light on hundreds of bipedal creatures at the ground level, and dozens of insectoid creatures skittering across the upper levels.

"They look like zombies," Pash said breathlessly.

Therrien shook his head fiercely, his voice nearly in a panic. "Not zombies. Zombies are slow and stupid. These are far worse than zombies."

The creatures on the ground level pressed closer, and the foursome could see that they were humanoid; hard, angular skull-like coverings adorned them, clamped on with teeth that encircled the crown of each victim's head. Bone-colored bands encircled the arms of the encroaching mob. The Clutchers guided their hosts swiftly, purposefully towards the four adventurers.

The realization of the city finally dawned on Larrik. "Elves! I knew that construction wasn't Dwarven. But what was a city doing so close to Solypse?"

Before anyone could answer, a shrieking noise like a thousand screaming children erupted in the chamber. The mobs on either side of the town stopped instantly.

Mikkel felt his stomach clench and the blood drain from his face. He looked around rapidly, and saw dozens of hungry Clutchers drop from the bridges on the sides of the cavern, skittering towards them at lightning speed. They continued shrieking as they advanced on the four companions. Pash's breath caught in his throat, and stood still, paralyzed with fear. The loud clattering of the claws of the creatures got louder as the creatures advanced upon them. Therrien blinked, unarmed and uncertain of what to do.

"Backs!" Larrik yelled. Mikkel and Larrik reflexively snapped into position, back to back with Therrien and Pash in between. They circled slowly in a counterclockwise motion as the Clutchers drew near. "Yer left!" A Clutcher darted out at Mikkel from just beyond Larrik's reach. Mikkel flipped has hammer low, and thrust back and around. The pointed pommel of his hammer caught the Clutcher through the center of its skull, the motion of his swing flinging it into a group of its companions. Larrik drew a second mattock from his belt, looping the corded end to his right wrist.

A Clutcher dove for Larrik's midsection; Larrik swiped it away with his right, slamming the point of his left into the brain pan of another to his side. He shook the creatures free just in time to swing his left mattock up and block one aiming for his face. *By the gods!* He thought. *They jump!*

"RIGHT!" Larrik heard Mikkel's shout just in time to see a Clutcher diving towards Pash's face. He hurled his mattock at it, the point of the mattock digging into a segment of the creature's spine. The barbed stinger at the tailbone of the creature twitched spasmodically as its spine snapped in half. Larrik jerked back on the cord, pulling the mattock back into his hand. Mikkel was a whirling dance of death, spinning his hammer as he circled Pash and Therrien like a lion protecting his cubs. He jabbed and swung in either direction, parrying attacks and bludgeoning the oncoming swarm. "There's too many of them! I don't know how much longer we can keep this up!"

Pash's mind was overcome by the horrors surrounding him. When he was a child, he remembered seeing other children cheering as a beetle was overrun and consumed by a colony of ants; today, they were the beetle. As he stood there catatonic, he saw a clutcher convulse, and fly towards him. His mind registered the rings of teeth, set into the fleshy underside of the skullcap, the teeth extended towards his face. Like a flash, he saw a mattock fly out in front of him, and the visage of death was gone. He blinked, and did the first thing that came to mind.

Therrien heard the strange words tumbling from Pash's mouth as the dwarves concentrated on beating back the waves of creatures. "Larrik, look ou-" Therrien's words were cut off as the wind was knocked out of his chest, a Clutcher slamming into him, and slamming it's poisoned barb into his diaphragm. Larrik saw the barb bury itself just above Therrien's stomach. He reversed his mattock and slammed the wedge into the creature. He yanked back with all his might, pulling it away as hard as he could, but it was too late.

Therrien collapsed to the ground, and the world erupted in a blinding spray of light. Larrik's jaw dropped. Pash stood between him and Mikkel, hands outstretched, his body a blazing beacon. Huge gouts of flame shot from his hands, blackening buildings as they consumed everything in their paths. The flames ceased nearly as abruptly as they had begun, and Pash collapsed next to Therrien. Where the zombified masses had once stood now lay an ashen path. The insectoid clutchers backed up, as if reconsidering their attack. Mikkel wasted no time. "Grab Pash, I'll grab Therrien!"

The dwarves holstered their weapons, and grabbed their companions. The creatures were at bay right now; that wouldn't last long. The dwarves sprinted through the ankle deep soot toward the cavern exit, their legs powered by pure adrenaline. Before they had cleared the town center, the creatures began to fall in behind them, chasing to press the attack. The ceiling turned to a menacing purple-black, the crystal reflecting dark and eerie shadows in front of them.

Dozens of buildings blurred by, blackened in the aftermath of Pash's spell. The dwarves began cresting the hill at the edge of town, their legs burning beneath them. "We can't run forever!" Larrik yelled, gasping for air.

"I have an idea," Mikkel panted, "but we're only going to get one chance."

"Well let's take our chances before the decision is made for us, yeah?"

"Okay, stop!" Mikkel skidded to a halt and dropped Therrien unceremoniously to the ground. He reached into his belt pouch and produced a scroll, and spun to face the shrieking horde that was only a few dozen yards away. Closing his eyes, he crumbled a piece of charcoal between his thumb and forefinger, waving his hand across the tunnel and rapidly intoning a prayer to Riordan.

Larrik waited with baited breath, watching Mikkel's back as he wove his spell.

Nothing happened. Mikkel cursed under his breath, the horde closing fast. He steeled his nerves, and reached into his pouch again. Clutchers scrambled in an indistinguishable mass of teeth and claws, scrambling over one another to be the first to consume and command him. He modified his inflection and re-read the scroll, casting his crumbled charcoal again.

A massive wall of flames appeared, spanning the entire width and height of the tunnel. The shrieking of frenzied hunger turned to the wails of the immolated, and the hissing and popping of incinerated carapaces. Mikkel trembled, and took a deep breath. He looked down to pick up Therrien, and recoiled at the sight of a bisected clutcher head at his feet. He kicked it forcefully back into the fire, pleased to hear the sizzle as it passed into the wall of fire.

"How long will it last?"

"Not long enough. We need to move, quickly, and attend to Therrien as soon as it is safe."

Pash sat up groggily. "Did we win?"

"Not yet lad, but we didn't lose yet, thanks to you. Methinks we need to talk."

Pash struggled to his feet. "Why does everyone keep saying that?" He looked down an saw Therrien. "Is he," Pash paused, trying to formulate the right words.

Mikkel struggled to lift Therrien. "Not yet, but we're all going t'be, if we don't get moving." Larrik leaned over and helped Mikkel lift Therrien. They pulled an arm on each of them and dragged his limp body between them.

"Can I help?" Pash inquired.

"Ye can help by saving yer strength. Now let's move." The companions moved swiftly away from the wall of fire for as long as they dared, before settling in a small open area along the tunnel.

Mikkel opened Therrien's tunic, and examined the wound thoroughly. He was got good. "Nearly got his heart. He's lucky, if there is such a thing with this."

Pash looked at the fiery red circle around the bleeding hole just beneath the ribcage. "Is he going to die?"

Larrik shook his head. "I don't think so; let's hope not. They paralyze so they can attach, but then they need their host to move around. It's said they can inflict a double dose of poison to kill their victims, but these clutchers seemed pretty hungry.

"So he'll wake up on his own?"

"He should wake up eventually, but he won't like it. When it wears off, the victims are nearly mad from the pain. The clutchers like it that way—just in case they don't attach to their victims in time, their victims can barely think, let alone run away."

Mikkel sighed a heavy sigh. "I wish I could fix him, but I wasn't prepared to deal with this sort of thing. Perhaps once we get to Solypse, the temple could see to him."

Larrik nodded. "In the meantime, there's a poultice I can prepare that will dull the pain once he wakes. It's mighty powerful though, and there might be some side effects."

Pash raised an eyebrow. "Side effects?"

"He might be paralyzed from the waist down until it wears off."

Pash looked at him in disbelief.

Larrik looked back at him defensively. "What? At least it helps a little bit."

Pash heard the knock at the door, regarding it with the same earnest disinterest that he held for most things after his coming-of-age. That which was supposed to be a joyous occasion -the most joyous occasion for him—had been dashed upon the floor at his father's pronouncement. The mood of the entire party had shifted after his father had spoken. The elder statesmen murmured amongst themselves, wondering at the political motivations that Gillas might have had for such a move. Pash's peers knew this was the last thing that he would have wanted. Those friendly with Pash clapped reassuring hands upon his shoulders; rivals cheerily speculated about why his father would want to doom his only son to celibacy.

Pash stumbled through the crowd in a daze, partly from confusion, and mostly from hard liquor. He wasn't even sure when he had gotten home, or how; all he knew was that his head was pounding steadily, much like the knocking at the door. He heard one of the servants open the door. He heard rising voices, politely yet firmly insisting on entry. Moments later, two robed clerics stood in the doorway.

"Go away. You aren't supposed to take me until tomorrow."

Brother Prival looked at the young man, involuntarily wrinkling his nose in disgust. Pash was seated at the end of the table in the main dining room, a rats-nest of unkempt hair showing as he rested his forehead on the backs of his hands. The reek of alcohol permeated the room, leaking out from every one of his pores. Brother Kern glanced at Brother Prival, and placed a steadying hand on Brother Prival's back.

"Begging your pardon Pash, we aren't here to take you." Brother Kern walked up and placed a gentle hand on Pash's shoulder. "We don't take anyone involuntarily at all, actually. We're here because we would like to convince you that you should join us."

"I thought my father already signed me away?"

Brother Kern sat down next to Pash. "You had your coming of age ceremony. No one can make that decision for you, not even your father."

Pash turned his head without lifting it, resting his temple on the back of his hands. "So I'm free to go. So are you, then. Helge can see you out."

Brother Prival stepped forward. "We know about what happened with the carnival."

Pash's lifted his head from the table, and looked up at Brother Prival. "So what?"

"We think you have a gift, one which we think we can help you learn to control."

Pash slouched back in his chair. "Go on."

"We all know your father won't send you to the tower. That much is understood. But you have a....capability that can be harnessed and controlled, if properly channeled."

"And of course you think that the proper channel is the Temple," he observed. "What is it that makes you think I would be a good acolyte?"

"Absolutely nothing", said Brother Prival, sighing.

Brother Kern pressed his palms flat against the table. "I can tell you do not feel called to the faith."

"Observant."

Brother Kern ignored him. "But you do feel a call to magical energy. We can help teach you how to seek control within yourself, which will allow you to control that energy. In your studies as an acolyte of the Temple, you will grow in your understanding as you grow in your devotion to Lethos."

"What makes you think I would want to go to the Temple?"

"Because prophecy foretells it."

Pash snickered.

Brother Prival strode swiftly up to the end of the table. He slapped his hand down on the table, startling both Pash and Brother Kern. "Pash, you can play whatever games you want, but one of the curses of nobility is that the freedom that you so hotly desire will never be enjoyed by the likes of you. Lethos blessed you with options, but the devil's bargain is the knowledge that the best one may not always be the most desirable. You cannot go to the Tower, that much is clear. But if you shoo away the Temple, what then? Your father would never allow you into politics. You have no tradecraft, goods, or customer network to become a merchant. What would you be then, a sailor or fishmonger, with those soft hands? A book-keeper, when you long for a broader view of the world?" Brother Prival paused, and leaned in close to Pash's face. "You see Pash, we all know that there is no other option that will make you happy. So you might as well take the chance that you might be happy. A leap of faith, as it were."

"What do you get out of this? Why try so hard?"

Brother Kern shrugged, then smiled. "Lethos led us to you. We are but his humble servants. Who are we to question?"

29. CILLAN HAS A CHAT

The inspector sat down comfortably at the booth in the loft overlooking the tavern, the one reserved for patrons who did not want to be disturbed. He tamped his pipe with smoke weed, imported from somewhere overland. He regarded the young woman across the table with mild curiosity. She had been a source of reliable information from unusual places, which was fortunate for him on one level. On the other, it raised curious and concerning questions about how she came about such information. He tilted the candle and lit his pipe, the candle glowing against his sallow, pudgy face.

The inspector's young partner sat back at the table, trying to conceal his excitement. He was new to this line of work, having recently been promoted out of the drudgery of chasing petty thieves in the merchant quarter.

The inspector looked at Cillan and smiled cheerfully. "Can I get you anything? A drink perhaps?"

Cillan shook her head. "No thanks. Not much to report though. I just got back from escorting a Temple contingent to a colony. Some interesting things happened there, but that will be filed in a formal report—nothing really unique about it to share."

The inspector nodded. "Actually, I didn't want to talk to you about the latest trip. I haven't had much time to thoroughly review your last few reports until just recently, and I wanted to go over a few things with you on them."

Cillan rubbed her eyes to conceal an eyeroll, and folded her hands to mask her frustration. The inspector was always insistent that she speak to him with every job that she did for the council.

"What I wanted to talk to you about isn't a big deal—just a little thing really. As I was cleaning up my files, I couldn't help but notice that very...interesting things seem to happen to you."

Cillan nodded. "Yes inspector, that's why I tell you about them."

"For instance, the last few times you have been sent on assignment details, you have been in fairly close proximity to unfortunate events." He folded his arms and looked at her through his pipe smoke, inhaling thoughtfully. She sat tight-lipped, saying nothing.

"We understand you have a special working relationship of sorts with Councilman Ellias. Did he ask you to, shall we say, take care of these things for him?"

Cillan glared across the table, not speaking. The inspector knew it was true; moreover, he knew that she was duty-bound not to discuss it. "No; I just report things because you ask me to. You ask all the guards to report anything strange."

The inspector's partner leaned in. "The thing is, none of them do. It would seem that all these strange things happen to you, yet no one else. Why would that be?"

She sat open-mouthed, confused.

"So we can't help but wonder... Are you just feeding us a little, to try to get closer to us and our organization?

She was flabbergasted. "That...is ridiculous."

The inspector leaned forward. "Is it?" He untied a binder of papers, and spread them across the table. "Shoal; one dead mayor. Councilman Rhetor at the theater, on a night you were on protection detail. Zixiz, an overland elf merchant when you were detailed to the quarter. And more."

She shook her head. "I do what I'm asked to do, and that's it. I tell you what's going on. How could I be so stupid to not see where this would lead?"

The junior investigator smiled wide. "But we don't think you're stupid, and that's the problem. You're brilliant, and you know it. So why are we here, having this conversation?"

"I don't know...why don't you tell me?"

"I think you know."

"I think I don't."

The inspector sat back and eyed her steadily. "Thanks for meeting us. We'll be in touch."

"Wait-what? We're done?"

The inspector nodded.

"What of this meeting? Will something more come of it?"

The inspector smirked. "If it does, you'll find out."

Cillan walked down from the balcony, numb. She was helping *them*, and they were tracking *her*. Ellias' words echoed in her mind. If she wanted to escape his grasp, it would take some drastic measures.

30. THE COMPANION'S JOURNEY

The three companions kept close watch over Therrien. They continued through the tunnels until they reached the Path, and found a suitable location for a campsite. Larrik built a low fire to both keep them warm and drive back the darkness. Mikkel volunteered for the late shift, falling asleep on his bedroll scarcely a moment after he lay down.

Larrik looked at Pash, then looked at the low embers of the fire. "Earlier, you did something." Pash caged his gaze on the embers, saying nothing.

"I wanted to thank ye, and tell you that you done right."

Pash sighed at him, exasperated. "How can you say that? This was supposed to be a pilgrimage, something to bring me closer to my faith, and now I haven't just blasphemed, I've done it multiple times. On top of that, I've let magic serve the role that faith was supposed to play. By my account, I did wrong. Very very wrong."

Larrik shook his head. "Lad, do you know why I don't like to be called 'Brother'?"

"Because you're not a full brother?"

He shook his head again. "It's more than that. I don't even follow Lethos. Think some of his teachings are quite daft, actually."

"So why stay at the temple?"

"They're good people, with good intentions; at least most of them are. Long ago, I found a brother in the tunnel, half dead and out of his mind. I got him back to the temple safely, and they said I was welcome to stay as long as I like. So I have."

"If you aren't a brother, why did they send you with me? Surely they didn't expect you to preach, did they?"

"No, but I know how to deal with the tunnels; many of them have never left Solypse in their lives." He paused. "Look this is about you, not me. I saw you light the whole world on fire earlier, and ye saved my life; heck, you saved all our lives. I don't know much about magic, but I can't imagine that what you did is some easy parlor trick."

"It just kind of...came to me. I was reading Therrien's spellbook earlier, and I kept reading the spells over and over, hoping that it would stick with me."

"Well, something did, that's for sure. You know Pash, you cast a spell from less than a day's reading... And I've watched you struggle with clerical magics for years without any big results. You should really consider what path you want to choose."

"My father—"

"...is not here. You are a grown man. Your decisions are your own."

31. THE ANGUISH OF LOSS

By morning, the collective carnage from the evening before left trickles of blood draining out of the cracks of the poorly constructed shacks in the huddled district. The overpowering odor of sewage and rotting fish that normally held sway over the area now had a new companion: the odor of gore and death. A stream of red blood smeared its way down along the gentle indentation that marked the middle of the street. Those who slept later than others woke to the sounds of bewildered sobbing and screaming; neighbors and friends wandered the streets, clasping each other in gratefulness and consolation. The soles of their feet were stained red with the life fluid of their neighbors and loved ones, the ground covered with the muddled red prints of feet and boots leading frenetically from door to door. All around, it was clear that something terrible had happened, but no one seemed to know why, or how.

After Lak'ail, the devourer had gone on a rampage. It had swept through Shantytown, devouring entire families that night. While the devourer fed, Gerrus rested and prepared for its return. He now stood in the middle of a perfect circle, described by a thick line of fine silver dust. Arcane runes surrounded the circle, enveloping the necromancer in a weave of protective energy. The Devourer now floated before him, pulsing with power and squirming in rage. It had never experienced strength like this before, such raw energy; and this mortal was going to take it away. The devourer seethed in rage, but could not shake the magical chains that held it in place.

"You would like to see me falter, wouldn't you?" Gerrus rasped. "If I gave you even a moment of weakness, you would consume me, just like the others." He placed his staff in the golden stand in the center of the circle, whispering words of power that surrounded it in a shimmering glow. "Last night, you fed; but this morn, you will feed me." He gestured toward the devourer with one hand, and the staff with another, his incantations both mellifluous and sharply punctuated at the same time. The devourer thrashed in protest, unable to stop the link. It felt the power it had amassed quickly draining away, siphoned into the staff. Screams of rage boiled through the devourer's psyche, across the planes, assaulting the necromancer in waves. The circle held firm, and the devourer weakened, the staff humming with power. "You know," Gerrus murmured, "It would never do for a vengeful beast from the planes to stalk me, would it?" The devourer launched itself violently against the mental chains that bound it. In one instant of realization, it lost all thoughts of vengeance, and redoubled its efforts on breaking its chains, trying to flee the withered half-man before it. Clearly it had underestimated what he could do. Gerrus smiled and grasped his staff, and felt a rush of the power transfer to him on contact. He pulled the staff from the holder, thrusting it through the circle and up into the mouth of the devourer. The devourer, a creature of a thousand epochs, let loose a scream worse than a thousand banshees then fell silent, its final epoch at an end.

32. THE WORM AWAKENS

He had been promised a manticore egg. He had been amused then, though not disappointed, when a baby gryphon had emerged from the shell. It was no wonder that it was sold for only a couple gold pieces; whoever had stolen it from the gryphon aviary in the wizards' tower likely wanted to get rid of it before someone found out. Nanong threw more corpse meat at the creature's makeshift cage, and went over the final steps in his mind.

He had circumscribed the well of flesh with arcane powders and traced the appropriate runes along the circle. He had set a makeshift wooden platform at the edge of the well, inscribed with another arcane circle around the cage. It was in this cage that the gryphon paced. The gryphon's tail twitched as it stared at him. Nanong dismissed the creature's angry display with a mock shooing motion of his hand, giggling.

Nanong took one last look around the room, ensuring everything was in place. He looked in the passage outside of the chamber; assured that he wouldn't be disturbed, he stepped into the circle beside the gryphon's cage. He pulled a piece of parchment from his sleeve, and read it aloud, causing the runes to glow dark blue as the scroll crumbled to dust. He closed his eyes and intoned ancient words of power, causing the air around him to hum with energy. The pool of flesh began to ripple, the shimmering colors reflecting the reddish glow emanating from the circle around his feet. He breathed gently in relaxation; the first spell, which provided protection from spiritual forces, had thus far held back the forces swirling in the flesh pool.

He continued his recitation, raising his voice to a shout, as the flesh boiled into a tower thrusting into the air, forming a clawlike hand, demanding a sacrifice. He opened the cage carefully, ensuring his hands were clear of the gryphon's reach. The hand grasped insistently towards the circle, green sparks arcing off of it as it came too close. The gryphon, however, refused to come out of its cage. Unwilling to speak, lest he break the ritual, Nanong thumped the top of the cage in frustration with his fist; still the creature did not budge. The hand snapped angrily at the circle.

The maelstrom in the pool would not be content much longer; without a sacrifice, the magical creature would collapse, and the bound demons who were supporting the ritual would be free. Nanong leaned over, tenting his body with his hands on the back edge of the cage, out of reach of the mighty paws of the gryphon. Nanong heaved with all of his might, sliding the cage closer to the angry flesh pool. The gryphon howled, startling Nanong. Nanong lost his footing for a moment; scrabbling for purchase, his foot slipped backwards, disturbing the circle.

The slight disturbance was all that the flesh beast needed. Raw flesh and energy reached through the circle, the protective magic now broken. Nanong broke his silence with a guttural scream, as the hand pulled him in. The hand flowed into many hands, which grasped his hands, feet, head, and stomach. The hands turned to mouths, and his screams turned to brief whimper, then silence. Freed and empowered by the creator that it had consumed, yet unfinished by its father, the flesh worm began to ooze out of the cistern, seeking a purpose.

Loose from the cage where it had spent its entire life, the gryphon was at a loss. It knew that it needed to escape, and that the only way out was through the doorway. Looking around wildly, he bolted for the door. He ran through the doorway to the far end of the massive chamber before turning around. Flowing out of the doorway from whence he came was a massive tubular mass of yellowed fat, red muscle, and connective tissue. An undulating slug comprised of human remains, it was over seven feet tall at its highest point, constricting down smaller to fit through doorways. It was already at least twice the length of the chamber from which it was oozing. The end was either hidden somewhere in the chamber behind it, or had yet to finish coming out of the pool. The gryphon fled down the tunnels that it recognized, then ones that it didn't, until it collapsed from exhaustion.

33. AN UNCOMMON ARMY

His body pulsed with power, limned with a yellow-green light. Gerrus strode purposefully past the high piles of bodies, bolstered by the energy that coursed through his body and threatened to consume him. He mounted the dais in the middle of the room. He raised his hands skyward, and green fire shot out from the dais to encircle the room in an eerie glow. The time had come.

34. THE RETURN

Mikkel roused Larrik and Pash after a few hours' time. Therrien had woken during his watch, and expressed his thanks to Larrik and Pash when they woke. Unfortunately, Larrik's warning had proven partly true: Though Therrien could feel his legs, he couldn't support his own weight. Mikkel and Larrik whispered prayers and massaged herbs into his wound, pressing yellow fluid out of the wound and into their makeshift bandages.

"Now that we're on the Path, Solypse isn't far from here," Larrik advised. "We need to get him to the Temple as soon as we can, to get him patched up."

While Larrik dismantled the camp, and Mikkel set about preparing himself for the rest of the journey, Pash sat with Therrien, discussing the clutchers.

Therrien breathed shallow, even breaths. He looked up at Pash and smiled. "Mikkel told me what you did."

Pash gave him a slight smile in return, and nodded.

"You have a gift, Pash. Do not squander it by following a path set before you by someone else. If Lethos had meant for you to be a cleric, you would be one by now."

"It felt...incredible."

Therrien nodded weakly. "I never succeeded in casting that spell, but I know of what you speak. Which brings me to the next thing I wanted to talk to you about. Can you fetch my spellbook for me please?"

Pash walked over to the mage's belongings, and rummaged until he found the runed red book. He carried it back to Therrien. Therrien reached up and placed a hand on the book, closed his eyes, and whispered arcane words.

He opened his eyes. "There. I have removed my binding from it, and I bestow it upon you. You saved my life, and I am in your debt."

Pash felt the breath rush out of his lungs in exhilaration. "You can't—I couldn't—"

Therrien dropped his hand to his side once again. "We were delivered from certain death because of you with that book. Even if you can't see that as a sign from Lethos, I can. And where I'm going, I won't be needing a spellbook."

Pash shook his head vigorously. "You're going to be fine. Larrik said that the poultice will cause some paralysis, but that's normal."

Therrien smiled thinly. "That's not what I meant. I think my calling is with the temple. I suppose you could say that it's an even trade of tradesmen."

Pash sat down beside Therrien's head, astonished. "If you truly mean what you say, then I am honored to carry your spellbook. May your journey to faith be strong and true."

"It is your book now; may it serve you well. As for me, there's something about nearly dying that seems to help a man see their faith for what it truly is... My way forward is clear in my mind."

Larrik walked up behind them, fists firmly planted at his waist. "Load up!"

They loaded Therrien up on the litter, and took turns carrying him. They were cheered by the appearance of occasional merchants passing them on the Path, happy for any sign of civilization beckoning from the road ahead. At long last, they reached the bridge, the silent deep elves still standing watch. They stood in line with the other merchants that were on foot, waiting for their turn to be processed. An old grizzled man with a stack of paper stood by the entrance, endlessly repeating "Name? Purpose of visit?" followed by scribbling, stamping a paper, and letting visitors through. They reached the old man, stopping to gently set down Therrien. With barely a glance, the old man monotone "Name? Purpose of visit?"

"Pash and Larrik, of the Temple of Lethos. Returning from mission work."

The old man looked up, glancing at Mikkel and Therrien. "Are you two with them?" Mikkel nodded vigorously. The old man looked at the pair of guards to his left. "Here they are. The other two are with them as well." One of the guards shouted up to the window above him, and a compliment of four guards came down through the door behind the old man. "You've been sent for. The guards will see to it that you get to your destination."

Larrik cleared his throat. "Thank you kind sirs for your help. Would you please take our friend here to the Temple while we are speaking with Council?"

The guards laughed. "The Council? What would they want with

the likes of you? The magistrate wants to see you." A guard kicked Therrien in the ribs. "Pick him up. I'm not your servant."

Their weapons removed, they were grandly marched up the ramps past the merchant district. Flanked by the guard compliment, they proceeded up towards the fifth tier. "This is bad," Pash muttered. "The lower courts are in the merchant district. If we're going up, we must be going to the high magistrate."

"What does that mean?" Therrien asked groggily.

"It means," Larrik observed, "that Cillan got here before us."

The companions and their guard escort arrived at the grand doors of the huge stone compound. Two guards hauled open the doors, and the companions headed through the courtyard.

They walked into the courthouse, roughly pushed through the doors by their escorts into a broad stone room with pillars on either side; the high ceiling disappearing in darkness over the deep red carpet on the floor. Light magically emanated from sconces set into the pillars, their steady glow contrasting with the flickering of the candles set beside the chair on the stone platform before them. In the chair sat a slight, balding man, his feet barely reaching the ground. He was elaborately clothed in colored silks and superfluous furs, procured from merchants who brought them from the overworld. His fingers were splayed apart from all the rings upon them.

"Kneel before the high magistrate." A herald slapped the back of their legs with a pole, knocking them to their knees. Therrien dropped roughly to the ground, much to the delight of the herald.

The magistrate looked appraisingly at them. Ellias had asked him to take care of the temple rabble. Indeed he would; he and Ellias traded favors back and forth regularly. Still, he couldn't help but wonder what a pair of dwarves, a young man, and an invalid could have done to raise the ire of a councilman. Theft, most likely; crime led to odd allies. Regardless, a favor was a favor.

"You stand accused of the murder of the honorable Mayor Nar'el of Shoal, and the attempted murder of a representative for a member of the council. How do you plead?"

Mikkel snickered. "Nar'el? Honorable?"

Larrik smacked Mikkel's side with the back of his hand, and the herald in turn slapped the back of Larrik's head with his staff.

Larrik spoke up. "Not guilty, magistrate. What council representative do ye speak of?"

"According to the report I have here, it appears your escort fled for her life."

Larrik snorted. "Beggin' yer pardon sir, methinks it was she that did the deed."

What was Ellias up to? The magistrate tapped his chin thoughtfully. "You dare attempt to cast shadows upon the integrity of the well-respected guards and representatives of this city's fine council? I think not. Why would a murderer flee your company, then report back to the council in fear of her life?"

"It was a setup!" Pash blurted.

The magistrate feigned surprise. "A setup? I would laugh, if it were not for the seriousness of your crimes. Now I see why Council-man Ellias was so concerned: murderers and liars pretending at being pious. Tell me...what could a fledgling cleric and his pet dwarf do that could possibly make a councilman interested in setting them up?"

"We...know about the murder?"

Larrik elbowed Pash. "Hush!"

The herald struck Larrik again, knocking him to the ground.

"Indeed you likely do. Very well, I'm sure." The magistrate looked to the guards. "Throw them in the dungeon. We'll decide what to do with them tomorrow." The magistrate smiled thinly. Ellias had asked him to get rid of them altogether; however, if the acolyte was to be-lieved, then perhaps they were worth a bit more yet... He might be able to command a higher price from his council friend.

35. CILLAN RESOLUTE

Cillan slipped into the tunnels as soon as she dared. Though shaken from her encounter, she had already begun to formulate a plan by the time she reached the tunnels; but first, there was unfinished business to take care of.

Cillan walked into the guild hall, greeted by an empty room. She liked coming in before midday; most work was done at night, and the rest of the guild was likely still sleeping off the previous evening's work.

She walked casually to room of assignment, locking the door behind her. She murmured the words of opening over the box, reaching in to scoop out the coins while she dropped in a note. She secured the box and put it away, and swiftly headed for the guild exit. Preoccupied with her thoughts, she ran full force into Thalen, knocking a full mug of ale out of his hand and on to both of them.

She cursed under her breath. "Hells upon you Thalen! What are you doing here drinking at this hour?"

Thalen laughed, and tossed her a bar rag. "It seems that someone has been swimming in our pool. My last mark was killed before I got there. I have no job right now, so..." he hoisted his tankard. "I thought I should have a drink."

Cillan dabbed ineffectively at the spill that covered her tunic and ran down her legs.

Thalen grinned. "So you're a town guard now? How's that working out for you?"

"Council business. You know how it is."

"Oh, don't I ever. Ellias speaks highly of you by the way. How was your jaunt down the Path?"

"Who said I was down the Path?"

He laughed again. "Ellias mentioned you were doing some work for him, and," he continued in a mockingly righteous tone, placing his hand over his breast with a flourish, "the whole government sector is abuzz about the shocking assassination of a beloved Mayor. It's terrible what the Temple is willing to stoop to these days to maintain their dominance."

"Yes, well...I just told Ellias that I'm not doing council work anymore. I'll put in a good word for you."

He bowed with a flourish. "You might have to, considering my last job didn't quite work out."

"So what happened with that?"

He shrugged. "I'm not sure. When I got there, it was a mess. There were pieces—and pieces of pieces—strewn everywhere. Gods, I would hate to be the scullery maid trying to clean kidneys off the walls."

She shuddered. "It sounds brutal."

He grinned evilly. "Oh, it was."

Cillan sighed heavily, and gave up on trying to mop up her clothes with the dirty rag. She tossed the bar rag behind the counter, bidding Thalen goodbye. She headed out the door and down the tunnels until they led to a sewer channel. She followed the channel until it merged with a flowing river of sewage, walking along the raised cobblestone path next to the river of filth. She was heading towards the lowest and most fetid part of the city, a portion of the tunnels completely devoid of life shy of rats and insects. The odor of fecal matter and decay were overwhelming; no matter how often she passed through this tunnel, her eyes would always water and bile would rise in her throat. Ironically, this particular locale was far too familiar to her. The guild often met clients or one another here, as it was both secluded and left few places to hide.

She peeked out of the end of the tunnel, ensuring there was no one present to witness her egress. She stepped out confidently, with the practiced air befitting one who was a member of the guard. Her pace slowed; something was amiss. Most days, Shantytown was nearly deserted, the residents having headed to the fishery, the warehouses, or the docks to beg for work. Today, however, the streets were full of people rushing back and forth. She picked up her pace, her heart beating in her chest. She could hear wailing and sobbing, and could see people cradling others in the street. She broke into a trot. When townsfolk saw the guard tabard, they began to shout and chase after her, demanding answers. She ignored them and kept running, until she came to a shack covered in flaking yellow paint.

Trembling, she reached out and pulled the door open. Reflexively, she ducked as a brick threw at her head. She tucked into a roll, clearing the expanse of the small, cluttered room, something heavy flying past her body and clanging off the door behind her. Her hand shot up and caught a wrist slicing downwards with a rusty blade.

"Mother! It's me, Cillan!"

The wrist holding the knife relaxed, the hand going limp and the blade clattering on the floor.

"Cillan! Oh dear. I was afraid you were someone coming to kill me!" Her mother began sobbing, collapsing in her arms as Cillan stood to catch her.

Cillan held her tight, running a hand gently through her mother's thinning hair, re-fastening the worn pink flower hairclip that held the wispy grey hair back.. "No one is coming to kill you, mother. You're just having one of your dreams again."

"No, this is different," she sniffled. "Just have a look around. People are dead everywhere. Blood...such blood. I can't get the floors clean no matter what I do."

Cillan looked down, and saw the red and pink stained floor. The stacked scrap that marked the walls kept little out; blood had seeped in and around the edges, running in smeared trickles crisscrossing the ground. Her mother leaned back and looked at Cillan's guard tunic approvingly. Cillan let her mother stand alone, and turned to a trunk at the back of the room. She stripped off the guard attire and crumpled it in the corner. She pulled on more comfortable clothes, black tight fitting leather armor with matching gloves. She packed some tools and clothes into a small knapsack, and snugged the straps tight against her back. She paused for a moment, then leaned over the guard uniform, pulling out the sack of coins, and dividing them in half. She wrapped half tightly in a swatch of cloth from her trunk, keeping them from jingling, and stuffed them in a side pouch of the knapsack. She pulled on a long brown stained jacket that reached down to her ankles, covering her knapsack and buttoning it to look like one of the local fish renderers.

Her mother's expression hardened. "I was hoping you had actually joined the guard. My mistake."

Cillan pressed the pouch with the remaining coins into her mother's hand, and kissed her on the forehead. "Don't worry, I'll be back soon."

Cillan slipped out of the shack without waiting for her mother to respond. She slouched over, her backpack beneath her jacket making her look like a hunchback. She kept her head cast down, glancing sidelong at the massacre around her. Blood and destroyed bodies were everywhere. Some had their viscera removed and strewn about like a child's forgotten toys; others had been decapitated, nothing left of the heads except misshapen piles regurgitated on the ground beside the bodies.

Whatever had been through the Shantytown clearly wasn't human. Cillan shuddered. She had seen men do many terrible things; however, this was something else entirely. She swiftly headed back in the direction from which she came, stealthily clambering into the tunnel mouth. Once inside, she doffed the jacket, rolling tightly and stuffing it into her backpack. She pulled out a pair of gloves and the mask served that served as both a symbol of her role and as a means of disguising her. As she donned the mask, her height and bulk altered. "Better," she croaked, her voice deepened into a sneering rasp.

After Cillan left, Thalen laughed. His mentor, though still young, was no longer as youthful as she once was. She carried herself with the demeanor of an old blade, past her prime and lacking the ambition to climb within the guild. *"Perhaps she is tiring of the life,"* he thought. He shrugged to himself, finishing his draught. *"All the more opportunity for me."* He wandered down the hall to the room of assignments. He had checked his book the night before, and didn't expect much; still, he was expected to check daily, and if he got it out of the way early, he would have the rest of the day to lollygag and entertain himself. He went through the usual ritual, and plucked his book from the shelf. He opened the book, and pulled a slip of parchment from it. To his dismay, his day was already ruined. He gathered his things in the guild hall swiftly, and headed down the tunnels.

Cillan waited patiently until she saw the glowing hands in the dark, signaling her that Thalen was there. "You're early," she growled, the mask obfuscating her voice.

Thalen was startled by the sound. Accustomed to communicating with the guild master by hand signals alone, Thalen had never actually heard him speak. He studied the figure across from him intently now.

Cillan switched to silent hand language. "Your assignments have shifted. You will report to Ellias and tell him that you will take over any work that he might have for the guild."

"What of Cillan?" he signaled back.

"Cillan is no longer in play."

Thalen pondered this. Apparently she was better connected than he gave her credit for. He had never refused an assignment. Indeed, never even heard of another refusing an assignment.

"It shall be as you say, sir." Thalen removed his gloves, causing them to go dark. He disappeared into a narrow cleft in the stone channel, standing still as stone, watching the guild master from the shadows.

Cillan slipped the gloves and mask off, hastily repacking them in her sack, then swiftly moved down the hall. She only had a few short hours before the guild hall would be fully populated again; with Thalen out of the way for a bit, she would have time to gather some equipment without arousing suspicion, but she would have to work fast. She darted down the tunnels, unaware as Thalen slipped from the shadows behind her.

As she neared the entrance to the final passages to the guild, she heard a sloshing noise coming from a side tunnel. She paused at the side tunnel entrance; the traps that surrounded the inner circle of tunnels around the guild would have stopped all but the most accomplished interloper, and this clearly did not sound like someone practiced in stealth. The sloshing got louder, and she waited until she heard the reassuring sound of the crossbow traps being triggered. Smiling contentedly to herself, she took a step away from the tunnel, then realized that the sloshing continued. Quietly, she crept down the tunnel, getting closer to her unknown prey. She pressed herself flat in a niche in the wall, unwilling to strike up a light source. She could hear her quarry more clearly now: the noise had to be made by more than one, though she couldn't quite place a number. Regardless, there were no lights. "*They must be native deep dwellers,*" she reasoned.

The sloshing got louder and louder, until it was next to her. It became apparent that there were more than simply two or three Dwarves ambling down the tunnel: there was a large force here, and she was about to be trapped. Beginning to panic, Cillan sprang out of her alcove, intent on falling back to the guild. Cold, clammy hands grabbed her arms and tangled in her hair. Fingernails scratched deep gashes through the armor on her arm. Cillan spun to the side, pulling her arm free of the piercing nails. She felt a a tense pull on the back of her head, She heard a popping noise, then was released, tumbling forward and narrowly avoiding falling into the flowing sewage. She ran full speed, abandoning stealth altogether, her head throbbing. She was nearly at the guild entrance when she realized that her throbbing head wasn't from an injury in the hall; slowing her pace, she reached up and felt a hand still tangled in her hair. Unable to suppress a shriek, she yanked hard and dropped it on the ground. She sparked up a torch, in the face of the normal rules of darkness in the assassin tunnels. She now understood what the popping was: The hand was attached to an arm, the arm dangling flesh and muscle like a leg separated from a well-cooked feast bird.

Cillan reached for a dagger, and halted mid-throw. The zombified arm wasn't crawling towards her; rather, it was crawling back in the direction from which it came. Cillan silently cursed her foolishness at having lit the torch, and tossed it after the arm. She fled into the darkness, away from the mob sloshing its way through the tunnels.

From his position several hundred feet away, Thalen had sensed the guild master struggling with something, and easily followed as they sprinted away. When he heard the shriek, he had dropped back, the sound of her voice providing a surprising new turn of events. He shrank back as she tossed the torch in his direction, content to smile in the darkness. The game was now before him; all he now needed was to play it carefully.

36. AN UNEASY ALLIANCE

Pash pressed his face against the bars of the long, narrow cell, straining to see down the dimly lit corridor. Smoothly cut stone reflected dim light from an unseen torch around the curve of the hall. No guards or other cells were in sight.

"There's not much to tell. It's a long hall with a tall ceiling. I don't see any guards, torches, or even any other cells around."

Larrik spoke up. "That's because there aren't any. We're condemned. They leave us here, forgotten, for as long as they see fit. They'll fish us out when they are ready. Try the door."

Pash shook the bars on the jail, surprised to find the door unlocked. He looked at Larrik questioningly. "Are these the halls of the forgotten?"

Larrik shook his head. "Nay, and be thankful for that. Here, at least there is a chance they will come get ye. Still, they leave the doors unlocked, hoping the other prisoners will save the council the trouble of having to go to trial."

Larrik gestured forward with a hand. Pash opened the door cautiously.

"I can tell ye what you'll find."

Pash ignored him, and stepped out of the cell. He quietly padded down the hall, out of sight. Moments later, he returned.

"Well?" Therrien queried from his spot on the floor. The guards had decided that being condemned was more than enough reason to ignore the fact that Therrien was lame, and they had thrown him in the cell along with the others. The lameness had worn off, but the poison had not, so he had elected to remain on the floor in his weakened state.

Mikkel looked at Pash expectantly. Pash shook his head.

"The light comes from above. At the end of the hall is a big round room with a trap door in the ceiling. It looks like we're the only prisoners here, so that's good at least."

Mikkel brightened his expression. "Any chance of reaching it?"

Pash shook his head again. "Even if we stood on one another's shoulders, we would still only be about halfway up the wall. No doors."

Therrien sat up. "That's impossible. They brought us in here somehow."

Larrik grunted. "Enspelled doors. We'll be here until they get us, or until we starve to death."

A voice echoed down the hall. "Or you could leave right now."

Pash rushed into the hall. Larrik followed cautiously.

When they rounded the corner, Larrik angrily pushed past Pash. "You venomous, self-serving daughter of a dragon! I'll kill you with my bare hands!"

Cillan deftly sidestepped Larrik's charge, spinning her leg in a low arc and connecting with Larrik's backside, sending him tumbling to the ground.

"I apologize for the predicament that I seem to have placed you in, but I need your help."

Pash raised an eyebrow. "*Need our help?* What makes you think we would help you?"

Cillan nodded sympathetically. "I understand your hesitation. The door is open," she gestured at the far side of the chamber, where a door was, indeed, open in the side of the wall. "And you are welcome to go on your own. However, you know nothing of the tunnels, or the traps. Not to mention you are unarmed." She paused, as if in thought. "Oh yes, and you are all wanted as enemies of the council. You probably don't want to wander through the downtown merchant district, do you?"

Larrik had drawn himself up to his feet, and was making a grand show of straightening out his tunic.

"Ye got us thrown in jail, but now ye need us?"

"Despite what you may think, my fondness of the council only runs as far as my coinpurse; these days, it even runs short of that. The person who put you in here is Councilman Ellias. I also have issue with the good councilman. We have a mutual interest in his...departure."

Larrik shook a stubby index finger in her face. "Near as I see it, yer the only reason we're down here. And based on Nar'el, methinks you are quite capable of handling his departure yerself!"

Cillan shrugged. "Look at it however you like. I was paid to do a job; if it wasn't me, it would have been someone else. I bear you no ill will; I never have."

"The lass has a point." Cillan looked up to see Mikkel standing by the hall, next to Therrien. "Anyhow, I don't see that we have any other options."

"There is also another problem. I'm not sure I know how to explain it, but I think Solypse may be in big trouble." Cillan recounted her encounter with the ambling horde underground, and the carnage of Wallenbrook. Mikkel grew concerned as Cillan brought their attention to the wounds on her arm and scalp.

"Zombies!" Therrien gasped. "I thought they were children's tales!"

Cillan raised her hands in puzzlement. "As did I. All I know is what I saw."

"Well," Larrik said, "If the arm crawled back to the rest of them as ye say, then they're after something. Which means someone is controlling them. Which is a problem."

Cillan took a deep breath, and exhaled. "So are you in, or are you out?"

Pash looked at Mikkel and Therrien quizzically. "Wait; she murdered one of your friends, and now you will have her as a trusted ally, just like that?"

Mikkel shrugged. "I wouldn't have counted Nar'el as a friend. Regardless, one becomes a bit more...practical about one's company, after a few years in the tunnels."

"Or in the company of mercenaries", added Therrien.

Pash nodded. So it goes then. "My family helped found this city. I can't sit idly by while something like this happens."

Larrik rolled his eyes. "If the boy is going, I'm going to have to go to keep his arse alive."

"Well," said Mikkel cheerfully, "I thought Nar'el was a dungheap, and Halail would kill me if I had a chance to fight zombies and passed it by!"

Cillan paused, looking at Therrien. Therrien looked back at her, fighting conflicting emotions.

"I- I think we can trust her."

"Are you in?"

Therrien sighed. "Yes. My friends will need my help."

Cillan gave a curt nod. "It is settled then. Let us get moving quickly!"

"What of our equipment?" Larrik retorted.

Cillan smiled broadly. "It's in the tunnel!"

The companions stepped single file through the door, until Therrien and Cillan remained. Cillan put a gentle hand on his shoulder.

"Thanks."

"It wasn't for you."

"But you're willing to trust me. Thanks for that."

"A little."

"Why?"

He shrugged. "Because. Because Cael." Therrien shrugged her hand off, and ducked through the doorway as she stood there, dumbfounded and confused.

***

In the relative safety of the access tunnels, the companions adjusted their gear and strapped on their weapons.

"Here, let me take a look at that." Mikkel tugged on Cillan's arm, drawing Cillan into a crouch and her arm eye-level with the dwarf. The cut was deep and straight, winking from beneath the torn leather sleeve. Mikkel took the opportunity to look at the scratches on the back of Cillan's head as well.

"Hm. You're lucky, no infection, from the looks of it. Hold still." Mikkel massaged Cillan's arm, whispering a prayer to Riordan. He pulled her hands away, revealing mended flesh.

"Wait," Pash said dubiously, "You mean you could have done that for Therrien all this time?"

"No; Therrien still has poison that courses through his veins. We need to get him to the Temple. Halail might be able to, but I'm nowhere near her skill."

Therrien shook his head. "You think they will heal a condemned murderer, now escaped from prison?"

"You have a point."

"What we need to do is get to the Wizarding tower. My old master, Kithe of The Black, would know what to do."

Larrik cocked his head to the side. "Do ye think that is wise? It's more'n likely well protected, and as ye said, we're not exactly welcome dinner guests."

Therrien let out a twinge of a smile. "We're wanted because we are being accused by the council of something. That alone might give him cause for merriment."

Larrik fixed his gaze on Cillan. "Except'n one of us actually *did* murder someone."

"He has a very...flexible view on things; I do not see that as a problem. Truly though, he is the only ally I can think of to help us. We dare not involve the Temple directly, as they govern alongside the council. Mikkel is a wanderer. That leaves me, and Cillan. If she had somewhere else to turn, then she probably wouldn't have broken us out of prison. So that leaves me, which means that leaves The Wizard of the Black."

"Supposin' we do go to the tower. How do you propose we get there? We can't just stroll down the market district now, can we?"

Therrien looked at Cillan hopefully. "Have any other tricks up your sleeve?"

Cillan stared upwards at the tunnel ceiling, searching her mind for the appropriate maps. "I can get us close, but I can't get us inside, not without someone inside to lower a very long rope. Of course, if we had someone inside who could lower a rope, then we could just have him open the door instead."

Therrien held up his hand. "Actually, that part I can handle. I used to live there, remember? I know the way in; it's just the getting there part that is the problem."

Cillan surveyed the group. The veneer of nervous excitement that had once been wrapped around Pash's soul was now gone, replaced with a taught grim visage. Larrik leaned against the wall, his fingers drumming against the head of one of his mattocks. Mikkel, unflappable, leaned against his warhammer, awaiting the word to move. Therrien look at him intently, fatigue and the effects of the poison etching deep lines of exhaustion into his face.

Cillan nodded sharply. "Okay. Getting there is the easy part. Let's move."

Hold up, said Therrien. "There's one more thing that you should probably know about The Wizard of the Black. He's partially possessed by a demon."

37. WORM ON THE MOVE

A thick legged arachnid, larger than a man, sat comfortably in its web, waiting for prey. In the distance, it heard a low grinding noise, and scampered up into roof structure of its tunnel. It could smell meat already. The spider saw the oddity below it, but didn't think much of it—it registered as food, which was good enough. It dropped down to seize the element of surprise and envenom its victim before it comprehended the sheer size of the beast. The spider tried to clamber up the wall, but the flesh worm pressed from side to side, ceiling to floor. The flesh worm slammed into the side of the spider, knocking it sideways and crushing half of its legs in the process.

Ligament, fat, and sinew crept quickly around the spider's body and limbs. Seconds later, the spider stopped struggling, and was absorbed into the thick folds of the flesh worm.

The undulating mass oozed through the broad tunnel and further into the depths. Though the fledgling necromancer had conjured life, he had lacked the skill to imbue the subtleties of intelligence upon it. The creature was only left with the most basic of primal impulses: *consume*. Fully emerged from the spawning pool, the undulating worm crawled down tunnels into the reaches of the deep.

Creatures not smart enough to avoid it were enveloped, then consumed by hundreds of nameless faces within before becoming fused as part of the mass. The sour, necrotic smell preceded it down the tunnels for miles; predators that drew close, hoping for a free meal, became meals themselves. With each creature consumed, the worm grew. A greater magician would have given it the ability to absorb the powers of the creatures it consumed; Nanong had only given the worm the power to grow, and that it did in abundance.

The worm slid its massive bulk at impressive speed, needing no pause or rest. Had Therrien stayed in Shoal, he would have been frantically preparing the guard for a massive threat on the move. Instead, Therrien crept through the tunnels under Solypse, a sinking feeling growing in his stomach as the wards he had placed triggered alarms in his mind.

38. THE UNDEAD DESCEND

Five tiers below the temple, one tier below the interest of most of the city, hundreds of corpses began to walk, clamber, and fall out of the pipe. The zombies moved at a slow, steady pace, filling both the main roads and alleyways.

The middle of Shantytown was still a mess. Chevil had been dragging body parts out of the road in front of him and tossing them into the nearby river of filth, hoping to restore some semblance of dignity to his otherwise undignified hovel. The halfling's hands were covered in grime and gore. He wiped the sweat from his forehead with the back of his hand, trying to avoid touching his brown curly mop of hair. He looked up, collecting his thoughts, and was frozen in place, his eyes wide and fearful. Zombies were pouring out of the sewage pipe, like a colony of ants on the march. Hundreds of zombies swarmed towards the people of Shantytown, all who were too enveloped in their own grief to notice. Chevil let out a strangled cry. He began to scream, another voice lost in the cries that had begun at sunup that morning.

The first victims of the horde, predictably, were those who were in the middle of the main road, tending to the corpses from the night before. Body parts joined body parts, and families fell with families. Cold, fetid hands calmly and relentlessly rent flesh and ripped limbs. Five of the horde, slightly more whole but otherwise unremarkable, did not participate in the carnage. They wandered the roads with the horde, seeking solitary targets in houses and sidestreets. Each of the five collected a live squirming resident, then dragged their prizes back out of town and up the tunnel.

***

Ellias folded his hands and gazed out over the city, collecting his thoughts. Word of the temple murder had begun to spread. Fortunately, word of the murder in Shoal had begun to spread as well; he had seen to that. The temple-dwellers had been arrested, and were likely either dead or soon to be. That left only one loose end to clean up on this gambit.

He summoned his attendant to him. "The last guard proved unreliable. I require a replacement."

His attendant nodded. "Shall we find a new company of mercenaries?"

Ellias shook his head. "They have proven themselves reliable in the past. One bad fish doesn't poison the pond."

His attendant bowed his head, and hurried out of Ellias chambers. Ellias had begun walking toward his balcony to resume his contemplation, when there was a loud pounding and his door began to open.

"By the gods! How hard is it to follow one order?" he snapped.

Brother Kern opened the door wide, giving a swift half-bow out of courtesy. "Pardon my brash entrance, honorable councilman. The temple has just gotten word that there are scores of zombies descending upon Shantytown as we speak!" Breathless and sweating, Brother Kern grasped the edge of the table, awaiting a reaction from the councilman.

Surprised, Ellias whirled to face Brother Kern. "Zombies? From where?"

"It appears they are coming from the sewers."

"Have there been any spotted in any of the other tiers yet?"

"No, honorable councilman. Just Shantytown."

"Isn't this...a matter for those of holy might?"

Brother Kern shook his head. "I'm afraid that is a blessing bestowed upon the houses of the holy good. Lethos, his name be praised, stands for commerce and balance, favoring neither good nor evil, therefore-"

Ellias cut him off with an upraised hand, fearing another lecture on the glory of Lethos. "So what you're telling me is that your god doesn't give you the power to turn these creatures back to the grave."

"That is what I am telling you, yes."

"Very well then, the council and the city guard will see to this right away. If you would please, send the guard outside in, and leave us. We have much planning to do."

"As you desire, Councilman. The brothers will head down to provide spiritual support and any comfort we can." Brother Kern turned heel and stepped swiftly out of the door. Moments later, the guard stepped into the room.

"Yes, honorable councilman?"

"It seems, my friend, that there are zombies invading Shanty-town."

The guard's eyes went wide with disbelief. "Sir?"

"It is of no great concern. Brother Kern assures us that the temple will handle it. Just to be sure, please send some men down to protect the fishing and warehouse districts. Brother Kern was very clear that the men are *not* to engage the enemy unless the zombies threaten the commercial area. If anyone asks, please assure them that the temple has promised to take care of the issue swiftly. Go."

"Yes sir." The guard bowed his head, and quickly walked out of the room.

39. THE UNDERGROUND AND THE TOWER

The companions walked through the abandoned tunnels, Cillan leading with a torch. "Tell me again why we are going to a demon infested magician to banish zombies, rather than the temple?"

"The temple of Lethos holds little sway over the undead," Larrik explained. "Think of it in terms of opposites and balances: light opposes dark, good opposes evil, and so on. Followers of Lethos preach balance—everything having a place in the world, in equal degrees. As Lethos cherishes trade and commerce, he sees a need for both greed and generosity as two complimentary functions of the same system. "

"But what does that have to do with zombies?"

"Lethos' interest in balance may manifest as trade, but the ethos transcends the mechanics of buying and selling. In essence, to oppose evil, a god would have to be opposed to it, rather than merely interested in a healthy regulation of it."

"So in the face of a zombie invasion, the clerics of Lethos are powerless?"

"Essentially."

"What about yours?" Cillan gestured at Mikkel.

Mikkel shook his head. "Danites are interested in both adventure and discovering the natural world of the dark. Most creatures—even the likes of the clutchers—aren't considered evil. They're simply doing what they were born to do. Zombies, on the other hand, are unnatural, and conjured with dark magics."

"So what you're saying is that you could be useful?"

"Perhaps a little, but not much; even so, I couldn't beat back an invading horde on my own."

"Which brings us back to part of the original question," Cillan continued. "Why are we going to a demon-possessed magician for help against zombies?"

"Wizard", Therrien amended. "Any spellcaster can claim to be a magician. A Wizard, which he is, is far above your average magician."

"My mistake."

"It is an easy mistake to make, but it is an important point," he conceded. "Also important is that he is only *partly* possessed. As I understand it—and I do not know the details—It happened around a hundred years ago. One rumor is that he was in the midst of a very complex ritual, trying to conjure a planar gate, and he failed to notice the demon lurking in the shadows of the weave. Another rumor has it that he summoned the demon himself, but lost control of it. Still another has it that he was in a mighty battle with the demon, and this was the only way he could control it."

"Which story do you believe?"

"Me? None of them. The Wizard of the Black is far too intelligent to be caught unaware. The one thing I do know is that however the demon came about, The Wizard of the Black used a ritual of binding to prevent the demon from being released into the world."

"But the demon got out and possessed him?"

"No. The demon is incredibly powerful. If it got out, it could lay waste to Solypse in a heartbeat. The Wizard of the Black isn't possessed, exactly; he's a vessel. He bound the demon with his own soul as the chain."

Cillan stopped walking and turned to face Therrien.

"His own soul?"

Therrien nodded and gave a faint smile. "THAT is the difference between a magician and a wizard."

Cillan resumed walking. "What happens when The Wizard of the Black dies?"

"Interesting question. He doesn't appear to age."

"But if he did?"

"I suspect we wouldn't want to be around."

She nodded mutely.

"The real question is," Pash interjected, "What can he do to help us with a zombie horde?"

Therrien nodded his head. "Another good question. Though he has power, his skills are not in the necromantic realm. I suspect that he will have a better idea as to what is going on, or at the least, give us some direction on how to combat it."

Cillan paused, holding up a hand, passing the torch to Pash. She crept down the tunnel towards a shaft of light in a dead end, cautiously looking up. Waving the others over, she leapt to the far wall, grabbing a metal rod affixed into the stone.

Cillan waved the others over. As they approached, their eyes began to water from the smell.

Pash looked at her. "*Really* Cillan?"

She grinned. "The squat hole network. It's the only way to travel in Solypse!"

One by one, they jumped across the gap, clambering up and over the lip of the hole. Though they stood in a narrow alley surrounded by high stone walls, there was no mistaking the stone structure that reached up into the evening shadows: They were next to the Wizarding tower.

Cillan turned to Therrien. "It's your turn to lead." Her face drew concerned. His skin had taken a pale hue, and his brow was beaded with sweat. "You don't look so hot. Are you okay?"

Therrien dismissed her with a wave of her hand. "I've been better, but I'll be fine. I'm sure that The Wizard of the Black will know what to do."

A voice issued from behind them. "I'm not sure that I will; I am, after all, a Wizard, not a nursemaid." Therrien turned with a smile to greet his old master. Even before the demon, Kithe of The Black had been an imposing figure. At nearly twice the height of the Larrik, and powerfully built, his imposing frame was punctuated by a face with a broad forehead and a strong jaw. He appeared to be in his prime years, though his face appeared lined with sorrow. As he stood observing the group, ghostly images of faces flitted over his, as if a gossamer thin mask were pulled in front of him momentarily before vanishing. Faces in torment, confusion, and decomposition flitted by, occasionally punctuated by an enraged demonic visage. "Ahem." The Wizard of the Black interrupted their thoughts and shook them free from their dumbfounded expressions. "My dear apprentice, I can surmise from the scent of you and your companions that you did walk here down the main thoroughfare. Might I suggest that we reserve gawking for another time, and instead retire to my chambers upstairs?"

Therrien smiled. "You are, of course, correct. I think that is a fine suggestion."

"Gather close." Kithe circled around the group, and spoke the words to teleport them into the tower.

The companions found themselves in a spacious yet functional room, filled with furniture for entertaining guests. Several doorways led off from the main room to unseen areas.

"So." He said crossing his arms, "Sit. Let's hear it." They recounted their tale. He leaned back in his chair passively listening, his face a shifting illusion of expressions. He listened without comment until they recounted their encounter with the clutchers. When they mentioned Pash's flames, he leaned forward very suddenly, startling Mikkel into leaping to his feet. Embarrassed, Mikkel settled himself back into his chair quickly. "Interesting." He looked at Pash. "You learned this from reading Therrien's book, you say?"

Pash nodded.

"How far would you say the flames reached, how wide? How many man-lengths?"

"Begging your pardon sir, I'm not sure. It happened very fast; I wasn't even sure it would work."

"It was far enough," Larrik interrupted, "that it cut through dozens of creatures on each side, more or less."

Kithe nodded. "I wonder what powers are hiding within you, my half elven friend."

Cillan looked at Kithe, then Pash quizzically. "Half Elven?"

Kithe regarded Pash curiously. "And what other secrets you might have."

"But yer ears..." Mikkel said curiously.

"I never thought it was important," Pash said simply. "And since I look more human than elven, it was easier to let everyone assume what they wished. My father's mother was human; but I don't see how it matters."

Kithe pondered for a moment. "You said that you were from a well-positioned family."

Pash's face reddened. "Yes. My father is on the council."

"Interesting." Kithe of The Black stared past Pash, out over the balcony at the far end of the room. A demonic face, mixed with surprise and delight flitted past his countenance.

Pash sat frozen in his chair.

Kithe stood up abruptly. "There is much to be done. Come with me." He rapidly walked to the balcony, his charcoal robes fluttering in the wake of the flurry of activity. The companions followed him onto the balcony, and looked out. The view was breathtaking. They were nearly at the top of the Wizarding tower, far above even the sixth tier upon which the temple rested. The balcony wrapped all the way around the tower, providing views down below of the temple to one side, and the Veil on the other. From the platform less than a hundred feet above the balcony, gryphons launched from their aviary and soared in circles above the city.

It was beautiful and dizzying at the same time.

"It is a lovely view, is it not?"

Mikkel nodded. "Aye."

"Look down below."

The companions swept their gaze across the vast expanse of Solypse, across the bustling merchant quarter and out across the bay that was filled with fishing vessels.

"What are we looking for?" Therrien queried.

Kithe didn't respond, waiting patiently.

Cillan let out a strangled cry. "The town-the-"

Pash looked at her curiously. Eyes filled with horror and brimming with tears, she pointed at Wallenbrook. Even at their great height, they could see the ceaseless stream of lumbering bodies climbing out of the sewer pipe. Wallenbrook's streets appeared dark black; moments later, it dawned on Pash that they were covered in blood. Two troop formations stood facing Shantytown from across the river of sewage.

"Why aren't they doing anything?" Cillan cried.

"Perhaps they don't want to get involved", Therrien offered.

Cillan shook her head fiercely. "Many of the guard came from Shantytown. Many still have families there."

They could see a long line of brown robed figures winding their way down the ramps of the many levels of Solypse, snaking towards the lowest tier. Larrik shook his head. "That's not right. They can't fix this."

"But you can." Kithe walked away from the balcony, the ghostly visage of his face a blur of rage, screaming, anguish, glee, and calm interspersed in rapid succession.

"There is only one thing that I can think of that could be at the heart of this, and we have precious little time to act."

He pointed at Therrien. "You need to get to the temple. I will provide you transportation and a writ of safekeeping. Without their healing and cleansing, you will not last the week." Therrien raised his eyebrows in surprise, but said nothing.

He pointed at Pash. "You were born to be magi. You will stay here with me. You have much to learn, and very little time to learn it."

He pointed at Larrik. "You must claim your birthright. If I am right, we may be able to stop him in time. If we do not, it may be the only thing left that can save Solypse."

He turned to face Cillan and Mikkel. "Larrik will need your help, especially yours, Dwarf of the Wandering Path."

Mikkel bowed his head. "Whatever is necessary. I have grubby faces I'd like to see again."

Therrien's head snapped up. In the flurried activity, he had forgotten about the wards going off. "Shoal's in trouble!" He told them of what he knew, and Kithe's face grew concerned.

"This is bad news. That means that he may have launched an offensive in two directions at the same time. If he can do that, then there's no telling how much power he has already. We must begin at once!"

40. RITUAL

The five zombies slogged up the tunnels towards the necromancer's lair, their arms wrapped firmly around their victims. Though the creatures were indifferent to the waist-deep river of sewage next to them, they walked the pathway on the side, as they had been ordered. Gerrus needed the people alive, and he didn't want to take chances on the walking corpses accidentally drowning them. Though the corpses were more intact than many of their peers, they had been chosen solely for their physical makeup; they were no smarter than the rest of the horde of mindless automatons, simply bigger and more intact.

Chevil struggled against the unnaturally strong grasp that pinned him to the creature's chest. Covered in blood and sewage, he writhed and squirmed, hoping to slip free; but it was no use. The creature's grip was like steel wrapped across his neck and torso. He turned his head to the side to ensure he could breathe and stopped struggling, his cheek resting on the creature's forearm like a child held by its mother. He could see that the others being dragged up the sewage tunnel had become similarly resigned to their fate.

The steady slap of bloody wet feet beat a rhythmic tattoo that echoed off the tunnel walls. The zombies turned down tunnels, ascended stairs, and ambled into hidden passages, leaving their passengers hopelessly lost in the fetid dark.

Chevil's heart skipped a beat; he thought he could see light up ahead. As they drew closer, he could see that there indeed was light, cast from hundreds of candles and several torches. He squinted as they entered the room, uncertain of what he was looking at. It appeared that they were in a vast temple of beautifully carved stone, ornately decorated. The flickering of the torchlight was reflected in a colored mosaic in the ceiling, a stone tapestry telling the tale of the Path and the partnership of Kerrick and Lethos. Stone benches were scattered to the sides of the room to make space for the big circle surrounded by torches at the center.

Gerrus looked at his decaying servants with satisfaction. He had converted the temple adequately in their absence, preparing it for the ritual. He gestured to the zombies and the star drawn on the floor, and the creatures went to work, pinning each person to a point of the pentagram with heavy slabs of stone. Chevil squirmed and kicked, prompting his abductor to drop a second heavy stone on his legs, crushing his knees and pinning him still. Gerrus stepped to the altar, casting down his sash, robes, rings, dagger, and other accouterments.

Gerrus shuddered involuntarily, his naked body shivering in the candlelight. His spindly limbs and loose skin was as unattractive as it was indicative of his physical condition; already he felt a chill settling into his body. He coughed hard, gagging on phlegm as he did so, the persistent, burning cough that enflamed his chest a constant reminder of his mortality. He steadied his breathing and willed the coughing spasm to depart. He arranged the phylactery in the center of the circle of symbols he had drawn on the altar, and lit the golden sconce beside it. He lifted his staff and the sconce, and stepped to the middle of the pentagram on the floor, ignoring the screams and fruitless pleas of the people pinned around the circle.

At the points of the pentagram, the abducted Shantytown residents writhed ineffectually. The zombies stood back from the circle at a respectful distance, waiting for their master's command. Gerrus stepped to the center, careful not to disturb the sigils inscribed around and within the circle. He began reciting the words to the ritual as he had rehearsed in his head a thousand times, gesturing with the torch at each point of the pentagram as he spun slowly in a circle. He raised the torch high, his voice raising with the gesture. Shouting a word of command, he cast the torch at his feet.

The spellcaster erupted in flames, as did the pentagram, and the victims staked around the circle. The agonized screams of the burning citizens comingled with his, as the magical flame consumed their flesh, freeing their souls from their bodies. Purple smoke issued from the flames and encircled his head, forming a whirling vortex. The cloud spun faster and faster, until the flames of the burning bodies started to flicker. One by one the bodies were extinguished by the whirlwind, until finally only the withered, smoldering husk of Gerrus remained. As the flames extinguished from the center of the pentagram, the smoke changed course, flowing toward the phylactery like water toward a drain, a stream of light from his staff pouring into the box like running water.

When the smoke cleared, all that remained of the sacrifices were piles of ash. In the center, Gerrus slowly came back to consciousness.

He experimentally flexed one hand, charred flesh sloughing off and revealing blackened flesh beneath. *Something wasn't quite right.* A dull ache throbbed through his body. He rolled to one side and sat up, his body overwhelmed in pain. *Impossible! He had done everything right!* He stood up and surveyed the pentagram carefully, and then he saw it: Next to one of the points, there was a second stone. Beside the stone, there was a nearly imperceptible smudge.

He bellowed in pain, the burning in his chest deeper than it had been before, the surface of his skin exploding with the heat of a thousand torches. In a blind fury, he reached for his dagger and thrust it swiftly into his stomach and up into his heart. He ripped the dagger out and dropped it to the ground with a clatter. In the span of a heartbeat, he paused. The Halfling may have disturbed the circle, but it wasn't enough to stop him; he had become unborn.

He slowly left the circle, trembling. He staggered forward and grabbed the phylactery, cradling it close to his naked and burned form. He leaned on the ornately lined stone portal and uttered a single word, walking through to the safety of the crystal cavern. Soon, he would wield unstoppable power; but first, he had to rest.

41. THE HAND

"**I** think the time has come for me to tell ye a bit about myself." He eyed Cillan. "It was my family that carved the path. And it was my father that hid Lethos' artifact. My father was murdered saving my life, and I swore that day to recover it and restore glory to House Gaerrorn. So far as I can figure, I am the last of my bloodline, which means it is my responsibility to right the lies still spoken in Bruemarrar. The mattock is indeed my birthright; I am the only one, save perhaps some elders at the temple, or" he cast a glance at Kithe, "a select few others, who know of its full power."

The Wizard of the Black nodded. "Indeed, I am aware of its power, and its rightful name. It is known as 'The Right Hand of Lethos', and it has a match, also lost to the world." He paused, noting the surprise on Larrik's face. "We have much more to speak of, friend dwarf, when we have time. For now, this quest must suffice. I do, however, have a gift for you." The Wizard of the Black reached opened a glass cabinet, and pulled a small, ornate box from the back of the top shelf. He gently brushed dust off of the top, and opened it.

Inside, a golden pendant hung on a thick chain. The center of the pendant was set with shards of stone that shimmered in the light, like fragments of opal infused in stone.

"This pendant was made from pieces of the Hand, when the Hand was first created. If it ever held secrets, they still remain hidden. I think, however, that it is best with you, son of House Gaerrorn."

Larrik felt a tingle of excitement shoot through his chest. He removed the pendant from the box with reverence. He lovingly rubbed his fingers across the stone fragments in the middle. He sighed, slipping the chain around his neck, and dropping the stone down the front of his tunic.

"Go now," Kithe urged them, "there is no time to waste. You must recover the Hand, and put a stop to whoever did this."

Mikkel cocked his head inquisitively. "Why us?"

Kithe gestured towards Wallenbrook. "If there is someone out there that can do *that*, then we need someone who can stop them. The only way that I know is to use the power of the Hand."

"But why not you?"

He shook his head. "I have other things that I must attend to. Pash, you will be with me."

Kithe returned them to the secluded alley beside the squat hole.

"Must we?" Larrik grumbled.

"Well," said Cillan brightly, "You can always walk down the main roadways. I'm sure plenty of guards would be happy to help you find your way!"

They lowered themselves down into the squat hole and climbed to the murky stream below.

42. THE JOURNEY INWARD

"So thief, where do we go?" Larrik asked wryly.

"I'm not a thief. I'm a-" Cillan pondered a moment. She was a killer; or at least she had been. Now she wasn't sure what she was.

"Ye broke us out of jail," interjected Mikkel, "I don't care if yer the queen of Shantytown. Yer good by me."

"We wouldn't have been *in* jail if it weren't for her!" Larrik reminded him.

Mikkel dismissed him with a wave of his hand. "If not her, someone else. As the path wanders, don't curse how ye got here, just be content that ye got here."

They carried on, arguing point-counterpoint for several minutes. Cillan, sensing this was no longer about her, turned and began walking down the tunnel, the bickering dwarves in tow, still unsettled by the previous exchange. She had been a thief when she was a child. She had learned to kill early on, and was good at it; it was what she knew. Still, as she matured, she had come to realize that there were consequences to her actions. There were always innocent victims of the aftermath, even if her targets were not. Perhaps she would go to the surface; see the sun for the first time without the Veil; see the forests and mountains that the bards sang about, and the giant beasts that roamed in vast, open spaces.

Her thoughts were interrupted as they reached the main sewage-flow. The passage was well traveled by her guild, and she knew every scrape and stone by heart. Across the canal, she could see that someone careless had passed by. She held up her hand, wordlessly halting the dwarves in their tracks. She walked stealthily across the stone footbridge that arched across the canal, and inspected the markings. "Someone was here recently." Larrik and Mikkel walked across the bridge to join her.

Larrik pointed at the footsteps, noting the drag marks and the uneven footstep intervals. "Whoever it was, they were either carrying something heavy, or lame in one foot."

Mikkel piped up. "Well, we do know that a zombie army just passed this way not too long ago."

Larrik shook his head. "These footprints are heading deeper into the tunnels, not out." Cillan walked cautiously up the pathway next to the river of sewage, taking note of the muddled footsteps, when something caught her eye. Drawing closer, she said, "it appears that there were three to five of them. I think—"Cillan inhaled sharply.

Mikkel looked at her curiously. Cillan pointed. On the ground was familiar pink hairclip.

"They took prisoners?" Mikkel guessed.

Cillan nodded, and stepped off without another word. They quickened their pace to keep up with Cillan, who was hastily walking as fast as she could. They followed the tracks towards the intersection of the temple conduit, and then followed them on a sharp right turn away from the main channel, into an area nearly blocked by bars, save one bar missing from the middle. As they continued, the running sewage changed to water, then decreased to a small stream, then a trickle, then none. The shape of the passage changed the further in they went, finally opening into a low, but well hewn hall.

"What is this place?" Cillan wondered aloud.

She looked back at her companions, and saw that Larrik's face was ashen.

"It's where a thousand good dwarves died, and I lived."

43. OUT WITH THE OLD, IN WITH THE NEW

Thalen walked in quietly, spying the councilman on the balcony in his usual position, looking out over Solypse. Thalen moved to the balcony and peeked over the councilman's shoulder. Down in the nether reaches of the city, there was a flurry of activity, with guards overseeing it from the other side of the sewage river.

"You sent for me?"

Ellias nodded without turning.

"It appears I have a loose end that needs tying up."

"How may I be of service?"

"I need you to take care of Cillan."

Thalen gasped out loud.

"That will...be a challenging task, honorable councilman."

"You will be well compensated, I assure you."

"As always."

"Twice the usual fee. I would hate for any old loyalties to get in the way."

"Half up front."

Ellias nodded again. "I expected that. It is on the salver by the door."

Thalen could barely contain his delight. "Is there anything further?"

Ellias shook his head. "You might want to avoid the base tier. It's a bit messy today."

***

Thalen stepped into the street with a bounce in his gait; fortune was certainly on his side. He strode purposefully toward a small utility building that housed yet another entrance into the tunnel system, smiling in spite of himself. He was glad he had stayed his hand when he had first recognized her voice; now he would not only be well paid, he would be able to assume the role of guild master assassin.

First, of course, there was the matter of actually getting rid of Cillan. Thalen glanced around; seeing no one, he ducked into the small building and slid down the ladder. Lost in his thoughts, he absentmindedly wove his way back to the guild hall deep beneath the city, deftly sidestepping the traps and wards. It was only natural that he run the guild; after all, who else had more prowess than him, shy of perhaps Cillan herself? Without her in the picture, there would be no one of equal measure to pose such a challenge. The only question that remained now was *how* he intended to attend to her. Poison seemed too neat, and not nearly personal enough. This was an art form, and he was an *artiste*.

44. THE REMAINS

The constant stench of sewage began to fade, mingling with the scent of molten wax and charred meat. Cillan's stomach churned with nervous anticipation. Cautiously, Mikkel crept forward ahead of the others, looking for the telltale signs of traps left for them. Instead of traps, however, he simply found the wet, dragging footsteps left from the walking corpses. "The way is likely safe," he reasoned aloud, "because otherwise the creatures would have set something off." Still, they proceeded with caution. They rounded the corner and came to a doorway.

Larrik looked at Cillan; even in the low torchlight, she looked grey. He felt a sharp pang in his heart; nowhere more than this place was he reminded of the loss of family. "I'll go first. Wait for me." He carefully pushed open the door, quickly looking around for the offending monsters. Seeing none, he crept up to the middle of the chamber, his heart racing. He had been here; over a hundred years before, he had been here. This was the temple to Kerrick, built by House Gaerrorn when the Path was first constructed. Beautiful stone mosaics told the story of his House. The ceiling was a beautiful mural depicting Kerrick shaking hands with Lethos, their godly arms forming the tunnel known as the Path. Within their embrace, tiny merchants traversed the miles; Dwarves and Men working in concert. The rest of the temple had been desecrated. The rows of stone benches meant for Dwarves to sit upon in their worship had been removed and piled at the edges of the room. The room was clear, save for mounds of ash scattered about, and a pile of personal effects by the altar.

He walked toward the center of the room, and saw that there were lines drawn onto the floor. The ash wasn't piled, he realized. As he drew closer, he saw the pentagram. The floor was blackened to an obsidian hue at each point, the clear outline of burned bodies showing against the flagstones below. Piles of cinder were heaped at uneven intervals by the columns, and the center of the pentagram was as dark as blackened glass.

"Is it safe?" Mikkel asked, his voice just barely above a whisper.

"Aye."

Mikkel and Cillan walked to Larrik. As she drew close to Larrik, Cillan clutched the edges of her tunic, her knuckles white from the pressure. She saw the blackened shapes on the ground and bit her lip.

Larrik placed a hand gently on her back. "I'm sorry lass."

Mikkel walked to the altar, respectfully avoiding the blackened spots that marked the last resting place of the sacrifices. "What's this then?" he asked himself aloud. At his feet was a black robe. He picked it up gingerly, and felt the hem catch. He tugged, and heard something clatter to the floor.

"By the gods, there it is!" Larrik gasped.

Mikkel knit his brow in confusion. "Is that what I think it is?"

Larrik nodded, swiftly skirting the circle to reach the altar.

"But what is it doing here?"

Larrik reached out a trembling hand. As he touched the tool, he felt a surge of energy shoot up his arm, taking his breath away.

Mikkel heard him gasp, and looked up at him, alarmed. "Are ye alright?"

Larrik exhaled slowly and nodded. "The Hand was crafted for the house of Gaerrorn. The Hand is me birthright; but more than just a weapon passed from me father down to meself, it's bonded to our house. The Hand just found its home."

"But what does that mean?"

Larrik shrugged, then smiled. "Methinks we'll have a chance to find out soon."

Cillan was slowly circling the center of the room, looking carefully at the outlines of those who had been sacrificed. She reached down beside a slender black silhouette, and gently rested the pink hairclip beside it. She smoothed her hand gently along the scorched outline of the head. She pressed two fingers to her lips and then to the breast of the blackened flagstones, and stood up with a heavy sigh. "I'm sorry, mother," she whispered.

Mikkel looked up at her, eyes brimming with tears and pity. "Don't worry lass, we'll get the monster who did this."

Cillan nodded and looked away, scanning the room rather than meeting Mikkel's gaze. "I need to get some things."

Mikkel nodded. "Shall we all go?"

Cillan shook her head. "It's best if I met you somewhere after. The alternative could be...problematic."

Mikkel nodded, his colorful past having left him intimately familiar with people who kept their own council.

"Let's meet down by the exit to the sewers, by Shantytown. Will ye be long?"

She shook her head.

"Good enough then. We shall see you soon." Cillan nodded and turned on a heel, a disappeared into the darkness of the tunnels.

"An interesting lass," Mikkel observed.

Larrik arched an eyebrow. "Harumph." He resumed inspecting The Hand, awestruck at its balance and beauty. The temple of Lethos had known how to win the hearts of the Dwarves alright. The tool was perfectly balanced. Though it stood nearly half his height, it weighed less than a smithy's hammer. The bottom of the handle was capped in an adamantine cap, ornately carved to resemble the tiers of Solypse. The head of the mattock was slender and pointed, with a razor sharp blade on the topside. Saw-teeth bit menacingly downward from the underside of the long side of the pick, with a short but vicious spike on the backside. The long thin handle was wrapped in a lattice of leather and made of enchanted metal that shone like white bone, yet conferred strength beyond steel. Small, intricate runes covered the entire length and circumference of the handle.

Larrik loosed his mattock from his belt and dropped it to the ground, not even looking to the clatter as it dropped. He placed The Hand on the altar and held his hand gently over its head, closing his eyes. A brief flash of light caused Mikkel to blink. When the spots of light cleared from his vision, a second mattock, identical to the first, lay beside it.

"Did ye summon its mate?"

Larrik shook his head. "It makes a mate for itself. It is only a shadow of the original, but it works just as well at cutting stone...and I would suppose flesh."

"How did you know to do that?"

Larrik shrugged. "I wish I knew."

They looked around for clues, but came up with no further answers.

Mikkel looked at Larrik, troubled. "We need to find out who did this, and fast. For the Cillan's mother's sake, if for no other reason."

"Aye, vengeance we shall have."

"Not just vengeance. I have heard of such rituals, though I have never seen one myself. If this be what I think it is, then her mother's soul is bound to this creature, bent to the protection of its foul essence."

Larrik's brow furrowed. "I don't think we should tell her."

"Agreed."

"Let's get moving then, there isn't any time to waste!"

45. A CHANCE MEETING

Thalen reached the guild hall and noted it was quite lively. The smell of simmering stew boiling out of the kitchen behind the bar, dirty wooden bowls on the bar top demonstrating that the stew had already won the affections of the patrons crowded in the guild hall.

Breezing past the crowd, Thalen casually walked toward the back.

"Thalen! Still nothing to do?" Thalen fought the rising panic he felt in his gut, and turned around casually.

He smiled at Cillan graciously. "Oh, something came up, thankfully. You know how I hate to be bored. And yourself?"

She smiled wearily and nodded. "Always busy, but busy means I'm getting paid. I was just stopping in to grab some things."

Thalen stepped to the side to allow her to pass; a deference, he reminded himself, that wouldn't be required much longer.

46. WHEN HOME FOUND THALEN

*A*driax hoisted himself up on the overhang beside the window. He had originally come to the inn with a proposition in mind: join the guild, or die on the spot. As he sat on the ledge beside Thalen's window, he contemplated his mark. Murderers were nothing new in Solypse, nor were sell-swords. Rarely, however, did actual assassins surface without the guiding hand of the guild. Adriax had been surprised then, when he had heard that not only was there someone rising in power, but was actually taking work from the guild. Giving the boy the devil's choice—join or death—virtually assured them that he would pledge loyalty to the assassin's guild. Unfortunately, it did not guarantee loyalty; much the contrary, it would place a deadly adversary in their midst, one that might unravel the guild out of spite. No, Adriax sighed to himself, the boy would have to be terminated. Such a shame though; such talent, wasted.

Adriax peered into the room. Through the wavy amber glass, he could see the boy sleeping in his bed. Adriax eased the window open, pausing as he saw the figure begin to roll over. Quietly, he eased the window up, and slid one leg, then the other over the window sash.

Before Adriax could turn, strong hands grasped his ankles and yanked him to the floor, banging his head on the sash and causing the window to drop as he fell. Adriax reached for his knife, but it was already missing. The figure tucked, and rolled across the room to the far side by the door. Adriax lept to a low crouch, hoping to seize the advantage over the figure before it was re-centered. Adriax charged forward, only to feel a searing pain shoot across his forehead, knocking him backwards. He reached up and felt his brow, his hand coming back with blood. He wiped his hand on his breeches and focused on his opponent; once again, he had lost the advantage over his adversary. He sidestepped left and forward, trying to circle toward the figure on the opposite side. He felt pressure on his head, and reached up with his hand: a garrote wire. "Wire. Clever." Adriax pulled a dagger from his boot, and swiped the air. His satisfaction at the sound of a sharp twang was followed by a high pitched rubbing noise, and realization of what he had done.

Thin, nearly invisible wires formed the mesh of the net that wrapped around him, drawing tight around his body. The figure on the far side advanced on him, *casually.*

"I wouldn't try to cut your way out. It'll just tighten more. You really don't want that."

Already, Adriax could feel blood trickling down from his skin where it made contact with the wires.

"What do you want?"

"You came into my room. What do you want?"

"I came to offer you a job."

"A job? Interesting. Most people use the front door."

"It isn't a front-door kind of job."

Thalen sat back on the edge of his bed, plucking the wire from the stuffed dummy beneath the covers. *"None of my jobs are."*

"I had to ensure you were as good as they say."

"I am, and more. What do you want?"

"Your work has caught the attention of my guild master. He would like to offer you a permanent position in his employ."

"Thieves?"

Adriax shook his head.

"Assassins?"

Adriax sighed. *"Here I was, thinking you were one a bit more in favor of subtlety."*

Thalen hopped to his feet, casually pulling a boot knife out, pointing it under Adriax' chin.

"The thing is, you're lying. I am competition. You are either here to kill me, or you are an unwitting test subject. I will give your guildmaster the satisfaction of neither."

Thalen reached into a pouch and fished out length of wire fashioned into a slipknot. He slipped the wire through the net and around Adriax' wrist, and fastened it to a sturdy wrought iron ring fastened into the mantle of the fireplace. He repeated the procedure with Adriax' other wrist, looping it through a metal hook on the far wall and tied it to the basket of rocks normally reserved for a doorstop.

The weight of the rocks caused the wire to bite deeply into Adriax' wrist, and Adriax grit his teeth to keep from crying out.

Thalen punched Adriax in the throat, causing him to gasp for air, giving Thalen the opportunity to stuff a rag in Adriax' mouth. Thalen shook his head as he secured the rag in Adriax' mouth with a length of rope. *"I like to work in the comfort of my quarters sometimes. I can't have you screaming though."* Thalen circled around behind Adriax and ran his finger gently down Adriax' spine until he got to the base. Thalen slipped his boot knife under the wire mesh and Adriax' shirt, ripping upwards with one continuous motion. The net held secure below Adriax' torso, falling away up top, and releasing his arms. The weighted wire pulled Adriax with a jerk, spreading his arms wide between the wires. His feet and legs, still bound, dangled at an odd angle from his body as his hands turned purple and the wire cut rivulets of red into his wrists.

Thalen grasped Adriax' waist firmly and stood him up firmly in the middle of the wires. Thalen faced Adriax' bare back. A thin bead of blood welled up in a line up his spine where the dagger had slipped past. He set to work quickly, carving his missive shallow enough so as to preserve his canvas, but deep enough that neither message would be missed. The first message, carved plainly into Adriax' back, simply read "I accept your offer." The second message, unwritten, was clearly communicated: No one would be his master.

47. INEVITABILITY

Cillan gave him a courteous nod, and continued on into the trunk room. With Cillan out of sight, he rushed to the Room of Assignment, a plan forming in his mind. Stepping inside, he left the door open, and quietly clambered up one of the rows of volumes, his soft shoes easily finding purchase on the old dusty wooden shelves. Nearly twenty feet in the air, he was well hidden in shadows on the tops of the bookcases. He took a long slow steadying breath, and began the patient wait of a spider in its web.

Cillan gave the utterance of warding on the trunk room, shutting the door behind her. The room was a large, but otherwise unimpressive stone hall. There were over five hundred nearly identical chests in the hall, though many of them were empty, and all of them were trapped. Each assassin was assigned their own personal chest by the guild master. Most contained the tools of their trade and some personal treasures. Cillan, being the Master Assassin, had two. Her first stop was at the master's chest. She pulled the mask and gloves from her knapsack, trading them instead with a folded velvet sack and a leather cap. She girded herself with a thin leather belt lined with small pouches, which disappeared into her waist as she finished buckling it. Finally, she tucked two thin silver daggers from the box deep into her boots, until the emerald gems topping the hilts were the only things left showing. She left the chest open, without bothering to arm the traps. Though quiet wars might be waged over the symbols of power she had left behind, she cared little for what happened to the guild after this.

Cillan moved to her personal chest. As she opened it, she grit her teeth as a wave of sadness hit her. Neatly folded to one side was the dress and comb she had worn to the guild on her first day. She had told her mother that she had gotten a job with the council; Unbeknownst to her, her mother had saved the meager scraps from her own paycheck for two months, and bought her the dress and comb. "You can't go in there looking like a wastrel, dear", her mother had proudly proclaimed. Cillan had been so struck with emotion at the gesture that she had never been able to bring herself to throw it out, even years after her mother had discovered her ruse. Blinking back tears, she gently packed the dress and comb into her knapsack, along with the few other personal items collected over the years. Exhaling with the force of finality, she closed and locked her trunk, and headed for the door.

She stepped into the hall, heading towards the room of assignment one last time. Entwined in a latticework of thoughts and emotions, she walked through the entryway in a haze, and secured the door behind her. She took a long look at the room from where she stood. She remembered her first time getting an assignment, barely blossomed into womanhood. Scared. Excited. She remembered when the guild had become hers, and the vast amount of power and information that came along with it. This room—and all its contents—were as familiar to her as an old favorite tome. Except there was something out of place. She couldn't quite place her finger on it; something was gnawing at the back of her mind. She walked casually down the middle row, glancing at the books as she walked by. She saw it now; the books one side had been pushed back just a touch.

She felt the light breeze on the back of her neck before she heard anything. Before Thalen's feet had hit the ground, she was already in a tuck and rolling forward and away. She used her momentum to come up on her feet. As she lept up, she launched a dagger toward her attacker in one fluid motion. Her motion came to a rest with her on her feet in a half-crouch, a short sword in one hand, and the dagger's twin in her other. Her eyes instantly recognized the figure in front of her.

"Thalen!" She hissed.

Thalen deftly dodged to the side, avoiding the dagger's flight. With a flick of his wrist, he launched his own at her in response. She darted behind a bookcase, avoiding the dagger and putting Thalen out of view.

Cillan calculated her options. She knew the room better than most, if not all members of the guild. She crept down the rows of book shelves, quietly crossing where she dared, circling back to where she had ducked behind the shelf. Carefully, quietly, she reached inside a pouch in her belt, pulling out an egg-sized object, wrapped in a gossamer thin cloth.

Thalen's eyes darted around uneasily. Quietly he crept forward, listening for any noise that might betray her position. Though she had years on him, he had spent the last several minutes studying the layout of the room from above. Most of the rows ran parallel all the way to the back; at the heart, however, there was a small room formed from shelves facing outwards, breaking up the symmetry. The back of the room was raised about six feet above the main floor, girded by a railing and reached by twin ramps that formed a triangle where they met in the front of the rails.

His initial plan, now failed, would have been the easiest, but he hadn't gotten to where he was without having backup plans. Quickly, he glanced in all directions, and spooled out a razor-thin wire with twin loops. He eased he loops over books on either side of the aisle at calf height.

Cillan took the egg shaped object and threw it as hard as she could at the ceiling, where it erupted with a loud pop. Thalen darted toward the source of the noise, looking around for her. He felt something gently brush his hand. He looked down, smiling. White powder covered the floor and dusted his hands. *Nice Try*, he thought, carefully rubbing the powder off of the bottoms of his feet.

Cillan crept through the stacks nearby. Though she did not consider him quite her equal, he was close; and "close" wasn't a risk she was willing to take. *"hursh"*, she whispered, and the lights in the room of assignment extinguished, plunging them into darkness.

From somewhere behind him, Thalen heard Cillan's voice in the darkness. *"Kisail."*

Suddenly, Thalen's world erupted in blinding brightness, his vision blurred with bright spots of color. From her vantage point, Cillan grinned widely. Thalen, covered in glow-powder, was like a beacon scurrying blindly through the rows. She easily followed him, closing the gap rapidly. He disappeared around a corner and she quickly followed, a dozen paces behind.

She felt the wire a moment too late; in her haste, she walked full force through it, stumbling as the books came free from their shelves. The glowing apparition before her whirled around.

Not willing to lose his other dagger in the darkness, Thalen instead rushed at Cillan. Though she had trained him, she had never fought him in earnest; he was good, and he was fast. As he lunged in her direction, he slung his arm towards her. She threw herself to the side, a heavy brass spike narrowly missing her skull. Thalen yanked his arm in an exaggerated sweep, and brought it down. She felt the thin metal wire connecting the metal bob to his bracer snap past her face. Reflexively, she thrust her dagger upwards, the flat of the blade flush against her throat. Thalen brought his arm down fiercely, causing the wire to pull rapidly across her neck. Cillan felt the cool breath of air on her skin, and warm blood seeping down the front of her tunic as the bob pulled the wire around her neck like a bolo. She bit her lip as she angled her dagger to cut into the wire, the backside of the blade biting into the side of her neck and face as well. She drew her dagger down and away, severing the cable. The bob clanged on the floor, pulling the cable back across her wound and deepening the cut further. Her cuts flowed freely now, veins pumping out lifeblood. Thalen took the opportunity to rush towards her and lash out with his other hand, punching her full force in the stomach, and smearing glowing dust on her tunic. Cillan tumbled over, nearly convulsing with pain as she slammed her head into the stone floor. Thalen's momentum carried himself past her kneeling form. Too late, however, he realized his mistake: in his zeal, he had underestimated her. Blinded by the pain, Cillan's instincts took over. As he stumbled forward, she swung a dagger up and back, and felt it bite home. Thalen felt a sharp pain in his bowels. He looked down to see the tip of a dagger protruding through the side of his stomach, Cillan's hand guiding it hilt-deep into his side.

Cillan pulled herself crouching to her feet, and spun to face Thalen. Before his momentum had finished carrying him forward, she pulled her dagger and thrust it through his other side until she felt it come through the other side and bite into rock, pinning him to the flagstones below.

She leaned down close, and whispered into his ear, close as a lover's caress. "It is yours for the having, but it was never yours for the taking."

She stood up, pulling the blade from the groaning form on the floor. She wiped the weapon on the front of her breeches and sheathed it, and left the room.

When she emerged in the full common area covered in blood, gasps and low murmurs passed in waves through the guild members there, though none dared meet her gaze. She walked purposefully toward the exit, ignoring the attention.

48. CLAN GAERRORN

"Since the girl's gone, can ye tell me a bit more about how ye got here?"

Larrik scanned the room quickly, making a show of inspecting the ornate carvings around the room. "Which part? Not much for tellin'."

"Ye may be able to fool the humans, but you and me are drawn of the same blood. Long ago, I hailed from Bruemarrar too."

Larrik stared intently at a spot on a carving. "Like I said, not much for tellin'. Me family dug a tunnel. Other dwarves came and slaughtered me family."

"That's the part that I'm wonderin' about. How did you live, and everyone else die?" Mikkel paused. "Were ye just a whelpling, hiding out of sight?"

"I did NOT hide while my family was slaughtered!"

"Then what really happened?"

"Why?"

"It might be important. Yer holdin' an ancient relic blessed by a god, and yer playin' at school-girl secrets. Out with it!" Mikkel crossed his arms in exasperation, and planted his feet firmly.

Larrik met Mikkel's gaze with his own look of defiance, then dropped his shoulders and looked away. "I suppose yer right. But swear by Riordan's harp that you won't tell a soul."

"You have my word."

He nodded and reached out to the wall, running his hands gently across a faded carving of a dwarf hard at work.

"It was the last of the last days. We had finished tunnels to the surface on the far side, the Path, all these chambers you see around you, and quite a bit more as well. With The Hand, we were able to make an amazing amount of progress, the likes of which neither humankind nor dwarfkind had seen. We were finished—we were getting ready to pack up our camp and head back to Bruemarrar one last time. The high houses of Bruemarrar had never expected House Gaerrorn to succeed, let alone so quickly; they knew that House Gaerrorn's success would put the high houses behind it in a most favored trading status with Solypse. The High Houses made a pact and banded together; three houses banded together, and marched on House Gaerrorn while it finished the tunnel.

Neither me father nor me father's father were fools. They knew the other houses would cause problems, and they prepared for it. They build a massive underground complex beneath Solypse for House Gaerrorn. Their plan was to finish the Path, march back and collect their belongings, and bid Bruemarrar farewell. With their success in Solypse, their status as a "Primary House" of Solypse was all but assured. And then they came..." Larrik's voice dropped to a low rasp. He swallowed and exhaled, before continuing on. "There were scores of them, dressed and armed for battle. Me clan was dressed for a quick trip back, all gathered on the path for the journey. We were only armed with digging tools. The Path was knee deep in bodies, and some of the side passages were ankle-deep in blood. I was a youngling back then, aye... Me father cut down row after row of them, The Hand destroying every foe in his wake... But me father, seeing the the tide of battle, grabbed me by the scruff of me neck, and dragged me far from the fray, to where I couldn't get back."

"Why didn't you follow him?"

"Couldn't. He used The Hand. I'll show ye." Larrik held The Hand up and whispered. He ran forward and grabbed Mikkel by his wrist. Before Mikkel could utter a word of protest, Larrik had dragged him through the face one of the rock walls of the chamber. He continued running with Mikkel's wrist in a vise-like grip, until they finally emerged from the rock in an open room.

He released Mikkel's wrist; Mikkel let his arm drop limply to his side, speechless.

"So ye see, when he pulled me away from the battle, he pulled me too far fer me to get back. He went back the way he came, and left me lost in a tunnel. By the time I came out, there wasn't a living member of my clan to be found, and The Hand was missing."

"How'd ye end up at the Temple of Lethos?"

Larrik shooed Mikkel. "Another time. "

"But what are ye embarrassed about?" he pressed. "Ye weren't given a choice."

"Aye, but his kindness was a prison. A dwarf with no clan ain't hardly a dwarf."

"You might want to rethink that."

Larrik paused, remembering Mikkel's story. "Beg yer pardon. But you of all people should know what I mean."

Mikkel shook his head. "Ye can let the world tell ye who you are, or *you* can tell the world who *you* are. Ye have a choice, friend. You have always had a choice."

Larrik regarded him thoughtfully. "Hrm."

He turned abruptly away from Mikkel and gestured about the room.

"What do you suppose happened in here?"

Mikkel looked around. The center of the room looked like a huge wading pool with evenly spaced holes that dropped several feet to stones further below. The ringed area, just over Larrik's height, was empty. A cage lay open on a platform overlooking the ring of fitted stones. A splatter of blood and yellowish white tissue covered the floor in a damp smear, leading from the stones to the doorway.

Mikkel tiptoed up to the stone edge of the pool and looked inside. Whatever had been inside was gone, though the congealing trail left behind indicated that it had been there within a day or two. He inspected the doorway, noting the gore smeared around the entryway.

"I have no clue, but whatever it is, it's huge."

Larrik peered into the next room. "It gets worse. It looks like it expanded once it got through the doorway."

They walked through the doorway, their feet gliding through the thick, viscous slurry. The trail indeed grew once it passed the doorway, to nearly twice the width, cutting across the cavernous room before them.

"As memory serves, this was the great dining hall." He gestured behind him. "That was the privy. He jerked his thumb to the right. That means that over there would be the cook's quarters, and over there," he gestured vaguely forward, "is where we would have just run from."

"So where did this creature go?"

"It looks like it headed off toward the main tunnels. There's the sewers in one direction, and a back passage out into the tunnels in t'other."

"We have to meet up with Cillan. Will this get us there?"

"Aye, and at a decent pace too. No sewage. The real question is, which way did this 'thing' go, and why?"

Mikkel started walking. "Dunno. I'm curious, but we have work to do, yeah? Let's get walking."

They walked through the smear through well hewn halls, until the hall split. "To the left," Larrik said, gesturing down the declining, curved path to the side, "Is off into the rest of the dark, where our creature oozed off to. Straight ahead leads to a passage that lets off near the docks. The door is concealed and locked; I should be able to still open it though."

"Unless something has changed."

"Everything has changed. Here's hoping something stayed the same."

They continued on the hall wordlessly, their Dwarven vision perceiving a hidden glow given off by rock, unseen by most creatures. Larrik's mind drifted to memories from his youth, of the halls and tunnels carved from stone. He remembered what it had looked like those last few days, filled with carefree dwarves proud of their accomplishment and giddy with the anticipation of emancipation from Bruemarrar, ignorant of the demise that was just around the corner.

Mikkel's thoughts wandered towards his newest home, in Shoal. They had just settled in, and had been planning to try to settle down in earnest. Neither he nor Halail truly believed it would last forever, but they intended to make it last as long as they could. His dear Halail, the water that bore his boat forward through countless adventures. He missed her. He missed their little minions too.

Their thoughts were jarred back to reality by a fierce screeching growl that stopped them in their tracks. Larrik drew the twin mattocks from his belt; Mikkel followed suit, bringing his hammer to the ready. Silhouetted against the grey glow of the rocks was a low figure, crouching against the wall.

"Well that's a tad inconvenient", Larrik muttered.

"How's that?" Mikkel whispered back.

"It's standing in front of the door."

"What is it?"

"Dunno."

Mikkel quietly cast a spell, summoning the brightness of a candle into his palm. The creature gave a low gurgling screech at the sudden brightness. Mikkel held his open palm up to his mouth and blew, sending the light floating toward the creature like a puffball in the wind. The creature stayed stone still. Chin-high to Larrik, it stared at them from the one eye facing them, the deep black eye rimmed in brown. The eye sat in a bold avian head helmed with light brown feathers, a beak the color of gold rubbed in amber protruding from the front. Beneath the poorly preened feathers was the body of a lion; or more accurately, a lion cub, with small wings lying flat against its sides.

Larrik's hands went limp, his weapons clattering to the floor. The creature let out another low growl.

"It's a gryphon", he said breathlessly, "a baby gryphon."

"That must have been what was in the cage."

Larrik dropped to his knees, and slowly extended a hand. The creature hissed at him, and backed further into the corner.

Larrik slowly reached into a pouch and pulled out some dried meat, leftover from their journey. He tossed it gently to within reach of the gryphon. The gryphon growled at him again. Larrik reached into his pouch once more, and produced some hardtack, and once more tossed it toward the creature.

It lowered its head carefully, not blinking or dropping its gaze until it was inches from the hardtack. As soon as it was close, it snatched the hard travelers bread up and swallowed it in a single motion. Larrik and the creature repeated this dance several times, pausing from time to time to appraise one another, until he ran out of hardtack.

Mikkel cleared his throat quietly. "Larrik, we need to get going. Cillan will be waiting."

Larrik closed his eyes and reached out his hand once more. "Come along little friend. We won't hurt you." The gryphon growled at him again, but took a small step forward. Larrik inched forward, and the gryphon instantly recoiled.

Larrik gestured Mikkel back. "I have an idea, but you need to back up."

Mikkel took several steps back. Larrik, never dropping his gaze from the gryphon, slowly sat down on the ground. He leaned backwards, eventually lying flat on his back. He closed his eyes and took slow, calming breaths; he knew this had the chance to end poorly.

Larrik felt a heavy weight as he felt the four paws land on his chest and stomach. He opened his eyes. The gryphon let out a loud screech, the sound issuing from an open beak inches from his face. Larrik willed himself to remain calm and motionless. The gryphon relaxed, its head drooping. It gently rubbed its beak alongside Larrik's face.

Larrik gently reached a hand up and placed it on the gryphon's side. The creature tensed; then it relaxed, and Larrik gently rubbed its side. A deep throaty purr issued from the gryphon, and it lay down on his chest, a paw to either side of Larrik's head.

"It looks like ye earned yerself a friend", Mikkel observed.

"Aye," he said quietly, "I believe I did. But how do I get up?"

"I dunno, but I'd advise ye to do it carefully."

49. WIZARDS

"What in the name of the gods are you doing?" Kithe looked at Pash quizzically, his visage shifting between confusion and silent mocking demonic laughter.

"I'm preparing. You said you wanted to teach me about magic."

"Indeed...though I don't recall telling you to sit on the floor and make strange hand gestures."

Pash's face turned crimson. "I was doing a Lethan trance ritual, cleansing my mind of errant thoughts. Is there a different way to do this if you are magi?"

"Get up."

Pash stood up obediently, his arms dangling limply at his sides. Kithe of The Black suddenly raised a hand, and slapped Pash firmly across the face.

Pash bit his lip.

The Wizard of the Black swiftly raised his other hand, and slapped the other side of Pash's face.

Pash gritted his teeth, saying nothing.

Kithe knit his brow. "Do you like this sort of thing?"

"No sir."

"Then why don't you defend yourself?"

"You didn't tell me to."

The human and the demonic face showed equally interspersed, and they rolled their eyes in unison.

"This isn't the temple, and you aren't a boy. You are a man, and you stand on your own two feet. Let's try this again."

Kithe swung for Pash's face again, but this time Pash caught him by the wrist before he could make contact.

"Good, now we're getting somewhere. Now it's your turn."

"You want me to slap you?"

"Yes. Either side. It's a better surprise if I don't know where it is coming from."

Pash began swinging with his left hand. Kithe screamed at the top of his lungs. Pash faltered, stopping just shy of impact.

"Did I tell you to stop?"

"No, but I thought-"

"So loud noises distract you? I told you to hit me!"

Pash quickly coiled a hand and swung it in his teacher's direction; but before he could connect, he was blinded with what felt like the light of a thousand suns on a clear day. He pulled his hand back, rubbing his eyes with his palms.

"You aren't very good at this. I. WANT. YOU. TO. HIT. M-" Before The Wizard of the Black could finish his sentence, Pash lashed out with an open palm. His hand froze in place, a hair's breath from the face of The Wizard of the Black. Kithe smiled. "All magic, to the uninitiated, seems like the product of old men in towers, salivating over dusty tomes. The reality is that magic, to those who truly understand it, is a reflex. It is part of who we are as wizards and sorcerers. There's much to be learned in books, for certain; but before you get there, you need to understand something thoroughly. You have to know and feel all the way in your core, that magic doesn't simply surround us. Magic permeates us, and everything else. If you *do* truly understand that, you will understand how to manipulate it with your will."

Pash's hand dropped to his side. "Is that why I was able to cast that spell when we were attacked by the clutchers?"

"Essentially yes. What that told me was that at some primal level, you comprehend how to wield magic. What I wish to do is try to unlock that primal understanding. Complex spells require more thought, more intricate understanding, more nuance. It is for that reason that we study. We do not study spellbooks because the words are magic; we study spellbooks because they explain the complex, deeper meaning of spellcraft."

"If magic is pervasive, and spells are more of an understanding of a recipe than magically learning how to shape a spell, then why are spells written in exotic inks, on rare parchment, and things of that nature?"

"Because the particulars of such things are part of the nuance. Tell me, have you ever walked into a room, and known that something was out of place, but you just couldn't quite figure out what was wrong?"

"Of course."

"Imagine that the components used in inscribing the spells essentially provide the opposite effect. That is, using the appropriate components clarifies meaning in a way that one can't quite quantify."

"What of magical objects then?"

"Magical objects...are merely containers for a magical purpose. Much in the same way that you can shape a spell, you can shape a magical container for them. Though you often see wizards with wands, such things are a mere convention. One could just as easily use a rock, presuming that one ensorcelled the rock with the same magical containment as one would have on their wand."

Pash nodded in understanding. "One might even use their own body to contain something."

A demonic smirk flitted by as Kithe nodded. "One might indeed." He turned abruptly, then glanced over at Pash with curiosity.

"So you hail from the temple."

"Indeed sir."

"You were not a Brother." It was not a question.

"I was only an acolyte sir."

The wizard raised an appraising eyebrow. "When did you join the temple?"

"Many years ago, sir. I'm afraid Lethos did not choose to bless me with clerical magics; they would not let me advance until I could demonstrate that I had favor."

"Several years. Hm." The wizard tapped his chin in contemplation.

"What will your family think of you leaving the temple?"

"They will be very upset." Upset was an understatement. Pash's father had moved rivers and mountains to secure his place at the temple. If Pash left, his father would be the black sheep of the council.

"Perhaps they will be comforted to know that you have been chosen to study at the Wizarding Tower."

Pash shook his head emphatically. "My brother died while in training at the Wizarding Tower."

"Died? That's impossible. No one has died in training here, not in many many years."

"He was older than me, but I'm not sure how much older; I was very young. My parents never speak of it; they refuse to. It is considered bad politic at the Council to discuss such things."

The Wizard of the Black raised an eyebrow in mock surprise. "The council? Ah yes, your father is on the council."

"Indeed. My father's name is Hielan. He is the fourth seat. After my brother died, they refused to talk about me entering an apprenticeship at the tower.

"Hielan, ah yes, I recall now. That was long ago indeed, but not so long that I can't remember. Would you like to hear about your brother?"

"You knew him?"

"Knew him? He was who gave me this!" The Wizard of the Black gestured at his face, which slipped between sadness, demonic mockery, and returned to sadness.

"I- Yes. I would like to know how he died."

Kithe gestured at the sofa. He poured two glasses of brandy, handing one to Pash before sitting down.

"So let me tell you the story of Gerrus Hielan."

"When I first saw you, I recognized your elven traits right away; nonetheless, you look far more characteristically human, which put me off on your age at first. Once you mentioned your father was on the council, and gave me your family name, it all fell into place."

"You are Pash Hielan, Brother of Gerrus Hielan, both sons of House Hielan of the Fourth Tier. Your father is seated in the fourth seat on the Council; your mother is the full-elven daughter of a modestly well-off merchant family. Your mother's family, incidentally, is from the surface world; though for whatever reason, that isn't something spoken of often, if at all.

Approximately one hundred and forty years ago, your father approached me. He had a son, he said, that seemed very magically gifted, and he wanted him trained in the Wizarding Tower. You must understand that the Tower does not allow requests; it would simply have too many. The Tower instead keeps a watchful eye on all of Solypse, and finds individuals that it considers exceptional. Such as yourself." Pash felt his face warm at the compliment, but he kept silent.

"Normally he would have been turned away; but this was a member of the council, which meant that he was afforded a different level of consideration. I took it upon myself to observe and assess your brother. As it turned out, he did indeed have a natural talent, a very strong one. Unfortunately, the Tower selects on more criteria than simply talent.

There are a good many reasons to want to become a Wizard, and power can certainly be a factor. Unfortunately, your brother had an incredible thirst for power, far more than most. It also became apparent as time went on, that he cared little about his friends and allies, as long as he reached his goal. I brought your father's request before the Wizards of the Tower, and gave them my honest assessment, recommending that they not allow him to study at the tower.

When word of my recommendation got back to your father, he was furious. He called your brother in front of the council, and had him demonstrate his capabilities. He privately let the Tower know that if they didn't accept his son, then he would have the Council perform an official inquiry into the Tower, focusing around their selection process and their use of city funds. The Tower's elders buckled. To further rub my nose in it, your father insisted that I personally take on your brother as my pupil."

Pash cringed. His father's temper was legendary; if his brother was power-hungry and cruel, there was no mistaking where it came from. Once, when Pash was young, his neighborhood playmate Teil had befriended a mother duck and her ducklings in the park that spread before their homes across the fourth tier. The ducklings used to follow Teil everywhere, even waiting for him outside of the Academy at the end of the day. Then one day, one of the ducklings, having eaten perhaps a bit much late in the day, had loosed its bowels as it followed Teil past the Hielan home. The very next night, Teil's family was invited to Pash's house for dinner. When they sat down to the table, a roast duck sat at the head of the table, with little roast ducklings set before each child's place setting. So afraid of his father they were, they both ate their meals, tears silently streaming down their cheeks.

The wizard paused, until he sensed that his new pupil was once more paying attention. "Your brother knew that I didn't think he should be there; worse, he knew that I had no choice." The wizard got a far off look in his eyes. "Had I not said anything at the outset, I wonder if things would have turned out differently...I suppose we'll never know." Kithe shrugged. "At any rate, your brother was a dazzling pupil; in other circumstances, I would have been incredibly excited at his innate ability. He was gifted at everything he tried. Unfortunately, he tried everything. Thaumaturgy, transmutation, sorcery, enchanting, summoning, demonology, haruspicy, necromancy...

After sampling the darker arts, he was hooked. He didn't try to hide it, though I tried to dissuade him and guide him towards more productive activities. At first, his dabblings never caused much harm, as unpleasant as they might have been." The wizard smoothed his hands slowly across his lap. "Then came the demon." A dark shadowy smile flitted across his visage.

"Summoning rituals weren't unfamiliar to him. We had practiced with minor interplanar creatures, and even an imp. He repeatedly asked about major demons, but I refused due to the inherent danger with dealing with such forces. He saw it as a personal affront, an intentional slight towards his talent, as well as me taking an opportunity to lord something over his head. One day, he decided to take matters into his own hands. Actually, he took it one step further: While I was away, he tried to summon a greater demon. He half succeeded."

"Half?"

"When I returned to my summoning chambers, I found it laid out for summoning in the manner as one would expect. The circle reserved for containing the demon however, was a different matter entirely. I'm still unsure as to what he did wrong. It could have been a smudge, a mis-marked rune, or a circle rendered imperfect by a single grain of sand. Regardless, it is academic at this point, and was beyond my focus upon my arrival. At the center of the circle was a portal to one of the lower depths of the hells. As a credit to Gerrus, his warding was good enough to restrain all but the strongest of the demons on that plane—and that is what he had tried to summon. Standing in front of the portal was a demon. It must have been fully seven or eight feet tall, with massive wings. It had Gerrus pinned up against it chest to chest, a lover's embrace, with his entire torso wrapped in tentacles. I tried to get his attention, but it was nearly too late. He was locked face to face with the demon, too weak to move. I knew I had little time and few options. Every moment that the tentacles remained wrapped around Gerrus was a moment closer to oblivion for him.

I cast a spell-blade. The tentacles split from the demon's body, and Gerrus dropped to the ground. Nearly as soon as they hit the ground, they began crawling up the demon's body to re-attach themselves. I had the full attention of the demon at this point." The Wizard of the Black leapt to his feet, anxiously pacing back and forth.

"I didn't have many options—any really. I had just returned from a long journey, and I certainly hadn't expected to encounter any demons. I was tired. I acted out of instinct. I cast the one spell I knew I could be sure of—a spell of containment, modified to be strengthened by my own life force. I had forgotten, however, that Gerrus lay nearly dying at my feet because the demon had drained nearly all of his vital essence. The demon unleashed a counterattack with his full bolstered power, nearly overwhelming me. I tapped deeper, chaining him with my own soul, anchored within my own body." The Wizard of the Black stopped pacing and took a deep breath, extending his arms wide. "And now, here I stand. Neither possessed nor a free man. And yet, had I not acted the way I did, when I did, I would not be here at all, and perhaps neither would Solypse. That comes not from book knowledge, but from *truly* knowing. Do you understand now?"

Pash sat dumbstruck, and gave a sharp nod of his head.

"After I closed the portal, I attended to Gerrus. Though he had never been athletic, he had always appeared to be in moderately good health. What I saw before me was not that Gerrus."

Seeing both glasses empty, Kithe poured more brandy. "The man before me was barely recognizable. His flesh hung from his bones, his skin ashen, his muscle withered as a victim of famine; it's a wonder that he hadn't perished. I dressed his wounds as best I could, and hurried to his home and spoke to his father—your father—right away. I told him of what transpired, and that I would be forced to recommend him for dismissal. I remember he said to me, 'It is a shame to lose a son in a tragic accident. I shall mourn him eternally.' Fearing I was unclear, I repeated that he was in my care, but that he would not be allowed to remain at the Wizarding Tower. He looked me in the eye, and said very slowly, 'On this day, my son died. Dispose of him however you wish.'

Though such things may be a pragmatic solution for one such as your father, I fear that I am not as iron willed in that regard. I nursed him back to health, only to return one day and find him gone, along with several of my tomes on necromantic magic."

Kithe sat down, and laced his fingers together across a knee. "So you see, that which is happening in Shantytown is of grave concern to me. And when you turn up on my doorstep by some divine providence, I can't help but think that we might be of some use to one another."

Pash swallowed, hard, as if it would somehow aid in digesting all the information. "You shouldn't feel responsible-"

"Responsible for this? Gods no! That boy began bad, and finished rotten to the core. No, I wouldn't say that I feel responsible for it. It is more that...it is the synchronicity of it all. As wheels of fate turn, they sometimes align with fantastically harmonious balance. When such an event in time occurs, the wise understand that they must play their part, or simply fall victim to great forces—like the foamy churn beneath a waterfall crushing a boat. It is not the waterfall's fault; only the fault of the ship captain who chose not to heed the warning."

"But a ship's captain can avoid the Veil, no?"

"Time does not stop because you try to hide from it. No, we are already in the foamy churn. Do nothing, and you will be crushed asunder. Play your part, and you may perish, or you may survive... But if you do not, you will most certainly perish."

"If this is a fated event, how am I to know my role? You have had over a century to prepare for yours."

"I have a friend at the Temple of Lethos will be able to help us. They are skilled in prophecy. We also have a need to see your friend Therrien."

50. PRAYER AND WAR

"**B**ut that isn't what we *do!*" Brother Thedd shouted into the wind. "You must do something to save these poor helpless people!" A fierce gale whipped across the harbor, bringing with it water from the Veil.

Thedd shivered. Raindrops stung faces like needles, as near-hurricane force winds brought driving rains down on the township and the troops alike.

Behind Brother Thedd, beyond the ranks of soldiers, chaos and carnage was flooding through the streets of Wallenbrook, borne on the tide of the driving rain. An unending sea of undead washed over the citizens; with no weapons to speak of, the creatures clawed, twisted and tore their way through every living soul they could find. The odor of death was thick enough to penetrate the fog of sewage stench emanating from the river between Wallenbrook and the town guard, the sewage and blood mixing with the torrential rain to form rushing calf-deep streams of blackwater flowing through the streets.

The town guard stood in formation along the length of the river, facing away from the conflict. Ghastly screams erupted behind them with such regularity that many of them no longer flinched at the sound.

The tall, thin man's weathered skin gave him the appearance of a seasoned fisherman who had weathered many storms. In a way, it was true. The son of a fisherman, General Karstin had weathered a great many 'storms' in his career before ascending to the role of Commander of the City Guard. "Brother Thedd, I have my orders. WE have our orders. We are to keep more townsfolk from entering Wallenbrook. YOUR orders are to go into Wallenbrook, and put a stop to this!"

"But that is what I am trying to tell you. Clerics of Lethos cannot turn the undead. Despite what you may have been told, this is not what we are here for. Thousands of people are dying while you stand by, idle."

A knot tightened in the General's stomach. Though his troops could not see the battle, he and his officers faced backwards towards the troops, back towards Shantytown. He knew Thedd was right, but what choice did he have? His orders from the Council had been very clear. He was to contain the threat at the border, and prevent people from coming in.

"General," said the priest in a low voice, "I see the conflict within you. This was your home, long ago; I know you haven't forgotten. You know it is the right thing to do."

"I have my orders."

The Captain paced nervously at the front of his line of troops. They had all been in the tunnels, and had been challenged by the creatures of the depths. Their swords were sharp, and their wits sharper. This however, was the harshest test of their mettle. As they heard the screams of their fellow citizens, friends, and kin, they restlessly shifted their weight from foot to foot. Silvius had never led them astray, and they trusted them implicitly. And that was what was gnawing at him. He could see the carnage beyond the ranks of troops, the blood freely running over the wall into the river. Terrible things were happening, and he had to do something.

"Sergeant Brabo, you are in charge of the formation. I must speak to the General."

Sergeant Brabo snapped a salute. "As you command, sir."

Silvius walked swiftly to General Karstin, ignoring the red-faced monk gesturing angrily beside him.

"General Karstin." Silvius snapped a salute. Karstin, relieved at the distraction turned to face Captain Silvius and returned the salute.

"What is it, Captain?"

"Sir, I understand that our orders are to hold the line, and protect the citizenry."

"You understand correct, my young Captain."

"Sir, might it be...prudent to send a patrol across the river, to assess the situation?"

Karstin stared at Silvius for several moments. Captain Silvius remained ramrod straight, unwavering, awaiting his reply. A small smile crept from the corner of his lips. He knew he liked Silvius for a reason.

"Captain Silvius, our orders are to hold the line."

"Yes sir."

"But we will not be able to effectively hold the line unless we know what manner of enemy we face."

Silvius grit his teeth, suppressing a smile. "Yes sir."

"Therefore, I believe that the proper course of action is for you to lead the Dark Veil across the river to assess the situation."

Silvius, unable to suppress it any longer, broke into a grin. "Yes sir!"

The general scowled. "Silvius!"

He stopped grinning. "Yes sir?"

"Be careful."

"Yes sir."

Silvius returned to the head of his formation, returning Brabo's salute without breaking stride. He raised his voice, projecting his voice with the full authority of a seasoned combat leader.

"Brabo, call the Dark Veil to attention!" The platoon stiffened and came to attention instantly. A murmur passed through the unit that flanked them, and their heads craned to look at Silvius and his platoon.

"Warriors! You have been tested in battle in the tunnels. You have guarded the gates. It is time to face the real foe, to defend those whom you love dearly. While you have stood here exemplifying proper discipline", he paused, allowing a quiet snickering to pass through the crowd, "undead creatures have been ravaging Wallenbrook. They have ravaged the township. They have taken men, women, and children, and ripped them apart. The streets are deep in gore and blood, the likes of which you have never seen."

"We are to go on a scouting mission, to assess our foe." He held up a hand to suppress the angry whispers that ensued. "We shall cross the bridge, and woe betide any creature that get in the way of our ability to *thoroughly* scout the situation. Platoon, forward...March!"

To the right, a murmuring ripple passed through the platoons, one by one.

At the head of the formation General Karstin watched the growing discord with unease.

"General," Brother Thedd said quietly, "Is it wise to send a lone platoon out to patrol? It is not an insignificant township, nor is it an insignificant foe. Perhaps support from others would be a bit safer."

General Karstin planted his fists on his hips and took a deep breath. He looked at Brother Thedd warily. "I'm going to regret this."

Brother Thedd smiled, placing a hand gently but firmly between the General's shoulder blades. "No you won't, General. If you live to be a thousand, you will look back upon this with pride, every day henceforth."

Karstin looked across his full brigade one last time, praying for their safety, knowing his prayer was futile.

"Battalion commanders, call your battalions to attention!"

The men stood at attention, and the air stood still.

"We are going into Wallenbrook. Battalion A, take the northeast. Bravo, you take the northwest. Charlie, you take the southeast. Delta, southwest. We're facing undead. We don't know how many of 'em there are, but they're killing people as I stand here flapping my gums at you. So figure it out, and figure it out quick, and take 'em out."

The general strode purposefully toward the bridge over the river. There would be hell to pay when he returned; but first, there was hell to kill.

51. THE WORM COMES KNOCKING

After Nar'el's funeral, life returned back to normal in Shoal fairly quickly. The residents, to intent on survival and accustomed to casualties, had little time to focus on intrigue.

Halail tended the dwarflings, reassuring them that their father's return was right around the next corner. Her work as the town healer had provided them with a decent nest-egg of cash; not that the residents would let them pay full price for anything. She set the final plate on the table, a fire warming the room. She looked up at the gleaming war staff above the fireplace mantle, a slight smile passing her lips. It hadn't been long since Mikkel had traded his hammer for a handful of forks and knives; now it was her turn for a while.

"Thinking of the good old days, ma?"

Halail threw her arm across Gavin's shoulders. "Not the good ol' days. Just different days. Every day is a new good ol' day, am I right?"

"I wish da were here."

"Aye. I wish he were here too." She patted Gavin on the back gently. "But he ain't, and we have supper to sup. Sit yer tail down. He'll be along soon enough. TEAGAN! LIAM! COLLIN! Get yer beardless faces to this table this instant!"

"But da," Gavin persisted, "I wish da were here right now. I miss him."

"Me too!" Teagan piped up.

"Now now, my minions. We all miss da. But I tell you what. Yer all gettin' on with yer writin' so..." She looked around cautiously, dropping her voice to a conspiratorial whisper. "I'll teach ye a magic trick."

Gavin's eyes went wide. "*Magic?*"

Halail nodded sagely. "We'll send some messages to da, carried to him by Riordan himself." Halail fished around on the cluttered counter beside the table, producing scraps of parchment and small shards of charcoal. "Now what ye do, is ye write yer message right in the middle.

Then you fold it in half just once, like this." She tented the paper, the words "I love you" facing into the table.

Teagan's brow furrowed in concentration. "I can't get my letters ma!"

Halail patted her comfortingly. 'That's okay. It's not what is on the paper, it's what's in yer heart when ye write it. Riordan knows what is in yer heart."

Teagan, mollified, made a crooked tent from her scrap of parchment, and rested it in the middle of the table to join the ones already placed there by her brothers.

Halail picked up small shards of flint from the desk now and placed them in a spoon. She heated the spoon until the flint glowed red hot.

"Stand back me minions!" Halail waved her free hand in front of the fire. "Abbaca chee, abbaca chail! Send our love to my dear beloved Mikkel!" With that, she scooped up the papers with her spare hand, and tossed the flint in the fire. The flint hit the stones at the back of the fireplace, exploding into sparks. Just as swiftly, she threw the papers into the fire. One by one, the flaming parchment pieces floated up the chimney, embers consuming them even as the smoke bore them away.

"And so, if ever ye miss someone, Riordan will bear yer wishes along the flames to their heart, just so." The dwarflings gathered around Halail and hugged her tightly. Collin sniffled, but held back his tears.

"I know that wasn't real magic," he whispered, his breath hitching in his throat.

"Then ye don't know nearly as much as ye think ye do," Halail said huskily. "Come on, then. There's no use spoilin' dinner."

52. TEMPLE BUSINESS

Pash paled. He had expected one of the brothers, or one of the high priests of Divination...but this was another thing entirely.

"You didn't tell me we were seeing Brother Kern," he muttered quietly.

"My dear Pash," he said lightly, "I am the high mage of the Wizarding Tower. Who else would I see other than the High Priest of the Temple?"

Pash looked up sharply. He hadn't contemplated what his new mentor's position in the Wizarding Order might be. He suddenly felt like an extraordinarily small pawn in a game of far greater importance than he cared to contemplate. Though he had originally been afraid of what the Temple might say when they learned of his defection to the Wizarding Tower, he now found himself more frightened as to why the High Wizard of the Tower had chosen him. And the first person to find out was the High Priest of Lethos. He felt very small indeed.

53. THE SLAUGHTER REVEALED

Mikkel let out a low whistle. "I've not seen the likes of this...ever." Larrik nodded. "Even when Clan Gaerrorn was murdered..." Larrik absentmindedly stroked the back of the gryphon's neck. The gryphon stared intently ahead at the carnage before them. The roads were no longer distinguishable as roads, shy of where the cobblestones broke the high-water mark of the blood sluicing its way towards the riverbank.

"So where do we start?"

Both dwarves turned at the sound of Cillan's voice.

"Gods girl! What happened to ye?" Mikkel began rummaging in his pack, while Larrik continued to look her over. Her fetching human face was marred with a massive black and blue welt that rimmed her right eye. Crusted and dried red-black blood crossed her throat like a grim necklace, a matching slice reaching up to her cheekbone. Her armor—exquisitely crafted chimera leather—was torn in a few places. Completing the picture was blood caked across her gauntlets and splattered across her armor. She looked down.

"Don't worry, most of it is his." Mikkel looked up from where he was kneeling by his pack. He pointed a stubby finger toward her neck. "That may be, but ye got lucky at least once. I dun' have time to fix it properly, but this should help." He tossed her a small vial, compact enough to fit in her palm. "Drink that, all of it. It'll fix ye up a bit. We can't afford for ye to be broken right now."

She downed the vial without complaint. Fiery liquid hit her belly and spread out across her body, tingling at her neck and head. Her headache subsided, and she felt a renewed vigor in her limbs. She nodded in thanks.

"I see you picked up a pet along the way."

Larrik nodded. "His name is Scanlon. Named him after a fierce warrior."

Scanlon growled appreciatively.

"Very nice. Let's hope that Scanlon has a taste for killing zombies."

Scanlon let out a blood curdling cry, half growl, half scream. Startled, all three adventurers took a step back. Scanlon growled low, and leaned in, nuzzling Larrik's hand.

Larrik cleared his throat. "All right then. I guess that's a yes—and I think he understands us too."

Cillan nodded mutely. "So back to the original question: Where do we start?"

They looked out across the town. From their vantage point, they could see that the city's guard had begun wading into combat in Wallenbrook, though by the time the first forces had crossed the bridge, a quarter of the town had already been saturated with the undead.

Larrik shook his head, gesturing with the Hand. "This would help, but I'm not sure how it would do against all that. And now the city guard is involved, and we're fugitives. Well, at least two of us are."

"All three", she amended, gesturing at her neck. "I can only guess that my offer of resignation was not accepted by Councilman Ellias."

Larrik raised his eyebrows in surprise, but refrained from comment.

Mikkel tugged his beard thoughtfully. "Well, we ain't an army, and an army they got down there, on both sides."

As the trio pondered their course of action, Scanlon growled and lept down from the pipe onto the ground below. They looked down to see the Wizard of the Black and Pash striding purposefully toward them. Larrik and the others jumped down from the pipe, and closed the distance.

"Didn't expect to see ye here anytime soon. What's news?"

"It would appear that Pash and I have a lot more work here than we had thought. We need you three to head to Shoal immediately!"

Cillan paled. "I'm not sure that's a great idea for me, all things considered."

"Oh, I don't know. I'm sure you could find someone to vouch for your innocence... The blacksmith's wife perhaps? I'm sure you ran across her when you were taking a walk at night. Perhaps you even walked together for a while. Young ladies walking alone are much safer in pairs, and you must have had wonderful stories to tell her about your travels."

"How did you- nevermind. It doesn't matter. As you say, Wizard of the Black, I shall accompany the dwarves on the route to Shoal. It can't be any less safe there."

Mikkel waved a hand from the back "Ah, 'scuse me, but we have a slight problem. Therrien said the wards were going off already. We're over two days' journey from Shoal; we'll never make it in time!"

Kithe nodded. "I am aware of this. Fortunately, I can help you with this. The three of you, stand close."

The trio crowded together, as Kithe opened a small leather pouch. Sprinkling fine silver sand in a circle, he began the ritual of teleportation. He paused, putting a hand on Mikkel's shoulder.

"Thank you."

"Er, yer welcome I guess."

As he completed the ritual, Scanlon bounded past him and jumped into the circle. The four of them faded from sight, leaving Pash and Kithe of the Black alone once more.

Kithe let out a heavy sigh. "What's done is done, and what is left...is much to be done. Let's get moving. We need to find Captain Silvius immediately!"

The wizard and his apprentice waded into town, hitching up their robes as they waded through the gore. The edge of town was eerily silent, the zombies having already plowed through, leaving only corpses in their wake. Ahead, they could hear the loud clamoring cries as the soldiers met with the army of the undead. The soldiers were heavily outnumbered, and it did not appear likely that they would prove much more than a momentary distraction to the army of corpses that soldiered through the streets.

"We can't destroy them all by attacking them head-on," the high wizard observed, "but we may be able to herd them into an unfavorable position. They shouldn't be intelligent enough to notice such things."

Pash nodded. "The next question then, is what do we do with them once we get them where we want them?"

"I was just wondering the same thing. We can nudge them in a particular direction, but the guard is still heavily outnumbered. Hacking them to pieces takes too long. Fire would work..."

Pash picked up where Kithe trailed off. "...But as dumb as they are, they're smart enough to avoid fire. And from the looks of them, drowning wouldn't do much either."

Their hurried pace quickly caught up with the Captain and his troops as the formation skirmished on the edge of town. Kithe hailed him as soon as they got within range. "Captain Silvius, I am Kithe of the Black, Chief Wizard of the Tower. Pash and I come from the tower to aid you and your champions in battle!"

Silvius halted the unit and rushed over to greet them. "I recognize you well, Chief Wizard," he said bowing low. "It is an honor to meet you and Wizard Pash. Your assistance will be most appreciated."

Pash opened his mouth, but stopped short of words as Kithe held up a hand. "The honor is ours, truly. Let us dismiss with formalities, and get down to business, please. You are outnumbered nearly ten to one, even with the additional forces that follow your unit into battle. The creatures you face are neither intelligent nor complete automatons. They grind through townsfolk like a butcher through meat. How do you expect to win against such odds?"

The Captain held up his hands. "I don't rightly know if we can, in time to save Wallenbrook. They are relentless in their assault. Fortunately, that also puts us at an advantage—attacking them from the rear, they continue their forward assault as if we aren't even there. I hope to kill enough of them to save the rest of Solypse, even if we can't save Wallenbrook. Wallenbrook is home for many of my men. They'll fight fiercely here, no matter the odds."

Kithe nodded thoughtfully. "It is a noble endeavor, but we need to slow them down. If we can get their numbers to stagger, we will have a better shot at taking them down piece-meal."

The captain nodded in response. "I think I have a plan. It might give us a chance to evacuate the remaining citizens, if everything works the way it should."

Kithe shook his head slowly. "Does it ever?"

The captain gave a grim smile. "Though a good point, we have no choice but to hope that it does. What will your part be in this?"

The wizard arched an eyebrow. "I will see what I can do about evening the odds."

Silvius grinned. "I like the sound of that." The captain turned and began barking commands at Brabo, then ran off to consult with the other commanders.

Brabo had been with the Dark Veil for almost as long as he could remember. He had been one of the founding members, one of the first to volunteer for the risky and foolhardy unit. The Dark Veil had been formed to scrub the tunnels around the Path and Solypse; though it was impossible to ensure completely safe passage, their rigorous cleansing did a good job of providing a substantially higher standard of safety. Over the years, he had led and lost countless men, half-elves, dwarves, and the occasional gnome. His stubby dwarven hands had been calloused from many years of swinging an axe in the tunnels against all manner of living foes. Living foes. This was a different matter entirely. His boys had been honed to a fine fighting edge in the tunnels, but they had never faced an enemy like this.

Each member of the Dark Veil was equipped for the three Cs of tunnel combat: cracking, crushing, and cutting. In their left hand, each wielded a flat-headed hammer with a conical spike at the back. In their right, each wielded a short sword. Their armor was thick leather, heavily oiled to allow maximum freedom of movement. Though painstakingly cared for, the armor was largely an afterthought to the warriors. The Darkened Veil wasn't known for being in a defensive posture very often.

Not far from Silvius' unit was the Council Guard, wearing heavy ornate steel armor and closed-visor helmets topped with scarlet plumes. Each guard bore a gold-rimmed scarlet tower shield with a golden gryphon emblazoned on the front. Brabo scoffed at their force. They looked formidable, but the meticulously polished armor, the shining shields, and the men beneath them had likely never seen a conflict greater than a verbal altercation. The longswords that hung by the side of each side were likely sharp, but he doubted that they were scored from having been drawn from their scabbards.

Behind the Council Guard were the rest of the rank-and-file city guard. If his men were nervous, then these soldiers were likely terrified. Though their routine duties involved thieves, fighting, and the occasional bloodshed, there wasn't much in life that had prepared them for the scene before them. Silvius found himself impressed with the novice fighters, still marching into battle against what appeared to be an insurmountable foe.

From a distance, Brabo saw Captain Silvius gesturing to the other commanders, giving guidance and describing what needed to be done. The Captain had been through countless battles, true, but never orchestrated one of this magnitude.

Captain Silvius trotted back and beckoned Sergeant Brabo over rapidly, shouting over the driving rain. "The City Guard is going to line the river, providing an escape path to the bridge. The main force is going to run into Shantytown and start building barricades with whatever they can—wood, rock, broken houses, whatever. They will remain on the other side of the barricades and cut down the creatures that make it through to the other side, while the citizens escape behind them. We will be behind the main attacking enemy force, engaging them from behind."

Sergeant Brabo did quick sums in his head. "Sir, our boys are outnumbered a hundred to one. Do ye think we can really cut through that many before they chew through the main city guard?"

Captain Silvius shook his head. "We just need to take out what we can. We sent a runner to the council requesting barrels of oil. With any luck, we can set the barricades on fire. The oil will float across the top of everything, and should catch some of the enemy force as well. Once the barricades are on fire though, they'll turn towards us. That's when we earn our paychecks."

"What happens if we don't get the oil?"

"Then it's going to be a very long day."

"Or a very short one."

"Yes."

54. WHAT IS NECESSARY

Mikkel's vision blurred, and he blinked rapidly, adjusting his sight to the dimness around him. He could see Larrik and Scanlon beside him, and squinted at a familiar voice.

"By Dan's beardless face! It's home!" He bounded through the door of his home, roaring at the top of his lungs.

From outside, Larrik could hear the squeals of delight from the children inside. He smiled briefly, a pang of familial loss deep in his heart. As if sensing his discomfort, Scanlon growled low in his throat, rubbing his beak against the side of Larrik's leg. Dwarflings poured out of the small house, running towards them. "A gryphon!" Teagan squealed, rushing up to pet him. Mikkel and Halail emerged from the doorway, arms and hands tightly clasped. Before the adults could raise a concern, all four dwarflings had crawled on top of, under, and around the neck of the gryphon. Scanlon suffered the indignity in stoic silence, only protesting when Gavin plucked a feather as a keepsake.

While the children were occupied, Halail and Mikkel walked up to Cillan and Larrik.

Halail looked Larrik in the eye. "Mikkel tells me something is headed our way."

Larrik nodded slowly.

"Ye have the hand of Lethos. I hope that's enough."

"I guess we'll have to find out."

"Listen to me, all three of ye." Halail raised her voice to a strangled note of authority, one usually reserved for a concerned mother warning her children. "I know ye are all going to fight. But ye truly need to fight with all ye have. Fight for this town. Fight for yerselves, fight for survival." She looked at Mikkel, tears brimming in her eyes, her voice dropping to nearly a whisper. "Fight for me. Fight for the children. Fight. Because I can'nae bear to think of losing you."

Mikkel cupped her hands between his, looking her in the eye. "I will fight. But even still, all journeys we take, we take together, whether we be near or far...."

Halail shook her head furiously, allowing a single tear to slide down her face. "Just come home safely."

"So it shall be."

Though Halail's hearth was inviting, the home was a bit cramped for the adventurers. Cillan and Larrik set up camp outside, playing with the dwarflings.

The dwarflings were thrilled at the mystical beast that had joined their company. They discovered, to their delight, that the fierce gryphon refused to eat meat. The dwarflings took turns tossing pieces of bread to him, until he had consumed two entire loaves.

When the creature had finally been sated, he lay down, stretching his massive paws in front of him.

"Come along, minions!" Halail said, clapping her hands together. "It is time that beasts and babes got their rest." Halail and Mikkel ushered the dwarflings inside, leaving Larrik and Cillan alone by the campfire.

"Ye know yer probably not too popular here."

Cillan nodded. "Not much I can do about that."

Larrik looked at her across the fire for several minutes. She kept her gaze cast in the flames, not meeting his eyes.

"I'm usually a pretty good judge of character. And for whatever reason, ye don't strike me as a bad person. But there's one thing that just doesn't square well with me. You're good at all this sneaking around bit; which means you've been doing it long enough to get good at it. Ye showed up battered in the tunnel, and I didn't question it—but there was a lot of someone else's blood on ye. Who are ye? How do we know we can trust you? What's to say you won't disappear?"

Cillan continued staring into the fire. At long last, she spoke.

"I'm the daughter of a whore and a fishmonger, or so my mother said. Given her profession, that couldn't have been much more than an educated guess. I grew up in Shantytown with my mother. My mother resented me, because my birth cut down on her ability to ply her trade. We lived off of whatever we could scrap together, and I swore that I would get out of there, and leave her and that filth behind."

"Did you?"

Cillan shrugged. "I could have. But I realized that for all my mother's failings, she had kept me alive, and refused to let me follow her profession. So there's that. Plus, I realized that nearly everyone is a whore; we're all just selling different parts of ourselves."

"Life doesn't have to be that way. You can choose your path, rather than letting your path choose you."

"Says the dwarf in exile." she retorted.

Larrik's face grew red in the darkness. "I aim to fix that."

"Yeah, well so do I."

"But the original question. How do we know we can trust you?"

Cillan's lip quivered. In the few short days they had been together, this group was the closest she had come to having friends since she was a child. Her life and the balance of her choices was a heavy mantle on her shoulders. "You don't." she said quietly, her eyes cast at the ground. "You shouldn't." She snapped her gaze up, angry that the dwarf had struck an emotional nerve. "I guess you'll just have to expect that I'll betray you when you least expect it." She stomped to the far end of the campsite and lay down on her bedroll, pulling a blanket up and rolling to face away from the campfire.

After much wrangling of squirming children, Mikkel and Halail finally got all of the little ones into bed and sleeping soundly. They sat at the table by the hearth with hot mugs of herbwort, a hot spiced beverage with a stronger kick than most dwarven stout. The drink was a staple for adventurers in the dark, who more frequently referred to it affectionately as "poison mush smash", or more succinctly, "smash".

"It's not good, Halail. I've never even heard of something like this."

"And it's coming this way?"

He nodded. "According to Therrien, it was setting of alarms he had placed around paths leading towards Shoal. There aren't many other places it could be heading."

"But why?""

He shrugged. "Why anything? We're the first real colony to thrive in decades, but what purpose could it serve?"

She shrugged. "Your guess is as good as mine. Then again, you know colonists..."

He nodded. "We have more than enough people here who have secrets they'd rather not share. I don't think this will change that either."

She nodded. They had both been on the road long enough to know that it was full of an equal number of people running towards and away from things. Colonies often provided the opportunity for a fresh start. None, however, were as large as Shoal, let alone thriving as well as they were. Large settlements attracted attention, which made them a rarity. "I'll call a meeting in the morn. We need to prepare for whatever this is. The townsfolk deserve to know about this, if nothing else." She paused. "Do we have any idea what it is, or even if it is worth worrying about? Perhaps it's just some spell gone awry."

"It may be that...but given the reaction of the Kithe of the Black, I'm thinkin' we should be very concerned."

"You met with the Chief Wizard?"

He nodded. He took her hands gently in his. "I don't say this often, but I am scared. But that doesn't matter. We need to fight this thing. Whatever it is."

She nodded. "The concerns of today are enough; let us deal with tomorrow...tomorrow. Sleep for thee, and sleep for me. Tomorrow will come too soon."

They stepped towards their bed, hugging each other tightly. He kissed her on the forehead, and they slipped beneath their blankets, both fast asleep nearly as soon as blankets hit their chins.

Morning indeed came too soon. Mikkel sat at the table quietly, looking out the doorway at his friends sleeping outside. Halail cheerfully prepared breakfast for the minions, nervously evading conversations of what the day might bring. After the children were fed, she quietly blessed Mikkel's war hammer. She left him and the children behind to wake Larrik and Cillan, and slipped off.

The children pounced on Larrik with gleeful abandon. With Mikkel roaring at them from behind, they raised a ruckus that woke Cillan on the other side of the encampment. Cillan rolled over and watched them play from heavily lidded eyes, feigning sleep. *"Family,"* she thought, *"hm."* The dwarflings' joy at assaulting Larrik fading, their eyes settled on their next target. Cillan watched them sprint across the open ground towards her. She waited until they were only a few feet shy of her, and she sprang up with her arms outstretched.

"Grrrrr!" she shouted, scattering the dwarflings amid shrieks and giggles. Mikkel trotted back into the house, emerging with two breakfasts that Halail had left prepared for the visitors.

"Halail's gone to call a town meeting this morn. We're going to need ye both there."

Cillan exhaled forcefully. "Is that really wise?"

Mikkel shrugged. "There ain't much choice. Yer here to fight, they'll see ye soon enough."

She nodded unhappily. "I suppose."

"Ye need to understand something about...traveling folk. They didn't come here because they were well loved somewhere else."

She regarded him curiously.

"That includes Nar'el."

She paused, still silent, looking confused.

"What I'm sayin' is, they may not like someone gettin' killed in the middle of 'em, but he wasn't popular. They ain't upset that he's dead, they're upset that he was killed, if you catch my meaning."

"I'm not sure that helps though."

Mikkel winked. "Maybe it wasn't you. Maybe you left for some other reason. Mayhap some invisible assassins came and took him out, and they're mysteriously gone now. Mayhap he was the reason that somethin' is coming here."

Halail walked up, smiling broadly. "P'rhaps you came back to warn and protect them. Ye just might be the hero that Shoal deserves."

Cillan shook her head in disbelief. "I guess we'll just have to see."

The full colony gathered in the middle of the cavern, shy of a handful of guards keeping watch. Halail stood atop the speaker's rock outside of Nar'el's former residence, gesturing for the crowd to quiet down.

"Friends, I thank ye for coming, for I have potentially dire news for us all." She waited until the crowd was silent. "Those of ye who know the name Kithe of the Black, know that he does not trifle with small matters. It is with that knowledge and his warning that I bring tidings of a grave threat looming upon us." She gestured to her left. "Ye all know Mikkel. He was sent here, with two companions, to help aid in our fight." She gestured at the doorway, prompting Larrik and Cillan to emerge.

"Larrik, Ranger of Riordan, and Cillan, bladeswoman of reknown, have come with to aid Shoal."

At the mention of Cillan, loud conversation erupted in the crowd. Cries of "murdress!" and "She can help by hanging!" rang out. Halail held up a hand, gesturing for silence.

"I know that there are concerns about what happened with Nar'el. But she assures me that she was not the culprit. Though her departure was poorly chosen timing, it was mere coincidence, not malice. I, for one, am willing to believe her, and accept her offer of assistance. Who else is willing to accept her gracious offer in our time of need?"

A man's voice rang out from the back. "I shall."

The crowd turned to look at the speaker, though his voice was known well enough to them.

"The young lady went for a walk late that night with my wife. They were together the whole evening. Isn't that right, Cael?" The blacksmith's wife, pale as a ghost, nodded her head vigorously. The blacksmith continued, his voice ringing out loudly over the silent crowd. "In fact, I offer my thanks to the lady warrior. One never knows what sort of trouble a young woman could wander into late at night, without her husband awake to ...protect her. We are all fortunate that neither of them ended up a victim to the treacherous assassin that felled Nar'el." Nervous glances were passed among the crowd.

Halail's voice rang out over the crowd, turning their attention back to the front. "Who would lift a weapon alongside her, in defense of Shoal?" Halail never got a proper response from the crowd, as horns sounded from the far end of the cavern. A loud din erupted from the crowd as the scrambled to alternately reach their homes, or rush towards the gate. Mikkel waved at the companions. "This way!" As they started off towards the gate, a calloused hand clamped down on Cillan's shoulder. She whirled around, dagger and short sword already in instinctively in hand.

"I meant what I said. I owe you my thanks. Pity what happened with Nar'el; I'm just glad that my dear wife is okay. She used to like going for walks late at night. Terrible for her constitution. Sometimes she would get confused, and not come home for hours..."

"But she's home now."

He nodded, giving her a shoulder a squeeze before dropping his hand. "That she is."

The companions were among the first to reach the gates, though a large contingent of the settlement was assembling and heading their way. Climbing the wall, they could see a massive tube of living flesh undulating towards them. Fully ten feet tall and nearly as wide, the creature relentlessly approached.

Deep within the mental recesses of the massive creature, a mote of consciousness screamed for control. Though Nanong could not quell the creature's relentless desire to devour -after all, that is what he had created it to do—he could exert his will enough to guide it towards his only chance at salvation. Physical destruction of this creature was nearly impossible; it would replicate, reform, do whatever it had to, just to survive. His only hope at wresting his consciousness from this creeping death was to have it magically dispelled, to have his consciousness forcibly ripped from the creature.

The clerics of Lethos were powerless to do anything, and the Wizards of the Tower would happily char the worm to a crisp. His only hope, therefore, was a depths druid residing with a colony several days' walking distance from Solypse. He was initially delighted when he discovered the supernatural speed at which the worm slid through the caves, in and around smaller caverns that no human could pass, cutting off several days' journey. His delight had swiftly transitioned to panic, as he felt his mental acuity slip with each passing moment. It seemed that each creature consumed emboldened the worm, and suppressed his psyche more. Worse, a lack of creatures to continuously consume would likewise drive the worm into a hunger frenzy, effectively muting his thoughts altogether until it fed. His mental tunnel vision continued to narrow. His psyche surged at the sight of the gate. As arrows began to strike the worm, Nanong began to register the pain. The distraction made it difficult to concentrate. He began to lose focus; then, out of the corner of the worm's vision, he saw a group rushing towards it. He saw a robed figure in their midst, and took a gamble. Summoning the sparks of his willpower that remained, he focused the worm's attention on the party that approached, willful rage guiding the creature toward the group.

He felt the worm scream, and his consciousness began to collapse into itself. His tumult of thoughts fell into a panic, as he realized his error too late: he had pushed the worm too hard, and its frenzied hunger consumed its thoughts. He saw a gryphon leaping towards it, and slipped into eternal blackness.

"What in the nine hells is it?" Cillan exclaimed.

"It looks like a flesh golem gone wrong", Halail panted, trying to keep up with the long strides of her human companion. Larrik and Mikkel trailed behind them, while Scanlon charged ahead.

Cillan furrowed her brow. A flesh golem normally looked vaguely humanoid in form. This looked more like a blob, held tenuously in a tubular shape by sinew and fat. Bones, and occasionally somewhat distinct limbs of humans and other creatures would protrude from the sides, only to be swallowed again by the doughy fat.

Archers rained arrows from atop the city wall. The worm soon became speckled by the arrows, but did not slow its approach. Ahead of them, Scanlon leapt to meet the creature. He growled and swiped with claws, only to discover that sinking his paw into the flesh resulted in the ooze surrounding his paw. He jerked back in alarm, and retreated to Larrik's side.

As they caught up with Cillan and Halail, Mikkel brought the haft of his hammer from his shoulder to his hand. "Ifn' it be alive, it can be killed."

Larrik nodded. "Well, we saw what it did to the gryphon. And those arrows aren't doin' much to slow it down either."

Halail nodded. If anything, the arrows had driven the worm into a frenzy, pushing it toward the open gate faster.

"Why is the gate open?" Cillan queried.

Mikkel shrugged. "No point in closing it. It isn't meant for much more than stoppin' men and goblins and the like. There's no way it could stand up to something like this." As if to prove his point, the worm began to squeeze through the broad gate, crushing the timbers and dislodging the stone on either side.

"claws ain't workin', arrows ain't workin'...now it's time to see about fire." Halail pointed at the parapets that topped the wall. Guards were hurriedly wheeling massive pots of oil towards the breached gate. The oil poured down onto the worm, covering it with the sticky, tar-like liquid residue harvested from the fireshrooms. Guards tossed torches toward the crawler, igniting it like a massive bonfire log. The entrance to the cavern began to fill with thick black smoke, with the cloying scent of burning flesh assaulting their nostrils. The worm began to lose its tenuous grasp on a shape, liquefying and running in streams down the entryway into the town. A cheer erupted along the wall, as the guard watched their foe diminish into a flood of flesh.

Halail shook her head. "I'm not so sure we should be celebrating yet." She muttered.

Larrik pointed at the river of flesh in front of them, as it began to swell. "Methinks yer more right than you know."

Halail nodded. "Fireshrooms were once alive, which means..."

"...that even if they're on fire, they're getting eaten by this 'thing'" Cillan finished for her.

The worm was already beginning to reform in the gates, growing larger and leaking oil like blackened pus.

"To the side!" Larrik cried, as the worm began its forward progression directly towards the town behind them.

The companions followed his lead, running to the left of the worm before it could march through them. The worm paused, and slowly reoriented itself towards the companions.

"Fan out, and back up," Mikkel advised.

"A fine time for our only mage to be out of town!" Halail shouted.

The companions spread wide. The worm, reformed, waved its ungainly front end in their direction, until it found the target that it sought. It rested back on the ground and began undulating toward Halail with a renewed sense of purpose. She ran backwards, zig-zagging her way through the cavern. The worm continued its pursuit, picking up speed.

55. GERRUS WAKES

He came out of his reverie slowly, as if waking from a dream. His entire body pulsed with a throbbing pain, a permanent reminder of what a single minor imperfection had cost him. He flexed his hand before his face and saw —or rather, perceived— his burned, sinewy hand flex and close into a fist. His mortal concept of vision had shifted into a hazy gauze that blended the spirit world and the material world, the souls of those not yet departed from the plane flitting past his vison. He reached out with his mind towards Solypse. He noted with some satisfaction that the carnage in Wallenbrook was almost complete; even ahead of schedule. He saw that the town guard had begun to gain traction with an organized resistance effort. He began to smile absentmindedly, but the burned flesh cracked and tore at the pressure, causing to grit his teeth in pain. Unwittingly, his vision pulled back to the darkened chamber in which he sat. No matter; he would be in Shantytown soon enough to remedy the situation, after one more task.

His left arm still cradled the phylactery that housed his soul. The first order of business was to place it somewhere safe, beyond prying eyes. Gerrus wove his way deeper into the cavern, down the rough-hewn corridor to the heart of the crystal cave. When he reached the center, he placed the phylactery on a broad, flat altar stone and cast a web of protective spells on, over, and around it. He backed into the tunnel from whence he came. He waved a hand, reciting the incantation in his mind. The ceiling of the crystal cavern collapsed, burying the precious treasure beneath thousands of colored crystals. He walked back up the corridor and through the wall into the Dwarven temple. He turned and faced the ornately adorned frame. He waved a hand and the artifice work disappeared, replaced with a plain wall of rock. He crouched down and lifted his dark robes, pulling them over his head. He cast his thoughts to Shantytown and prepared to transport himself there. Somewhere in the back of his mind, he registered something out of place. He pushed the thought down and away, and focused on the next phase of his plan.

56. ENDLESS BATTLE

"Two Hundred!"
    "If yer still countin', yer' behind, Captain!"
"You wish, half-a-man!"
"None-a-man, but twice the man you wish to be...sir!"

A huge pyre illuminated Sergeant Brabo. His back was to the blaze, into which soldier after soldier tossed hands and heads, leaving the rest of the bodies to be hacked into ineffective pieces. The attack was proceeding well; they had fought through the evening and into the night, and through the morn. The Veil's light was already past peak, but the onslaught was finally starting to ebb. Even as the corpses staggered onward towards the retreating townsfolk, the Darkened Veil swept in behind them, crushing heads and hacking limbs. Already the numbers of the undead army had thinned substantially; the rest were getting tangled in the barricades, and being cut down piece-meal as they stumbled through to the other side.

Captain Silvius was most impressed with the Council Guard; they had performed admirably. They had executed far past what he would have expected from what he had always considered to be little more than a ceremonial guard. Behind them, hundreds of townsfolk had already escaped across the bridge and were already flooding their way through the warehouse district and up through the merchant district. Huge mounds of foes lay in a fleshy wall before them, their body parts forming unnatural barricades for their undead brethren who followed.

Silvius' self-congratulatory introspection was interrupted by a ball of light that caught his eye, hovering above the writhing masses. The light expanded and grew brighter, until the brightness threatened to blind him.

An unnatural voice surrounded him, seeming to come from everywhere at once. "Hold, my children!"

Silvius could see from the bewildered looks on the battlefield that he was not alone. The creatures halted their activity at the command. The soldiers did likewise, out of confusion. All eyes were on the burned remains of a man hovering above them.

Captain Silvius looked up. A skeletal figure in black robes levitated above the crowd, not far from the Dark Veil. The man—if it could be called that—had a voice that was seemingly everywhere and nowhere at once. Charred flesh, like blackened leather, stretched tight across the hands and skull of the creature. The definition of his features had melted away with whatever infernal heat that had claimed his humanity.

The creature spread his hands face down before him, gesturing for silence. Combat slowed to a halt, and was replaced by quiet murmurs as the groups of soldiers and citizens slowly turned to face the source of the sound.

"Citizens of Solypse! You despise those who you consider lesser than yourselves. You conceal your prejudices with talk of trade and money. You look down upon those you consider beneath your station, and you keep them in their place. Your arrogance and selfishness shall be your undoing. You ignored the slaughter of Shantytown, and even refused to save them."

He paused. "So much weakness, slaughtered. But today, those you deem weak and unworthy shall have their day."

The death's head rictus of a smile pulled back from parted blackened lips, and he raised his hands above the sea of corpses in Wallenbrook.

"Citizens of Wallenbrook, rise and serve your new master. Tear asunder those who oppressed you in life. Let them taste the power of a man made into a god!"

Soldiers began looking about wildly as the deep blood-pools of the streets swayed and churned with movement. From the near and far reaches of town, the corpses of the recently deceased townsfolk and soldiers rose to answer the call.

At the edge of town, the Wizard of the Black was shaking his head, muttering to himself. "This is bad. Very well, I accept your terms." He began the incantations of a teleportation spell, drawing Pash near.

Above the town, Gerrus swiveled his attention to the rippling magical energies at the corner of his perception.

"Chief Wizard! Leaving so soon? Abandoning the people of Solypse as you did me? Tell them! Tell them how you made me who I am!"

Kithe ignored the taunts and finished his spell, vanishing with a flash.

Gerrus looked down at the massive army assembled beneath him.

His next words sent an involuntary shudder through Silvius' body. "Attack, my children. But leave me pieces that I can use."

57. THE DEPTHS OF HELL

Halail's legs and lungs burned. She looked back over her shoulder to see the worm gaining on her, its massive body undulating and slick with brown-black oil. She weighed her options. She was in a cavern with only two exits; She could reach neither in time. She called a spell to mind, and ran for a steep pile of rock. She began to scrabble up the surface, loose stones slipping out of her hands and bounding into her shins and knees. She scrambled as fast as she could, oblivious to the cuts and scrapes she was tearing into her hands and arms, intent only on escaping the enormous pile of flesh that pursued her.

Sensing impending victory, the worm sped its pursuit towards its prey, gliding up the face of the climb with ease. As its prey reached the top, the creature paused, fanning out the front end into a wide fleshy blanket. It couldn't remember why, but this was a meal to be savored; it would envelop it whole.

Halail saw the worm fan out, ready for the kill; but she was quicker. She lept full force off of the pinnacle of her perch, shouting the words to the spell that would buoy her up above the ground below, and just beyond the reach of the worm.

The worm howled with rage, lurching at her form bobbing in the air. The lunge brought the worm past the precipice, causing it to teeter and fall to the stone cavern floor below. The companions reached the flesh pile as it began to reform, drawing itself up to try and reach Halail. From her vantage point, Halail could only see a pile of undulating flesh, inching closer to her feet by the second. She quietly whispered a prayer to Riordan, praying for the safety of the dwarflings. She took a long, steady breath, preparing for what might be the inevitable end.

A loud, visceral howl caused Larrik and Cillan to whirl around. Mikkel charged past them, swinging his hammer with supernatural force and speed. Flesh exploded outwards from the creature, as if hit by a mining charge, leaving a scarred hole where it had struck. The worm screamed in pain, its instincts pivoting from hunger to rage. The worm collapsed into a thick mess on the floor, the scar from Mikkel's hammer visible on top. The worm began to reform facing Mikkel, and still he kept swinging, searing flesh from flesh. The ooze retreated from his hammer, sinking to the floor, and surrounding him. Cillan cried out to warn him, but he was in a berserk rage, oblivious to all but his surroundings. Mikkel swiped at the creature, blazing channel after channel in the flesh.

Larrik and Cillan charged in, cutting and flattening the creature as it tried to surround Mikkel, but any damage they caused to it healed over almost as soon as they dealt the blow.

Larrik shook his head angrily. "He'll never be able to take the whole thing down before it gets him." He looked up to Halail. "Is there anything ye can do to help?" Her eyes, wide and frightened, gave him his answer.

She had spent her time healing the sick, and caring for the needs of the colony since Therrien had been gone; she had never anticipated something like this. She was completely unprepared, and could only watch with tears in her eyes as this ravenous creature consumed the one she loved. Mikkel was wrapped from foot to chest now, and began to struggle with his swings. His face slowly changed from rage to a look of pleading panic, all the while swinging through as hard as he could.

A swirling mist formed next to Cillan and Larrik, and rapidly coalesced into familiar faces.

Cillan's face lit up. "Pash! Chief Wizard! You must do something quickly!"

Without looking at Cillan or the others, Kithe of the Black walked swiftly up to Mikkel. The creature parted around him as if he were a block of ice sliding through fire.

As Halail watched from above, it was as if the world had come to a standstill. Kithe leaned down and whispered in Mikkel's ear. Mikkel shook his head vigorously. Kithe whispered into his ear again for several minutes, the creature in stasis as he spoke. The panic slid from Mikkel's face, replaced with sadness. He slowly nodded his head. Mikkel tilted his head back, tears already streaming down his face. She was too far up to hear him, but she could clearly read the words on his lips: *I love you.*

Halail screamed and fell from the sky, landing on the ground unconscious. Kithe of the Black staggered backwards as Mikkel crumpled to the ground, the wizard's body collapsing against a boulder.

Fire erupted from Kithe's chest. He grasped the edge of the rock with white knuckles as his rib cage split open, birthing the demon from the flames and his viscera. He fell to the ground, and the demon fully emerged, shaking off Kithe's entrails as he pulled his last foot out.

With a subtle flick of the wrist, the demon sent Halail's motionless body skittering across the ground several hundred paces, where it finally slid to a halt. The demon stretched his arms wide, the black-red bruise colored flesh rippling over corded muscles and leathery wings. Towering nearly twice Cillan's height, it crossed the gap from Kithe's body to Mikkel's in two strides. Flinging Mikkel's lifeless form aside like a child's toy, he roared with a ferocity that forced the companions back a step. Larrik struggled to find his footing, only to discover that the ground itself moved beneath his feet. Pash stumbled over to Kithe's body, while Cillan braced herself on all fours. The rumbling was joined by a loud cracking sound, and the ground split open.

The worm writhed uncertainly, confused by the turn of events. It sensed that it was facing something that should cause it to flee, and reformed itself to pursue that cause. Before it could escape, fissures opened up, and flaming arms reached from within. Blazing bands wrapped around the worm, searing it to the core. It fought mightily, but every movement caused the bands to sink deeper. More fissures opened and more bands issued forth, wrapping the worm entirely in flames.

The demon laughed, the blackened mirror-shards of teeth in his broad mouth reflecting the fire light. "Feel the power of a true immortal!"

The rumbling subsided, and with it, the shifting earth. The blazing bands cooled to a smolder, the flesh of the worm blackened to a char. Towering above the companions, the demon flashed a wicked smile. It extended its arm, pointing a sharpened claw at the end of a long black finger at Halail. "She lives. Wake her."

Larrik hesitated.

"NOW!"

Larrik leapt at the sound of the demons voice, and rushed to Halail's side. The demon turned to face Pash.

It made a chopping gesture with its arm and a rift formed, as if he had torn the air in front of him. He grabbed Pash and pushed him tumbling into the rift. The demon followed, the rift disappearing behind it.

58. DESPAIR

In the span of an instant, the tide of battle shifted, as the sheer quantity of new corpses instantly beginning to overwhelm the exhausted and dispirited city guard. Silvius signaled Brabo over to his side.

"We need to fall back and protect the evacuees, then get the devil out of here! Send a runner to the other side of the barricades, tell them to fall back to defensive fighting positions until the townsfolk are gone, then have them retreat immediately."

"Sir, there's a solid army between us and the main body of the city guard. It's a suicide run."

"Options?"

Brabo shook his head. "Can't send a runner to the city guard, they're too busy fighting for their lives. The runner would have to run upstream against the evacuees. Most likely he'd never make it in time."

"So it sounds like that isn't an option."

"Right. So the only option left is a runner, up the middle, and pray to the gods that he makes it, since they're facing the other way."

"Sounds like." Silvius shook his head. "We've lost enough men. I don't want to send someone on a possible suicide mission in vain."

Brabo nodded. "But you know it's the only hope we have."

Silvius hesitated, the anguish painted clearly on his face, then nodded his head once. "Probably true. Then who?"

"I'm thinking Brug."

Silvius furrowed his brow in confusion. Brug was a brilliant troop, but far from the most athletic. Sending Brug on the run removed the word 'possible' from 'possible suicide mission'.

Brabo smiled wide. "The boy is smart, and I'm too old to think I'm going to live forever." Before Captain Silvius could respond, Brabo turned heel and plunged headlong in to the rear compliment of the undead army, his diminutive stature swallowed up by the crowd nearly the moment he stepped away.

His legs pumping, Brabo plowed through the crowd of undead with relative ease. Though dwarves weren't known for their speed, their endurance made up for it over the long haul. Conditioned from long marches and tireless patrols, Brabo plunged past the thicket of legs faster than the simple-minded creatures could register his presence. He elbowed his way through, swinging his hammer and removing lower legs at the knee as he passed by.

Silvius allowed himself a brief as he watched Brabo's path through the army. Though he couldn't see the dwarf, he could see the undead collapse in a straight line, indicating Brabo's swath of destruction. His chuckle was short lived, as the line rapidly filled back in behind Brabo, reminding Silvius of the task before him. "Brug! Front and Center!"

Brug stepped out of the formation and ran to the Captain, his oversized helmet slightly askew.

"Yes sir?"

"Brabo is off on a mission. You are now my second. I need you to send a runner to the council guard leadership—they have the red flag at the mid of the line—and tell them we are working a 'collapse and evac'. They will know what we mean."

Brug's eyes went wide as he registered his new responsibility, and his orders.

"Yes sir!" He turned on a heel and barked out a command. A junior member of the Veil stepped up, and Brug quickly explained the orders. The runner snapped a quick salute, and disappeared in the direction of the city guard.

Silvius sized him up. "We're outnumbered by an insurmountable sum, though the enemy is surrounded on three sides, with water on the fourth, for all the good that will do. Cutting them down isn't going fast enough. What do you suggest we do?"

Brug looked at the teeming horde. "Fire would work. But we would need a lot of it."

Silvius smiled, and slapped Brug on the back. He pointed at the bridge, as a wagon train made its way toward them at a breakneck pace.

"Fire by oil it shall be!"

Brug smiled widely, and cast his gaze at the sky, doing quick calculations. "If we just light the back here where we are, it won't slow them down enough—half of the army is in front of us. We should run a line down next to the council guard line, then cut across to the barricades."

Silvius nodded. "That just might work, at least long enough to evacuate the townsfolk."

"But what do we do after that?"

"Then it's in the General's hands. Let's focus on the task at hand."

Brug nodded, stepped back, and saluted. Silvius returned the salute. As Silvius turned back to survey the battle before him, Brug ran to intercept the wagon train and explain the plan. It had to happen quickly. The troops were staggering with fatigue. The adrenaline of battle gone hours before, something had to happen before despair took hold.

59. AFTER THE WORM

Her unceasing sobs echoed across the cavern. Halail knelt on the ground, Mikkel's head cradled in her lap. She had survived torture, exile, and near starvation. She had watched an entire adventuring party of friends cut down, then consumed by trolls; but never in her life had she imagined this much pain or desperation. Gone. Forever. She gently brushed a careless curl of brown hair off his forehead, her tears landing on his closed lids. She caressed his bearded face with a trembling hand, willing him to wake up and tell her all would be okay. She tried to think of the children, but all she could conjure in her mind was blankness and grief. When images of the children came, it was of him tossing them in the air, or playing with Teagan's hair. She sobbed harder.

Cillan had tried consoling her, to no avail. Larrik made eye contact with Cillan and slowly shook his head. Scanlon sat quietly at Halail's side, occasionally rubbing against her leg.

Behind Larrik, the body of the Wizard of the Black lay split apart like a barrel fallen from a wagon. While Larrik and Cillan kept a silent watch over Halail, the body parts began to retract back into the body, until they were once again in place. The body's ribcage slowly closed, and the flesh above it knitted together. Kithe groaned, and slowly stood up, his robe in tatters. A bright purple scar drew a line down the middle of his torso.

At the sound, Larrik spun to face the new threat. As he saw Kithe rise, he grabbed for the mattock at his belt.

"Hold!" shouted the wizard. Larrik stopped in his tracks, his jaw dropping. Cillan whirled around to face Kithe. Even Halail looked up, confused at the sudden animus of the Wizard.

"You were—How?"

"The Demon and I reached an accord." He took cautious steps forward, walking gingerly to Halail.

He crouched down and looked Halail in the eyes. "He saved us all, you know."

She looked down at Mikkel's face, his head in her hands. "He died protecting me, while I was lying useless in the corner."

Kithe shook his head. "You could not have prevented his death; it was his destiny to die this day."

She shook her head violently. "No! Had I been conscious, had I thought about it sooner, maybe- Oh, I don't know. I just don't know. He didn't deserve to be consumed by this hideous thing. We were supposed to grow old, watch our dwarflings grow, teach them...teach them how..." Halail lost her breath into convulsive sobs.

Kithe put a gentle hand on her shoulder. "But my dear, he wasn't consumed by the worm. Here he lies. The worm wasn't what claimed him."

Halail continues sobbing, hugging Mikkel's head to her chest.

"Do you understand? His spirit lives on in this realm. He was destined to die this day, it is true; but he did not die to the worm. He voluntarily sacrificed himself in Riordan's name."

Larrik shook the enchanted pickaxe at Kithe. "Confound it! Ye wizard types speak in riddles. What in all the hells are ye talking about?"

Kithe regarded him thoughtfully. "What, *specifically* in the hells I am talking about, is that Mikkel rides the demon T'izz'ikel now."

Halail looked at him, horrified. "He sacrificed himself to a demon? He would never—" Her eyes grew wide. "No! Not for me! NO!"

Kithe shook his head rapidly. "T'izz'ikel and I came to an accord. He renounced evil in exchange for his freedom. He swore an oath of fealty to Riordan. Mikkel voluntarily gave his life to be the guardian of the demon's oath. He was not sacrificed to T'izz'ikel; quite the opposite."

"So he lives on, in the demon?"

Kithe smiled gently. "In a sense. He is truly an extension of Riordan himself now."

Halail took a deep breath, and wiped her tears from Mikkel's face. "So he's...gone."

Kithe nodded. "From that vessel, yes. Celebrate what was; do not mourn what could be, for this is all that ever was going to be. Celebrate the joy he brought you and the dwarflings, and let your heart be full knowing that he fulfilled his purpose—both in life and in death."

Halail nodded slowly. "We shall have a funeral."

Larrik nodded, contemplating the arrangements that would need to be made.

Cillan looked at Kithe quizzically, her head cocked to one side. "If the demon got his freedom, what did he give you in exchange?"

Kithe looked up at Cillan with a twinkle in his eye, and smiled.

60. THE BATTLE RAGES ON

The wagon train reached the Darkened Veil just as the zombies began to overwhelm the force. The horses jerked painfully in their bridles as a wheel gave out. Still, the well-trained animals dragged the cart the last hundred paces, until finally the wagon came to a rest beside the warriors.

The soldiers at hand immediately went to work. The smaller kegs of oil were punctured and sent off lashed to the backs of their fastest runners, trailing streams of fuel in their wake. The larger barrels were handled by pairs of men, rolling or carrying them behind vanguards of fighters wedging their way through the undead. Upon reaching the barricades, they unleashed their cargo, flooding the line.

Silvius paced nervously. He knew they only had a few moments before all the oil, floating on the surface of the flow of blood and rainwater heading toward the river, slipped away. Worse, he had no way of knowing if Brabo had even made it. He raised a hand. Brug, unloading the wagons, paused and raised his arm. Silvius raised his sword in his other hand, and Brug brought a horn to his lips, bellowing a single note across the field. A dozen horns answered him in unison.

Brug blew two long notes then went to work, striking flint and steel over dry bits of string cupped in an oily rag. His hands were trembling, and slick with sweat. Spark, spark, fizzle. Spark, spark, fizzle. He frantically scraped his dagger across the chunk of flint. The blade slipped off, biting deep into his hand and causing him to drop his tinder. He pressed his hand to his sleeve, blood seeping out of the deep cut. He squeezed his eyes shut to steady himself.

"Brug, you did it! Light something!"

Brug's eyes snapped open, and he looked quickly at his barrel hauling partner. The young man gestured down at the small flame that was threatening to consume the oily rag. Brug quickly scooped up the precious flame and set it afloat in a nearby stream of oil cascading down the cobblestones. The fire took on a life of its own, zipping down the stream of oil into pools that had gathered, spreading outward and onward through the undead horde. The undead—while not wholly intelligent, comprehended the danger that the fire presented.

The fire raced down the street, a blazing trail in its wake. The ambling corpses to either side, already liberally splashed by the cask bearers, caught flame. A cheer went up among the refugees, who had all stopped moving to watch the spectacular immolation.

At the far end of town, Brabo was slapping, swearing and pushing. He compelled the crowd forward toward the chute of guards as best he could, shouting above the rain and combat. Begrudgingly, people slowly shuffled forward while craning their necks to watch the spectacle before them. Brabo forcibly pushed people toward their exodus route. Mindful that they might not get everyone out before the flames died.

"Damn ye! Get moving, before it's too late!" he yelled, shoving yet another person toward the chute.

The flames hit the barricades. The barricades, covered in oil, flamed to the heavens like dozens of bonfires. A collective cheer went up amongst the remaining townsfolk, as wagon after wagon rolled in and unloaded their casks.

"It's not over! Move! Quick!" Brabo hollered at the crowd.

Atop the roof of a warehouse cross the bridge, General Karstin watched the events unfold through a spyglass. He nodded to himself with a small measure of satisfaction. "Silvius. Good boy."

Brother Thedd took the glass from the General, and looked for himself. "General, you may have just saved thousands of lives."

The General shook his head. "It wasn't me. That son of a"

"General..." Brother Thedd clucked disapprovingly.

"That fine young man in the middle of things—that's where the credit rests. And I'll see to it that he gets it, when things are settled."

General Karstin's satisfied contemplation was interrupted as the cheers from across the river turned to panicked screams. He snatched the spyglass from Brother Thedd, peering at the evacuation line. He groaned, slapping a hand to his forehead. *Why hadn't he thought of that?* The flaming oil, floating atop the fluids pouring toward the river, was gradually making its way toward the river. Unfortunately, the evacuation route was somewhere between the flames and the river. From their vantage point on top of the warehouse, they could clearly see that the firewall creeping slowly but unceasingly toward the heavily armored council guard that served as the barrier behind which the survivors were evacuating. He could see the guards shifting uncomfortably as the flames approached; he prayed to the gods that the fire would burn itself out before it reached them.

In the middle of the fray, Silvius and Brug had just come to the same realization, as had the commander of the Council Guard. As the flames approached the wall of soldiers, the commander turned from his position and plunged through the flame wall.

"Captain Silvius!"

Silvius snapped his head in the direction of the voice. A giant of a man, completely covered in red plate mail stood in the distance. His armor was blackened and battered, as was the tall white shield with the red griffin emblazoned upon it. Sergeant Major Ferrin raised the visor of his helmet.

"Sir! The line will hold!" The Sergeant Major snapped down his visor and plunged back through the flame wall.

On the other side of the flames, the Sergeant Major barked out a series of orders, and the men crouched shoulder to shoulder, their shields presenting a solid wall rebuffing the floating river of liquid fire. Small streams of oil slid between the shields and clung to their armor, before getting whisked away with the turbulent waters churned up by the evacuees. In front of the shields, the oil and flames lapped its way higher, heating the shields to glowing hot. In the middle of the line, a guard fell forward, his shield opening a gap that allowed fire to pour into the evacuees, prompting a chorus of screams.

"Hold the line!" the Sergeant Major yelled. His frenzied shouts of direction continued until they reached a weakened crescendo, and then fell silent. One by one, the guards collapsed from the heat; each time, their companions would crush in on them, propping up their bodies and shields. By the time the flames had subsided, not a single member of the Council Guard had survived; but the line had held.

61. SCORCHED EARTH

Captain Silvius surveyed the battlefield. He had withdrawn from combat to formulate a plan, though he wasn't sure that it was of much use. Smoke hung thick in the air. He could taste the greasy char of burned oil and corpses with every breath. It appeared that most, if not all refugees had escaped, though the battle persisted. The corpse army had lost half its number to fighting or fire, but it still outnumbered the surviving army by nearly two to one. An orderly retreat might allow the surviving soldiers back across the bridge.

"But what then?" he mused. They would still be outnumbered two to one, with an exhausted force facing a tireless enemy. Evacuating a few thousand people was challenging enough; evacuating all of Solypse would be impossible; even if they did, there was nowhere to go. They could march several days until they reached Bruemarrar, but there could be no guarantee that they would be granted admission, especially in such numbers. It was more likely that the dwarves would seal their massive gates and wait for the threat to pass, be it a day or a century.

He shook his head as he calculated the odds. It wasn't worth the retreat; fighting here against mindless foes was of as much value as fighting in the streets. *"Best to let the soldiers die on their feet, rather than hacked to death in the middle of a rout"*, he observed unhappily. *"Let them die with a glimmer of hope, rather than a heart full of defeat."*

As Captain Silvius' shoulders drooped, a figure in deep azure robes coalesced into being beside him.

"Wizard Pash! Please, tell me you have good news. I fear we can't take any more of the bad." Pash opened his mouth to speak, but was interrupted by a bright flash of light and the sharp crack of thunder a few feet away.

"Well look at this!" Gerrus smiled at Pash and Silivus through the twisted and charred skin pulled back from his gleaming teeth. "My brother who went to become a brother. So nice to finally meet you." He looked appraisingly at Pash's robes. "I *thought* that was you with the Black. I see that he has taken you into his tutelage. Perhaps he feels he needs to make amends for failing his charges in the past?"

Pash looked at the blackened creature before him, split between revulsion and amazement. For years he had heard whispers of his brother, dead long before he was born. For years, he had wished that he had just one chance to meet him.

Gerrus watched his expression, guessing his thoughts. "Ah yes, father *wished* me dead. Especially after I left with a ...*not insubstantial* amount of money. Still, he was always far more interested in himself than in me, and I suspect he was just as happy to see me gone. Had my skills with the dark magics reached the ears of the rest of the council, his political career would have been over."

Pash continued to stare at him his mouth slightly agape.

"You know," Gerrus said contemplatively, "I didn't know you were interested in the arts. You don't need to follow that old traitor. We might be able to come to some sort of an...arrangement. My former apprentice seems to have gone missing recently."

Pash slowly shook his head. "I'm not interested in what you have to offer."

"Why? Because I look like this?" Gerrus lifted his arms, his robes sliding back to expose the sinew grafted to his bones. "Don't be short sighted. This body is nothing, compared to the power I wield."

Gerrus narrowed the skin around his hollow eye sockets, as if squinting. "Don't think you can defeat me."

Pash shook his head wearily. "I can't. I brought an old friend of yours though."

The air beside Pash rippled and distorted, darkening and stretching until a vertical slash grew long enough for T'izz'ikel to emerge.

"No." Gerrus whispered.

T'izz'ikel grinned, causing Gerrus' horror to be reflected the obsidian shards that served as the demon's teeth.

T'izz'ikel threw his head back and laughed; he threw his arms wide and up, pulling ropes of hellfire from the ground.

"Don't think you will escape from me this time, *apprentice* Gerrus. You are not the master here."

Gerrus hastily began casting spells of warding and protection, only to find himself thrown to the ground by T'izz'ikel. The bands of hellfire wrapped around Gerrus, searing into his already charred flesh, probing at his mouth and eye sockets.

Pash turned to Captain Silvius. "You would be well advised to have your men retreat as soon as possible, for their own safety."

Silvius shook his head in disbelief. "You control the demon?"

Pash smiled. "No; let us say that he and I are...allies. Truly, you must evacuate. When T'izz'ikel purges the undead from this area, it will not be a safe place for you and your men."

Captain Silvius spun and faced Pash. "They'll be smashed to bits if they can't stand and fight."

Pash bowed with a flourish to T'izz'ikel. T'izz'ikel grinned again, brought his hands together, then pulled them apart rapidly. The bands of hellfire sliced through Gerrus like a roast wrapped in garrote wire, then laced around the pieces until they were blackened to charcoal. The undead, having lost the will of their commander, staggered listlessly about, animation without a motivating force behind them.

Captain Silvius glanced at the massive demon, then back to Pash. Hastily, he gestured Brug over to his side. "Sound the retreat!"

Brug trembled in place, his eyes wide at the sight of the demon.

Silvius grabbed him by his shoulders and shook him roughly. "Sound. The. Retreat!"

Brug raised the horn to his lips, and sounded the clarion call as if his life depended upon it.

"Go! And do no stop sounding it until you have reached the other side of the bridge!"

Pash nodded at him, satisfied. "As for you Captain, you may return with your men, or you may remain with us while we clean up a bit."

Captain Silvius surveyed the troops running, walking, and jogging as fast as they could toward the bridge. Some carried their weapons; far more carried their friends and fellow soldiers.

"I think I would prefer to stay for this."

Pash nodded, and intoned a spell quietly. A glow appeared beneath their feet, and Pash placed out a steadying hand on Silvius' shoulder. T'izz'ikel held a fierce look of concentration as he began weaving a spell, and the three began to float in the air on a glowing translucent disk, far above the remains of Wallenbrook. T'izz'ikel's voice boomed loudly as he neared the completion of his spell. He slashed his hand violently downward, and a rift opened up in the earth, a scar opening up to a pool of lava and hellfire. He slashed his hand again and again, tearing the ground repeatedly until the whole township looked as if it had been set upon by a thresher. Lava oozed from the cracks; where the undead hadn't already fallen in, they caught fire and burned to ash when the lava reached them. Soon, the entire township was a molten red sore, the heat causing the water in and around it to rise up into a shroud of steam. T'izz'ikel sank to a knee, his eyes drawn closed, a placid smile pulled tight across his mouth.

62. A DAY OF HEROES

Brug stood at the crest of the bridge with his horn still dangling from his fingertips, looking back at Wallenbrook. All that remained of Shantytown was a glowing plain, the chaotic mess incinerated in a red sea of quiet placidity.

"Was it you who summoned the retreat?"

Brug nodded slowly, barely giving the speaker a half glance.

"You are to come with me, by order of General Karstin."

Brug absentmindedly fastened the horn to the side of his pack, and turned to follow him. The soldier who led him was scarcely older than himself, but sported red epaulets that indicated his position on the General's Staff. *Likely a political appointee*, he guessed; son of a councilman, perhaps, being groomed for a command. He put the thought aside and trudged wearily after him, the adrenaline of the past two days' battles finally taking their toll. Walking through the refugee crowd was like walking through a briar thicket of conversations; little bits snagging the recesses of his interest as they faded behind him; still, it was a soothing hum compared to the sounds of battle.

They came to a half-circle of guards emplaced to ensure the crowd stayed at a distance from the front of a warehouse building.

The aide glanced at Brug. "If you can do anything to make yourself more presentable, now is a good time to do so."

Brug glared back at him in response; the aide shrugged and turned back toward the building. The guards parted and allowed them to pass, and they headed inside.

Brug walked in, and scanned the group assembled inside. On the floor there was a massive map of Solypse that was wider than he was tall. Several high-ranking officers were using sticks to push small colored stones to different places on the map. To the side, a person he recognized by uniform as the General was deeply engaged in conversation with a priest of Lethos.

The young aide in the red epaulets strode purposefully forward and stood before them with his hands clasped behind his back, his feet slightly apart, waiting for his opportunity to speak. The General finished speaking and turned his head to acknowledge the aide.

"General, this is the person that called the retreat."

The General eyed Brug. "You look pretty rough, soldier."

The aide blushed. "Apologies sir, he didn't...feel the need to freshen up."

The general dismissed the aide with a wave, not taking his eyes off of Brug. "This man doesn't need a boy to make excuses for him."

General Karstin nodded slowly, and lowered his voice, noting the crest on Brug's tunic. "The Darkened Veil."

"Yes sir."

"How did you fare?"

"The survivors are evacuated sir."

"How did the *Veil* fare?"

Brug shifted uncomfortably. "Many survived sir."

"Silvius?"

He shook his head. "He... Elected to remain behind, sir."

"Brabo?"

"Unknown sir. He was gone, and I was made second. I did not ask."

General Karstin sighed. He had hoped—against all odds, he knew—that they would survive. He regarded his army like his family; The Veil, his old unit, even more so. The only thing harder than losing his troops was knowing that he had ordered them to their deaths.

"Stand at ease, son. And tell me everything." He looked up quickly at his aide. "Two chairs; water."

The chairs arrived. Brug sat down uncomfortably, and began to tell his story.

63. FUNERAL

A stack of dried fireshroom logs lay crisscrossed on the ground and stacked to half the height of a man. Across the top of them lay Mikkel's body, dressed in the simple cloth funeral garb of Danite tradition. His hands were folded together at his waist. Beneath his arms and tucked beneath his hands were tokens of affection from his loved ones: Teagan's favorite doll; a walking stick that Colin had made for their cavern walks; Gavin's toy hammer; and a drawing of the family from Liam. The small township gathered in a circle around the pyre, paying their last respects to an old friend. The companions stood in the center of the circle alongside Halail and the children.

For now, Halail had run out of tears. There had already been many, and there would be many more to come. Mikkel's passing left her feeling queasy and alone, like someone set adrift in a boat in the middle of the sea. But for now, she had a purpose, and she could focus on it. For now, there were minions that needed attending, and rituals to be performed.

She reached up with a trembling hand and lay her farewell token—a fresh loaf from the hearth—atop his chest. She felt miserable about it; she had cast about for something more meaningful all night, reaching for something profound. All she found was a feeling of profound loss. She had given everything to him, and he in return to her. Now, half of her everything had been taken, and no 'token' could change that.

The dwarflings drifted about aimlessly, alternately looking lost and oblivious. Their tears had been brief, but she knew that they would come in abundance in the coming weeks. She crouched down, gathering them all together and whispering. They nodded, and gathered closed to one another.

Larrik lit the torch and held it out to Halail, sympathy in his eyes. Her eyes welled up, and she cast her head down. She cocked her arm to one side to toss the torch atop the pyre, but thought better of it. Halail timidly crept up to the side and lay the torch next to him

"Goodbye, my love." She whispered.

The fireshrooms caught instantly, and the pyre became engulfed in a ball of flame. Halail stepped back to the children, each holding their piece of paper. She picked Teagan up first, and took a step toward the inferno. Teagan thrust her arm awkwardly forward, and the paper caught on the updraft, catching flame as it climbed toward the roof of the cavern until it was out of sight. She repeated this ritual with each of the children. After she set Liam down, she reached into a pocket of her robes and pulled out a carefully folded piece of paper. She stepped as close to the fire as she dared, and tossed it gently into the flame. The carefully folded paper spread as it caught fire. As it floated above her head, she saw her words the words from their wedding vows on the paper as it went up in flame, then faded to black.

She stepped back, her lower lip trembling. Cillan rubbed her arm comfortingly, Larrik bowed his head to her. "A perfect offering token it was."

"It w-was just a stupid loaf of bread."

Larrik shook his head. " 'Twas something more. Ye took a bunch of simple little things and made something amazing out of them. You warmed them by your hearth to make them rise, tempered them with flame, and something beautiful emerged. And when the time came, you let that beautiful thing go, because it was the right thing to do." He shook his head again. "No, 'twasn't silly at all. Methinks it was inspired by Riordan himself."

64. AN UNLIKELY GROUP

General Karstin leaned back in his chair, letting out a long, slow breath. "I knew that young man was made of a tougher mettle than most, but never did I expect...this."

The General shook his head and Brug looked dumbly into his hands. The General's aide ran up to them. He snapped to attention and tried to catch his breath with his mouth closed. His face flushed and his nostrils flaring, he stared at the general, waiting for acknowledgement.

"He delivered us into victory. We shall see that his memory is honored. As for Brabo, hm." He shook his head again. "There's no doubt that he succeeded, or we wouldn't have a few thousand refugees outside. But we aren't out of the mist yet. There's still a demon to contend with."

"Sir!"

The general glared at the aide. "Dammit! I don't care who your father was! He should have taken you over his knee years ago so that I don't have to!"

"Sir! It's about the demon!"

The general stood from his chair, glaring at the soldier. "Therox, would you get to the damn point?"

Therox swallowed. "The demon is here, and he's with Captain Silvius."

"He has Captain Silvius?"

Therox shook his head so violently, that Brug thought for a moment it might come off. "No sir, he's *with* Captain Silvius." He paused for a moment, and hastily added, "and a mage."

The general motioned for Brug to follow him. Therox led them towards the door of the warehouse. Outside the door, the crowd had already turned inward and was trying to peek past the guards. Captain Silvius stood in the protective half-moon of space by the entryway, flanked on his left by Pash, and on his right by T'izz'ikel. Captain Silvius came to attention and saluted.

"Sir, I am pleased to report that the enemy has been vanquished."

The general looked from Silvius to T'izz'ikel, and back over to Pash, his mouth agape. "This creature...is under your command?"

Pash smiled. "No sir. He is under no one's command but his own."

The general pondered this for a moment. He turned to address T'izz'ikel. "And you help us of your own free will?"

T'izz'ikel gave a half bow at the waist, smiling shards of glass at the General. "At your service."

"Well then." General Karstin paused. "Perhaps we should go get things sorted out with the Council."

Captain Silvius nodded at the General, guiding his gaze to the left. "I'm not sure we have a choice." General Karstin turned his head to see two guards, wearing the ceremonial garb of the Council Guard, several paces away. Upon making eye contact with him, they rapidly closed the distance.

"General Karstin and Captain Silvius, you are hearby under arrest, by the order of the Council."

General Karstin sighed. "Therox. May clutchers eat his eyes."

65. A REWARD FOR HEROES

The gavel fell with a loud crack, bringing the murmurs of conversation to a close.

"The special session of the Council has been convened to preside over the trial of Captain Giles Silvius, Commander of the Darkened Veil." Ellias fixed his gaze on each council member in turn, ensuring they were paying attention.

"The charge is high treason; the penalty is death."

Councilman Cyrus glared at Ellias irritably. Ellias had ascended to a position of authority, but he was still a weasel. "Treason? On what grounds?"

"Disobeying a direct order. Contributing to the deaths of innocents and soldiers. Desertion."

Silvius, still standing at a position of attention before the council, turned crimson, his face expressionless.

General Karstin, however, did not remain as composed. "They're calling him the Savior of Shantytown, and this is how you repay him?" The General's face purpled with disbelief, his hands balled into fists at his side.

Ellias casually raised an eyebrow. "General, please restrain yourself. The council reminds you that you serve at their pleasure, much as the alleged traitor here."

"Traitor?" the General shouted. "The Captain was under my command, and under my orders. He disobeyed nothing. His actions alone saved thousands. I'll not stand here and listen to you sully him before your peers, or anyone else."

Silvius remained at attention. His face a mask of indifference, his gut churned and his head swam with the volley of accusations and defenses.

Councilman Cyrus squinted at the General. "If what you say is true, then what of the desertion charge." He turned his head to regard his peer. "What of that, Ellias, from what does that stem?"

Ellias casually regarded his peer, "After the battle, he was nowhere to be found, according to the General's report."

"What report? I gave no such-"

Ellias folded his hands and smiled pleasantly. "Your aide was kind enough to supply us with a summary of the events. I didn't want to trouble you directly."

"What the *boy* failed to properly document was that the good Captain was overseeing the final stages of battle. He did not *desert* the force."

Ellias turned to fully face the General. "So let me understand this properly. You were given express orders to remain on the mainside of the bridge, yet you gave orders for your men to cross the bridge."

The General furrowed his brow, tight-lipped.

Ellias continued, his voice rising to a shout. "So you sent scores of troops across the bridge to Wallenbrook, knowing that they were marching to their DEATH, against express orders to the contrary, is that correct?"

Cyrus looked steadily at General Karstin. "Is this true, General?" he asked softly.

General Karstin looked at Councilman Cyrus. He straightened up defiantly. "Yes sir, it is. And if I lived to be a thousand, I would sleep comfortably every night with that decision, even as I mourn the fallen."

"With the blood of thousands on your hands! You are guilty of disregarding the will of the council, and will be tried in the Captain's stead." Ellias crowed.

Captain Silvius leaned forward, struggling against the guardsmen restraining him. "Sir! It was my doing, I-" Cyrus held up his hand, and Silvius stopped mid-sentence.

"Explain yourself, General."

"Sir, the Temple of Lethos was ordered to intervene, when they cannot; we were ordered to hold, when our duty is to the people of Solypse. If it is the will of the Council that the people of Solypse be slaughtered, then I freely admit that I defied the will of the council. And I would do it again."

Councilman Cyrus leaned on one arm, thoughtfully regarding Ellias.

"Councilman Ellias, I happen to have a little insight in this matter. A fortnight ago, Brother Kern visited me, expressing concern that the Council had asked them to perform in a manner that not only conflicted with their religious ethos, but was in fact beyond their capability. Further, he alleged that he told you of their inability to aid in the fight, yet you persisted in telling your messenger to the guard that the Brothers would be able to handle the situation."

Ellias laughed. "I'm sure there was a misunderstanding on the soldier's part."

Councilman Sha'el sat up smartly in his chair. "I believe the council would benefit from a full explanation, Councilman Ellias."

Ellias narrowed his eyes at him. "*Junior* councilman, though you may preside over this hearing, I suggest you pause a moment to remember who in this room is on trial."

Councilman Cyrus tented his hands, tapping his fingertips together lightly. "Now then, Ellias," he said smoothly, " I'm sure there's a perfectly plausible explanation for this; let's just get it out of the way."

He smiled thinly at Ellias.

"Did you tell the Brothers to head down to the river?"

Ellias sighed and rolled his eyes. "Yes."

"Did you tell the soldiers to head down to the river?"

"Yes."

"Did you send orders that the guard was to refrain from crossing the bridge?"

"Yes."

Cyrus turned to General Karstin. "Did you understand those to be your orders?"

General Karstin's face flushed. "Yes."

"Did you order, or otherwise permit by direction or intentional omission of prevention, the crossing of the bridge by Captain Silvius?"

"Yes."

Cyrus turned to regard Captain Silvius. He paused for a moment, studying the young man. Still covered in blood and ash, the Captain stood at a rigid position of attention. Cyrus could see that he was trembling ever so slightly. *Fear?* He mused. He dismissed the notion; for all this man had gone through, trembling before the Council was almost laughable.

"Captain, did you take command of the forces that crossed the bridge?"

"Sir, they asked for direction. I willingly gave them a plan."

"So you led them?"

"Yes sir."

"Which is to say, you took command of the forces."

"Yes sir."

"When was that?"

"In the morning, sir."

"After the first wave was defeated?"

"No sir, before the first wave."

"So nearly three days ago."

He paused. "Yes sir."

Cyrus gestured at a bench at the side of the chamber. "Captain, surely you are exhausted. Please have a seat."

"With all due respect sir, I would prefer to stand beside my General."

Cyrus arched his brow in surprise. "If you so choose."

Cyrus regarded General Karstin once again. "General, did the assault work?"

"Sir?"

"Did you stop the creatures from crossing the bridge?"

"No sir."

Cyrus folded his hands on the table, looking back and forth at the individuals arrayed before him. "Forgive me, but I find myself a tad confused. We do not have an enemy encroaching upon us, do we?" He frowned, noting the look of frustration on Silvius' face. "Oh fine, out with it Captain. What?"

"Sir, it is true that we successfully evacuated the township, but there would have been no victory without the help of the Wizarding tower. A wizard of the tower appeared, accompanied by a powerful creature. The creature enspelled the area such that cracks opened up, spilling lava into the invaders of Wallenbrook."

"Well this is news. How much of Wallenbrook was affected?"

"All of it."

"When you say all of it, you mean-"

Silvius exhaled sharply, drawing a reproachful look from Cyrus. Silvius took another, calming breath. "Sir, what I mean is that when the sorcerer and the demon were done, all of Wallenbrook glowed red, as if a smithy had spilled the contents of a crucible across the entire town."

"Did you say a *demon?*"

"Yes sir."

"So now we are being invaded by *demons?*"

"No sir, he seemed to be somewhat controlled. Perhaps by the wizard."

"I see", Cyrus said skeptically.

Cyrus looked at his fellow council members, who were either murmuring about demons or staring at Silvius with unabashed amazement. "Ahem," he said, clearing his throat.

"It is clear to me then, that by his own admission, the General ordered Captain Silvius into Wallenbrook. Accordingly, Captain Silvius is exonerated. Also accordingly, he is not guilty of the crimes with which he is charged." General Karstin allowed himself a small smile, and gently elbowed Silvius.

"However, also by his own admission, General Karstin violated a direct order from a member of the council. This violation resulted in the deaths of thousands of soldiers. Such a violation abuses a position of high trust, and is tantamount to treason. Treason has but one punishment; that punishment is death."

General Karstin nodded curtly, his jaw clenched. Ellias tried to hide the hint of a smirk, unsuccessfully.

"With the impending demise of the General, the leadership role will be vacant. Given his strong leadership ability and heroic actions, I think it fitting that the hero of Shantytown be accorded full honors, and promoted to the rank of "General of Solypse Forces.""

"But he has no experience! Surely you set him up for failure! Beyond that, what of violating the *will* of the council?" Ellias protested.

Cyrus feigned surprise. "My fellow councilmember, perhaps you are right. The boy is a bit inexperienced for such things. " He paused, seemingly lost in thought. "Accordingly, General Karstin's punishment is delayed. He shall function in his current role until such time that the council feels that the Captain has reached a level of experience equivalent to that of the General."

"But the General could be dead by then!"

Cyrus shrugged. "I suppose that could happen. If so, then the will of the council will have been fulfilled. Speaking of the will of the council... You presume to think that your actions speak for the will of the council. In the charter for the council of Solypse, countersigned by the original council and the Temple of Lethos, it states that our duty is to care for and tend to *all* the residents of Solypse. You instead ordered the guard to allow the citizens of Wallenbrook to be victims of genocide. *Your* intentions are counter to the will of the council; further, your orders equate to attempted murder upon all the residents of Wallenbrook. *This* is treason. As previously indicated, there is but one punishment for treason." He paused, offering the other council members a moment to process the information. "Fortunately for you, we do not execute members of the Council. Unfortunately for you, and perhaps all of us, you will be permitted to live...in the Cells of the Forgotten." Cyrus leaned forward. "*That*, Councilman Ellias, *is the will of the Council.*"

66. A MUTUAL UNDERSTANDING

Cillan rolled onto her back, her head gently cradled by a heavy feather pillow. The Pilgrim's Rest was an occasional luxury that she enjoyed; this time, the appropriate nature of the name was too good to pass up.

The humble name was an ironic reflection of the opulence inside. The Pilgrim's Rest was one of the oldest inns in Solypse, and had grown in reputation and stature over the years. Cillan smiled in the dark amidst the tousled nest of her hair, still damp from her bath the night before. The coals in the hearth emanated a low red glow, driving away the damp breeze borne in from the inn perched on the cliff wall above the warehouse district.

She rolled back toward her side, catching a glimpse of a glint out of the corner of her eye. Without slowing, she reached under her pillow. In one fluid motion, she pulled her dagger from under her pillow and rolled back to the opposite side, cutting the gossamer thin metal wire that was stretched taut mere inches above her head. She let the momentum of her roll carry her off the bed to the floor, where she landed on her feet with cat-like grace. Before she landed, she had already spotted the source of the cable that now lay limp, dangling from the wall in two pieces.

"Thalen. You're getting sloppy." Thalen was slouched the plush armchair beside the hearth. One many-buckled leather boot rested easily on his knee, while his hands were folded across his stomach.

"It's about time you woke up", he complained, "I've been sitting here for *hours*." Cillan slowly straightened up, tensing as he swiftly sat up in his chair. He held up his hands in mock surrender. "So jumpy. I was just going to throw a log on the fire." He leaned over the arm of his chair and reached out of sight, then held a log up. "See?" He tossed a log into the fire. A handful of sparks blazed up the chimney as the log landed. The bark caught fire, illuminating both of them. "Ah, still sleeping nude, I see." Thalen pulled a blanket off of the back of the chair, and tossed it at her. Cillan didn't move, letting the blanket fall at her feet. "Suit yourself. But please," he gestured to the chair across from him at the hearth. "Join me." Cillan leaned over and picked up the blanket with one hand, knife still in the other, not taking her eyes off of him. "Oh please, Cillan, can we dispense with this? If I wanted you dead, I would have done it hours ago."

"I could kill you now..."

Thalen smiled indulgently. "If you were going to kill me, you would have done it in the hall of assignment." He paused. "Actually, you very nearly did. I was lucky that I had a potion of healing on me."

"Tube in a small pocket, on the left side, near your lower pocket."

"So it was."

Cillan sat down on the chair across from him, laying the blanket across her lap and the dagger upon it. "So what are you doing here?"

"I wanted to talk."

"So talk."

"The guild is mine. As I presume you intended it to be."

She nodded.

"But it seems that there's something missing."

Cillan shrugged.

He frowned. "I just find it hard to believe that a guild with such a long and storied history as ours has no treasury. No riches. No amassed wealth. Nothing.'

"Did you check with the bank?" She suggested.

"Cute."

Cillan gave him a half smile.

"The thing is, I know we must have quite a hoard. And I'm sure that you know where it is. And I'm sure that you will go back for it someday. And when that day comes, I will know. And I will know where it is. And then I'll have no more use for you."

She smiled coquettishly. "It's a shame. I can still think of a use for you."

He grabbed the booted foot on his kneed and lowered it to the ground, and raised himself to standing. "Is that right?"

She stood up slowly, letting the blanket and the dagger slide to the floor.

"That's right."

Thalen reached up and slowly began to unfasten his leather tunic.

Cillan raised an eyebrow. "Does that mean you still have a use for me too?"

67. THE TEMPLE PEACE

Pash, Kithe, Therrien and Brother Kern

The four men sat cross-legged on cushions, sipping tea. A young brother with a shaven head refreshed their cups and set the pot down on the squat table between them. A small monkey ran down his arm and deposited a bowl of sugar and a spoon beside the teapot, then ran back up his arm. As the young man departed Pash looked at Therrien. Though it had only been a little over a week, Therrien looked to have made a remarkable recovery. His youthful vigor had returned, though there was a weary look behind his eyes, one that only came of facing one's own mortality.

"Acolyte Therrien, you are looking well," Pash commented.

Therrien blushed. He hadn't contemplated the Brotherhood up until a few days prior, and he still wasn't quite used to hearing the appellation attached to his name. Still, it seemed to fit in a manner that 'wizard' hadn't, even after several years.

"My thanks, Wizard Pash. I am disappointed that Brother Larrik couldn't be here, but it is good that you and the Chief Wizard could join us."

Kithe nodded. "Our thanks to you for your service. Without your assistance, Pash would have never made it back to Solypse in the first place. Though I think Larrik and Scanlon could have made a good home here, I think they are better served by carving their own path."

Brother Kern cocked his head. "Scanlon?" he queried.

Kithe nodded. "It seems that Larrik picked up a pet Gryphon somewhere along the way. Named it Scanlon, after a brave warrior he once knew."

Brother Kern started coughing until he choked on his tea. As he recovered his breath slowly, he broke into a wide grin. "Scanlon isn't a fallen warrior. Scanlon is the name of the young man that just served you tea." Brother Kern stifled a laugh. "A few seasons ago, he named his monkey Larrik, just to taunt the old dwarf."

The four erupted into a chorus of laughter.

Pash inclined his head in the direction of the doorway. "I think Scanlon got the better end of the deal."

Brother Kern smiled. "I would tend to agree. Speaking of bargains, by the way, whatever did happen with *your...*" Brother Kern searched for the right words, as he regarded Kithe. "...companion?"

"The demon?"

Brother Kern nodded.

"T'izz'ikel and I came to an agreement, you could say. He gave me my freedom, and I gave him his."

Therrien's eyes went wide with alarm. "Do you think that is wise?"

A blackened haze of smoke coalesced behind Kithe, until it solidified into the form of T'izz'ikel.

T'izz'ikel smiled his unnerving bladed smile at Therrien. "Why is that, Brother Therrien? Do you not *trust* me?"

Therrien sat petrified, unable to take his eyes off of the towering red and black creature.

T'izz'ikel laughed a deep, demonic laugh, and knelt down beside Kithe.

"I came to realize that power is a purpose unto itself. Evil can be crushed under my foot as easily as anything else. My purpose is not dissuaded by disavowing evil as my method."

"So power for power's sake?" Therrien looked at Kithe accusingly. "Are you mad? What is to keep him from killing us all right now."

T'izz'ikel looked at him smugly. "Your friend Mikkel says hello."

Therrien, wide-eyed, looked back at Kithe. "What-"

Kithe shook his head slowly. "Mikkel went voluntarily. He rides the demon now, for Riordan. Therrien, he saved Shoal." He paused. "T'izz'ikel walks among us now, here in Solypse."

Therrien looked at T'izz'ikel quizzically. "Will you stay here long?"

T'izz'ikel nodded slightly. "For a bit. I have chosen to serve Riordan, and Mikkel rides with me to ensure I live up to my part of the bargain." The demon shrugged. "It remains unnecessary. A new master is a master all the same, whether it be Riordan or someone else. Our goals align, and thus I choose to serve him."

"But you are now bound to him, with Mikkel serving as the chain on that bondage."

"It matters not. There is always a master. There is always one greater. This much I have learned living with this one over here." He nodded in the direction of Kithe; Kithe gave a faint nod in response, lost in his own thoughts.

Therrien looked to Pash. "And you?"

"The Chief Wizard has invited me to study under his tutelage at the tower. I'm looking forward to it quite a bit. Here's hoping I'm a better Apprentice than Acolyte."

Brother Kern smiled gently. "I think you may be surprised at how much more success you have in life when you follow your passion, rather than the path that others have set before you. For this at the least, you have my blessing, and that of the Temple. Besides," he continued, "I think the two professions have made a trade that Lethos himself would be pleased with. Acolyte Therrien is a very welcome addition to our family. You are, of course, always welcome to visit or attend worship with us."

"You are too kind, Brother Kern. I will certainly be here to visit old friends, if nothing else."

68. MAID SERVICE

H e woke to a rapping noise at the door. Groggily he looked over, seeing a young woman averting her gaze as she knocked on the open door.

"Does the Sir need some help?"

He tried rolling over, but thin wire bit into his wrists and ankles. *Cillan.* He looked down, and realized he was fastened to all four bedposts, a blanket casually tossed over his loins.

"What kind of help did you have in mind?"

The young lady blushed and set down the breakfast tray on the bedside table. "Compliments of your lady friend" she murmured, looking away blushing. "I'll send up the innkeeper."

Thalen sighed. *Women.*

69. ELLIAS AND HIS NEW HOME

The barred false window was worse than having no window at all. Ellias sighed, peering up the tall airshaft that led down to the 'window' in his room. At noon every day, a solitary shaft of light would make its way all the way down to illuminate his window ledge for a brief few moments, as if a mocking reminder of where he was, and then it would slowly recede until noon the next day.

He wasn't sure how many people had been thrown in the halls of the forgotten. There were no records of who had been put in the halls; after all, as the reasoning went, the people there were meant to be forgotten. Likewise, the prisoners there were given the kitchen waste, rather than food. This ingenious tidbit had actually been his idea. It not only saved money, but also emphasized that "the forgotten" were truly alone.

Ellias hadn't spent much time studying the halls, despite having sentenced dozens to exile in them. He did, however, recall that they were the remnants of Dwarven ruins discovered deep beneath Solypse. Few outside of the Council were aware of the Dwarven ruins, especially since the broad tunnel leading out of the halls had collapsed decades, if not hundreds of years before. *Not ruins*, he corrected himself, *abandoned Dwarven city*. True Dwarven craftsmanship would never fall into ruin, even after hundreds of years' time.

I am alive, he thought. *It's a start*. Ellias watched the sun beam fade, and used a stone to scratch another line in the wall to match the ones he had left before. He had started doing it to track the date; now he did it to remind him of the inescapable passage of time.

In the days following his exile, he had rarely left the small window, waiting for the single beam that brought him hope. As time wore on, so did his spirit. After a few days, his thirst and hunger drove him to explore outwards. He stepped over the cooled bodies of dead humans, their lack of sight in the lightless tunnels having turned the halls into a quick spiral of dark despair, followed by dehydration, hunger, and death. He eventually found a small band of half elves jealously guarding a minuscule trickle of water issuing from a rock, a small treasure cache in the middle of their circle. He waited, watching them for days, as they set camp guards and went foraging. Finally, half-mad with thirst, he stole into their camp while after the posted guard was asleep. He drank long and deep from the water, oblivious to the danger of turning his back to the camp. When he turned back toward the camp, it was still silent. His empty belly whispered promises to him, and he snuck to the cache unminded by the sleeping guard. As he reached into the pile to pick up a lump of not-quite-spoiled meat, he heard a grunt behind him. He froze.

"Well look at this."

Snoring to the side stopped. "What?"

"We have a thief among us."

"Kill it. Let me sleep."

The half elf guard stood in a low crouch. "You heard 'im. Stay still, I'll make it hurt more if you run."

Ellias stood up and turned around, his palms facing up. "My apologies good sirs. Perhaps I can make it up to you."

"Perhaps I can make yer head into a bowl for soup."

Ellias held his hands up in front of his chest. "I suppose you could do that, but...perhaps you would prefer to know how to get out of here?"

The drowsing companion sat up, and kicked their third. "Abraxis, hold a moment." His eyes narrowed. "If you knew how to get out of here, why haven't you left?"

"I need your help. Or someone's help. There's a way out, but it is more than I can manage to get to on my own."

"What's to keep us from killing you once we get there?"

He shrugged. "Once we get there, there's a magic door, and only I know the password."

"And why would that be?"

"I used to work for the council as a scribe," Ellias lied, "One of the records that I kept was of the Halls of the Forgotten."

"Then how'd ye end up here?"

Abraxis shooed his companion. "Those council dogs are dirtier than anyone in the Halls down here, and you know it too Shal. He likely saw something he wasn't supposed to."

Ellias nodded emphatically. "That's exactly right. I stumbled upon one of the councilmen bribing a court judge. When they saw that I knew what was going on, my sentence was swift. And here I am."

"Sounds like a convenient story for someone with pointy ears who doesn't want to die."

"Fair enough. But what do you have to lose?" He paused, then added timidly, "Besides, perhaps, a little food?"

Shal smiled and gestured at the cache behind Ellias. "I suppose it couldn't hurt, we have plenty enough to share."

Ellias turned and squatted, greedily shoving bits of meat in his mouth.

"It is exotically spiced, I am surprised. Where did you get such things down here?"

Abraxis laughed. "That's what we said. As near as we can figure, he must have been a spice merchant."

"Come again?"

"Come now, you don't see any cattle down here, do you? Meat is meat."

Ellias felt his bowels clench at the realization of his meal. He steadied himself against the cool stone floor, and took another bite.

70. CILLAN BEGINS

The cool breeze gently caressed her face. She closed her eyes, the sea-spray and telltale droplets from the Veil dotting her face.

"First time beyond the Veil?"

She opened her eyes, and looked at the man beside her. The lean, tan skin of the adventurer belied his experiences roaming the surface world, the variety of scars hinting at tales that eclipsed those of the average travelling salesman. They stood at the bow of the merchant vessel, heading toward the grotto that led to the surface path.

He shrugged and turned back to look at the Veil disappearing from sight around the edge of the cavern wall. "No shame in it. Most haven't; they say they have everything they need in Solypse."

"But do they have everything that they *want?*"

"Does anyone ever have that?"

Cillan shrugged, staring into deep waters as the bow of the vessel pressed incessantly forward.

***

ABOUT THE AUTHOR

Paul Neslusan grew up enchanted with the way books could transport him anywhere. He began the Solypse series to try to create a world as immersive as the ones he loved while he was growing up.

He lives in Central Massachusetts with his extremely patient wife and three children. This is his first novel.

Made in the USA
Middletown, DE
26 December 2020